Praise for
Alyssa Brooks's novels

"A wonderful debut story!"   —*Romance Junkies*

"Once again, Alyssa Brooks creates an enchanting and erotic tale."
—*The Romance Studio*

"Alyssa Brooks has written a charming, bewitching romance."
—*Romance Reviews Today*

"Alyssa Brooks has earned herself not only a few red fingertips from the flames she has produced, but also four Angels!"
—*Fallen Angel Reviews*

"Wonderfully sensual, erotic . . . will leave you wanting more."
—*Romance at Heart Magazine*

Berkley Heat titles by Alyssa Brooks

COME AND GET ME

HIDE AND SEEK

HARD TO GET

HARD TO GET

alyssa brooks

HEAT | NEW YORK

THE BERKLEY PUBLISHING GROUP
Published by the Penguin Group
Penguin Group (USA) Inc.
375 Hudson Street, New York, New York 10014, USA
Penguin Group (Canada), 90 Eglinton Avenue East, Suite 700, Toronto, Ontario M4P 2Y3, Canada
(a division of Pearson Penguin Canada Inc.)
Penguin Books Ltd., 80 Strand, London WC2R 0RL, England
Penguin Group Ireland, 25 St. Stephen's Green, Dublin 2, Ireland (a division of Penguin Books Ltd.)
Penguin Group (Australia), 250 Camberwell Road, Camberwell, Victoria 3124, Australia
(a division of Pearson Australia Group Pty. Ltd.)
Penguin Books India Pvt. Ltd., 11 Community Centre, Panchsheel Park, New Delhi—110 017, India
Penguin Group (NZ), 67 Apollo Drive, Rosedale, North Shore 0632, New Zealand
(a division of Pearson New Zealand Ltd.)
Penguin Books (South Africa) (Pty.) Ltd., 24 Sturdee Avenue, Rosebank, Johannesburg 2196,
South Africa

Penguin Books Ltd., Registered Offices: 80 Strand, London WC2R 0RL, England

This is an original publication of The Berkley Publishing Group.

First edition: July 2008

Library of Congress Cataloging-in-Publication Data

Brooks, Alyssa.
    Hard to get / Alyssa Brooks.—1st ed.
        p.   cm.
    ISBN 978-0-425-22175-4
    I. Title.
    PS3602.R645H37 2008
    813'.6—dc22   2008014758

PRINTED IN THE UNITED STATES OF AMERICA

10 9 8 7 6 5 4 3 2 1

As always, to Larissa Lyons, for all her priceless writing support; to my husband and family, who carry me; to my editor and my agent, for all their wonderful efforts; and to my fans—this is for you!

HARD TO GET

one

"*Rumor* has it you're the Queen of Dildos," her unwelcome suitor shouted over the blaring music.

Not again. Standing with her back to him, Lizzy straightened and picked her martini up from the table. Her sister, Elisa, sat on the other side, grinning like a drunken fool. Such familial support.

The olive swished in the clear liquid, and Lizzy debated turning around and throwing the drink in the jerk's face. *Nah.* She really needed to consume every last drop at this point.

Darn it, she should have stayed hidden in the ladies' room. The supply closet was looking mighty fine at this point as well.

"Shouldn't you be picking on the bachelorette?" What had possessed her to throw this party? Oh, right. The rum-consuming bride-to-be still laughing at her from across the table *was* her sister, after all. Siblings got special treatment, even when it came to forcing

Lizzy to deal with men. "Careful, officer. I've been known to kick a guy out of my club for hitting on me."

He moved a little closer . . . too close. "Play is *your* club?"

Freakin' guy smelled like a cologne factory.

"What? Can't a woman own a kickass club?"

"Kinky and fiery," he murmured, brushing his lips across her ear. "I like it."

Lizzy whirled around, trying not to inhale as she glared him down. Tall, blond, and very *healthy* looking, the "cop" stripper Jayson had been presented to her earlier by her well-meaning—but also inebriated—friends, who were attempting to set her up with yet another man.

They should have known better. No, they *did* know better. *God.*

Well, at least she'd have fun getting rid of him. Screwing with cocky boy toys was always a little entertaining. She enjoyed taking them down a peg or two, fooling with their heads.

"Sure you want to keep messing with the Queen of Dildos?" Reaching out, she squeezed his butt firmly. "You never know what I might do with one of my toys."

She allowed her fingers to roam dangerously close to his crack, waiting for him to pull away. He didn't.

And he thought she was kinky? Whoa. Better pull out the big guns.

"You know, sometimes I like to watch," she told him. "Nothing sexier than two guys rolling around in bed."

She shuddered to think . . .

Especially when Jayson didn't even cringe. In fact, he grinned like a kid in a candy store.

"You know, touching each other. Exploring . . ."

"Toys included?" the son of a bitch asked.

Double, no triple, whoa.

Okay, it was official. She was out of her league with this one. Men usually flew the coop at that suggestion, but he wasn't, and playtime was over. There was nothing left to do but be mean.

Withdrawing, Lizzy crossed her arms and tapped her foot impatiently. "You just won't take a hint, will you?"

"Oh, I've got a hint. In fact, you gave me three." Colorful disco lights beamed across his face as Jayson flashed a smile meant to melt inhibitions. "You're quite the naughty girl. I might just have to arrest you." He motioned to the cuffs at the waist of his very fake uniform. "You've the right to remain sexy, the right to—"

Oh boy. Lizzy took a measured sip of her martini and looked away, blatantly displaying her indifference. When would her friends understand? She wasn't interested. Not in men. Not in women. She didn't even own a pet, she disliked the idea of relationships that much.

She tried to make her unavailability clear in her appearance, but her frizzy pink hair, black clothes, and combat boots didn't seem to be working. Nope, she was just attracting weirdos now. Maybe it was time for a change. Perhaps she'd go blue, or maybe lime green.

At any rate, Jayson had heard correctly—she was the Queen of Dildos and for darn good reason. Far as she was concerned, they provided everything a woman possibly needed out of a man, so there was no reason to be bothered with sex. She didn't find it rewarding anyway.

Not that it was Jayson's business. And crap, why did he seem to keep gravitating closer and closer? She was practically gagging, and if he moved another inch . . .

"Hey, sweetie, you seem tense." Jayson reached for her shoulder, and she shirked away.

Like she'd seemed loose a minute ago?

"So I guess the rumor is true?" Jayson pressed, clearly too cocky and empty-skulled to get the point. "Do you prefer toys to the real thing?"

And just who had told him, anyway? Elisa, the damn drunk, no doubt.

"Jayson, you should know I consider gossip a disease." Lizzy's voice was even and constrained. "I swear some people have diarrhea of the mouth. They just keep talking and talking and never pay a damn bit of attention to what they're saying. Do me a favor, *shut up!*"

Beside her, Elisa barked with laughter. "Another one bites the dust."

Lizzy shot her a look. "So give up. Both of you."

Elisa's deep blue eyes glistened with amusement. She looked like a dam about to burst—liquor, not water. "One day, yooou'll meet a man and I promish those walls of yours will be demolished. You're too sweet not to love, Lizzy."

Sweet? Hardly. Love? Yuck. She'd opened her heart once . . . what a mistake. She should have known better in the first place, if her real parents were any example.

Elisa, technically being her adopted sister, might know some of what she'd been through, but she had *no* understanding, no grasp of what Lizzy really thought of relationships. She couldn't. To someone like Elisa, the fear and pain experienced in Lizzy's past life were incomprehensible.

Elisa's parents hadn't taken her in until she was fourteen, and life ever since had been like a fairy tale. But happily-ever-after or not, Lizzy's past wasn't simply erasable. It was alive in her and at times, all consuming. She tried to ignore it, but she could *never* get past it.

And even if she were on the market, she wasn't falling for this idiot in uniform. He wasn't even worth a lay.

Ah well, her sister was having a little too much fun, but she would let it slide, given Elisa was getting hitched in a few days and Lizzy would be all too glad to see her change her mind, even if that decision was invoked by a booze-induced blunder.

While Elisa's fiancé had won a teeny measure of her respect, Lizzy wasn't keen on the idea of seeing her sister be hurt by a man.

And what man didn't hurt?

This party was Lizzy's one last chance to ensure that Elisa wasn't making a mistake. The flocks of gorgeous men she'd hired weren't an accident, they just weren't meant for herself.

"Have another drink, Elisa." Lizzy released a frustrated breath. "I've said it once if I've said it a hundred times, *so* not interested."

"Oh, come on, baby. Don't you want some of this?" Jayson had the audacity to stroke his erection right in front of them. "I can make you throw those dildos out, baby. Me and—"

"Why don't you and whoever just go have some fun and forget about me?"

"Seriously?" Poor guy looked like he was in complete disbelief. A woman turn him down? The shock! The audacity!

"Seriously, Jayson." An irresistible smile tweaked her lips. He had gall, she'd give him that. "Sex toys are my addiction. I don't know of any better way to get off."

"Ever try a real cock?" Sneaking his arm around her, he wasted no time attempting to grab her butt. "I've got one you'll love."

Unfortunately for him, in cases like this, persistence should *not* be rewarded.

"Men," Lizzy snorted, giving him the shove he deserved. "No. Thanks."

Sighing exasperatedly, Lizzy plopped down in her seat and waved to the waiter for another drink.

"So you're into women?" Instantly cynical, Jayson spat out the unoriginal insult. "I shouldn't be shocked. You *look* the type."

No surprise. She'd dealt with this sort of reaction more than once. Thankfully, she had a shell harder than a turtle's. "Sorry, I'm not a lesbian, so you can squash those fantasies. And how old are you? Sixteen?"

"I've been tryin' to convinch her tha' men aren't *alllll* bad," Elisa interrupted, the increased slur of her words proclaiming she'd passed "slightly inebriated" three drinks ago. Practically falling backward in her chair, she popped the cherry from her piña colada in her mouth, then gulped the remaining drink. "Like my shweet Maxim."

Uh, no. Maxim might make Elisa happy, but he wasn't exactly *shweet*, definitely no angel, hence her apprehension about the impending marriage. As far as Lizzy was concerned, *no* guy was worth the trouble he'd eventually cause.

"Men suck," she told them both. "Some quite literally, some in an abstract sense, but I for one—"

The loud disco music skidded to a stop, quickly replaced by a blasting country song, and the colorful laser lights transformed into white beams flashing across the stage.

Good. Just what she needed—an interruption. It was about time the dancers she'd hired got to work anyway.

"Ladies, are y'all ready for a *real* cowboy?" The stripper hollered from behind the curtain. "Yee haw, here I come!"

The cowboy's words slammed into her chest, plastering her to the backrest of her chair.

That voice! It was deeper, more Southern than she remembered—probably on purpose for the part—but unforgettable. Oh God, her body recognized the drawl from her head to her toes, through and through. Her skin prickled in immediate awareness, her heart echoing in her ears.

Ty?

Here? Now? *A stripper?*

She had to be mistaken. Imagining things. Going crazy. Ty Black was out of her life, *for good*, and surely fate wouldn't be so cruel as to dump him in her club, *taking his clothes off.*

The curtain swung open, and to her utter shock and dismay, heartbreak himself danced out in cowboy boots and a hat.

*M*oney was Ty's biggest turn-on, and when he danced, that's all he thought about. Cash: cold, hard, and simple. He wasn't interested in the women ogling him, wasn't interested in banging a single one of them. The only female he'd ever wanted was gone, vanished from his life like dust on the wind. Sometimes, he wondered if Elizabeth had ever existed, but then, if she hadn't, he wouldn't be here now, yanking off his clothes in hopes of one day being something more than a nameless dirt-poor cowboy.

"You darlins want a ride?" He thrust his pelvis in the air in short rhythm, enticing squeals and clapping.

A more eager watcher tossed a bill his way. "Come here, baby!"

Maybe he wasn't on the hunt for a relationship, but he worked hard for his cut body and didn't mind having it appreciated, especially not when the attention was building his bank account. He had college to pay for, bigger plans than this shit.

Money—hell yeah, he wanted it, and he knew just how to get it. Some fools just got up and danced, but he knew what these ladies wanted—a cock in their faces, swinging round and round.

If he wanted to score big today, he needed to play the crowd. He needed to lavish attention on each and every last drunken gal.

The club wasn't close to being full—he'd wager there were only twenty or so partygoers in attendance—but nonetheless, folks from Aspen had money to waste. Starting at the left of the room, he focused his attention on a thrilled woman, careful not to touch her as he mock humped her leg and ripped his flannel shirt from his body.

"Yee haw!" he shouted, giving the shirt a whirl before tossing it aside. Clapping and shouts encouraged him, and he bucked his hips like a wild animal fucking the air, though he knew better than to give in to their pleas for him to take it all off. That wasn't legal . . . and what clothes were coming off were doing so *slowly*.

"Now where's that purty lil' bride I heard about?" Following pointing hands, he gradually made his way around the room until he reached the center of the *U*-shaped crowd, where the lucky lady was seated. On the way, he ripped his white undershirt off, leaving him wearing only a crotchless, backless pair of brown leather chaps and an uncomfortable pouch that confined his cock.

He turned around, bending and shaking his exposed rear. Cheers ignited through the room, and he whirled back around, ready to collect some tips.

That's when he saw her. Elizabeth.

Holy mother—was it possible to die and not know it? He had to have.

His heart sure wasn't beating—but maybe he just couldn't hear it over the screaming disbelief in his mind. For the first time ever onstage, his steps faltered. He didn't know what to do. To think. What the hell had happened to reality?

Sitting directly next to the bride was *his* Elizabeth, with *pink* hair. Gone was her sweet, innocent appearance . . . she looked like a hellion in boots. Short, colorful, frizzy hair framed the angelic face he remembered so well, her eyes a strange violet when they were supposed to be blue.

Was he imaging her? Maybe this stranger in burgundy lipstick just resembled Elizabeth.

No. Maybe their hue was different, maybe they were caked in black, raccoonlike makeup, but he knew those haunted eyes, knew them straight to the soul.

Jesus, what had life done to her? He'd hoped, prayed, searched . . .

Finally kicking back into gear, his heart slammed in his chest.

Fuck.

Mouth dry, Ty inspected the rest of her. She wore a short, black skirt and a polka-dotted blouse, both of which hugged curves that had filled out incredibly, though she didn't look as if she'd gained an inch in height. She was still as tiny as a doll, but she no longer looked like one. She looked like an ass-kicking bitch and had on the footwear to prove it.

Why? God, he hated the thought of her being so hard, so hurt. After a childhood like hers, the woman deserved—

More than he'd given her. More than life had given either of them.

He was too stunned to react, too stunned to breathe. All the years he'd imagined finding her again and *this* was how it happened? He'd wanted to discover her happy, healthy . . . still his.

But one glance at her and he knew that wasn't so.

Their eyes connected, her poignant purple gaze shining with tears. One thing was certain—she recognized him, though she didn't look happy about it.

And why would she be? He'd just shaken his ass in her face.

Cheers demanded he dance, and knowing he had no choice, he slowly, methodically, tried to continue. He moved toward her, instinctually needing to be closer to her. To touch her.

Elizabeth bit her lower lip and put up her hand, clearly asking him to stop.

He couldn't. He couldn't help approaching her, and he couldn't please the crowd a moment longer. Screw the money, screw the job, this was *Elizabeth*! His hip swings transformed into determined strides as he stalked toward her. The music screeched to a halt, all eyes on them.

Oh God, what was Ty doing? Approaching her?

Why? Why *now*?

All these years wondering what the hell had happened to him and *this* was how he'd ended up? A cowboy stripper working her sister's bachelorette party?

No, no, no. This couldn't be right. Maybe she'd been the one who had drunk too much and she'd passed out and this was all some crazy booze-induced dream.

It couldn't be real. Ty couldn't be here.

Hell, he better *not* be!

After what he'd done to her, he should be disfigured or maimed or dead—not looking like every female's dream come true and getting paid for it.

Ty had twice the body mass she remembered and had grown taller by several inches. His jaw was harder, *he* was harder, and he'd never been boyish to start with. She drank in his tanned, weathered skin, his sun-bleached hair, his full, kissable lips. His deep brown, almost black, eyes returned her dead stare, devouring her, hungry and unyielding.

In record time, Ty's long strides covered the short distance between them. Her mind kept telling her to react, to run for God's sake, but she couldn't move, couldn't think straight.

"Elizabeth?" He stood directly before her, enticing murmurs from the crowd. All eyes were on her, but she knotted up.

God, how she needed him, needed to love him all over again. He was so close. All she had to do was reach out and touch him.

Of course, strippers were hands-off . . . unless you were tipping. Maybe she should stick a five in his underwear.

But he didn't deserve even that from her.

Lizzy couldn't look away, yet she couldn't stand the sight of him. This was the type of moment to fear. Her vanished lover, come to life at the most unexpected moment ever, and everyone was witnessing it.

Elisa leaned toward her. "Lizzy?" she whispered, teetering in her chair, noticeably fighting to pull it together. "Ish everythin' okay?"

A murmur ran through the crowd and Lizzy swallowed, barely able to nod. "That's one hot cowboy," she eked out.

Elisa clutched her arm, her slurred voice growing louder. "Why's he starin' at you like that?"

God, she hoped Elisa wouldn't remember this in the morning.

Lizzy's heart tensed painfully, scorching hot embarrassment flooding her face. The knot in her throat burned and tears slid uncontrollably from her eyes. "Beats me."

She needed to get a grip. Why react this way? She was over him. He was over her. There was nothing to be upset about . . . nothing that mattered.

So what if he'd stolen her virginity, her heart, then left her cold and alone on the dangerous city streets? His abandonment had made her stronger. Better.

"Lizzy?" Elisa asked again.

It felt like a hundred pairs of eyes were burning straight through her. Seeing her pain. Viewing her secrets.

No!

Lizzy leapt to her feet and ran from the crowded room. The pounding of his footsteps followed her as she burst through the emergency door in the back and ran into the snow-dusted alley behind Play.

Hiccupping and fighting chest-burning emotion, she ran. She couldn't flee fast enough. It felt like her world was moving in slow motion, closing in on her, slipping right out from under her feet, all at the same time.

A hand clasped her upper arm. Wailing, she stumbled to a halt, jerking and twisting against the strong grasp. "Get off me!"

"Elizabeth!" Ty whirled her around and pulled her dangerously close. His dark eyes bored into hers, locking her to him. "My God, don't run from me."

"It's Lizzy," she spat, acutely aware of the way his nearness affected her, despite the way she fought the betraying feelings tooth and nail. All she wanted to do was melt in his arms, hug him tight, and rejoice in his presence.

Instead she glared at him, feigning hatred. She should feel repulsed, abhorrent, but couldn't.

She soaked in every detail of her long-lost lover, her childhood best friend, from his bare, freezing feet to his bare-ass leather chaps, to his meaty cock restrained in the ridiculous pouch he wore, to the desperate look in his eyes. "Well, if it isn't Ty Black, the *one* mistake I ever made—messing with a guy from the wrong side of the tracks."

"I was your neighbor, remember? Guess you aren't exactly from the right side, either." His free hand snaked around her neck and his fingers tangled relentlessly in her hair. To her dismay, he pulled her even closer. "And I don't remember any railroad tracks in our small town."

"And why should I care?"

His touch sent shivers racing along her scalp. "I do remember a creek though. Do you remember the creek, Elizabeth?"

The weeping willow tree, where they swung from branches and hid from summer storms. The sound of rushing water, crickets chirping in the evening . . .

Her mind slipped back in time, to the place where she'd run off whenever her stepfather was on another bender. The creek was where she and Ty shared their first kiss, where their love had bloomed. Her safe haven, *their* place.

"I don't know what you want me to say," she breathed, her heart in agony. "All of that was a long, long time ago."

"It was yesterday." His mouth hovered over hers, his hand still twirling the strands and exploring her head. "Pink hair, Elizabeth Victoria? It's a little over-the-top, don't you think? You used to be so sweet."

Sweet? That part of her was dead, dead as her real parents were to her.

What was she doing, letting him touch her like this? Torturing herself?

The knot in her heart erupted into her throat as she noted the sweat glistening on his forehead from the exertion of dancing.

Damn it, Ty was a stripper! *A stripper!*

Lizzy jerked back, wishing she actually could shoot bullets with her eyes. She'd put one right through his heart.

"You used to work with your pants on," she scoffed and tried to free herself from his grasp, jerking her arm. "And I said it's Lizzy, now get off me."

"Let you go? *Now?*" He held her even tighter, pulling her closer. "I don't think so."

Pushed to emotional limits, she shoved against him. "Fuck you! Haven't you hurt me enough?" She crushed his bare toes with a heavy black boot. "You lousy bastard!"

"Whoa!" Ty winced from the pain, but didn't ease his grip. "I'd never do a damn thing to hurt you and you know it. All I've ever done is attempt to save you—"

"Oh yeah?" Searing anger poured through her, making her chest burn, and she actually considered her urge to kick him where it really counted. Save her? He should have *saved* himself the trouble. "I was better off, safer, with my stepfather. At least he'd—"

"I'm sorry." Ty swore under his breath, his nose nudging her cheek. "God, I'm sorry."

"Ty, please, just—"

"I'm not letting you go, so we can either fight or talk." His fingers scraped over her scalp once again, tugging gently, pulling her to him despite her resistance. "God, Elizabeth." He lowered his head, so that his lips brushed hers gently, yet even that slight contact created fireworks, bombs destroying her will. "Or kiss," he whispered, his breath warming her.

Their noses touched, their hearts . . .

It was as if a super magnet pulled their chests together, locked them close when she would've pulled away.

Despite her intent to resist, her muscles went limp. She melted in his embrace, fell into his hold, yearning for that kiss so desperately, she could scream and plead for it. Pant like a bitch in heat.

"Oh, Elizabeth," he murmured.

Ty . . .

She couldn't fight him, couldn't fight herself. She didn't question the safety of her body, only the danger he was to her heart. Her lips.

"Ty, please." Lizzy wasn't a beggar, wasn't some weak girl, not anymore. She was a kickass woman who took what she wanted and dished out controversy like candy. But here, now, in Ty's arms again, she felt like a kid, a hopeless, helpless scared kid who *needed* him, who had no choices, no voice. *"Please."*

"Damn it, Elizabeth." He practically squeezed the air from her. "God, I've missed you."

Untangling his fingers from her hair, he grasped her chin and lifted it. He stared in her eyes, searching, asking.

But she had no answers. Only questions. "Where have you been?" She had to know.

"It's a long story," he told her, his voice oddly devoid of emotion.

She narrowed her gaze, calculating. "And now?"

"I live in Denver."

"That's three hours from here."

She hadn't even glanced at the company's address when she'd

called them. They'd had the biggest ad in the phonebook, came highly recommended from a friend, and their high initial fee had told her they weren't some fly-by-night amateurs.

"The company you hired for the party serves all of Colorado." He shrugged. "Normally, I don't work this far out myself, but I'm doing a favor for my boss. Worth it, when you consider the money you folks from Aspen throw around."

The money *she'd* thrown around. "I knew I should have asked for a firefighter."

To her surprise, he chuckled. "Thank God you didn't."

Without warning, his lips claimed hers.

Through his laughter, through her tears, he kissed her fiercely, making up for the eternity since they'd seen each other.

Back then, their love had been sweet, juvenile, but now the abrupt passion between them was explosive. Dangerous.

His tongue stroked hers, searched her mouth and seemingly, her soul. She couldn't help but answer. Couldn't stop the way her body cried out. God, when she thought back to those love-filled days . . .

Instantly, she was lost, kissing him back in spite of her resistance, her anger. Her mouth fought his, battled for control.

He clutched her, sealing their bodies together. "I swear, Elizabeth—"

"Don't," she told him. She didn't want to hear his excuses, not now. "Don't."

She kissed him back with everything in her, wanting him, needing him so much. Needing what she'd never had, never would . . .

Suddenly, she no longer cared about anything but *more*. Biting his lips. Sucking his tongue. Exploring his body.

Him, exploring hers. God, she needed that . . .

She latched onto his tongue, pulling as she fondled his bare ass, tweaked each cheek. Ty's grip on her chin tightened and her body shuddered, tingles racing over every inch of her skin.

"Touch me," she whispered, resting her cheek against his palm. "Ty . . ."

His other hand drifted south, settling at the base of her spine, molding her ass as he devoured her mouth and lifted her, raising her up on tiptoes, literally sweeping her off her feet.

She sobbed in his mouth, and his kiss gentled, his lips working hers, his tongue sliding along her teeth and inner cheek, tasting the recesses of her mouth.

So sweet, so perfect. Beyond her every fantasy, long denied as they were . . .

A sudden squeal filled the air, jerking her from the moment.

"Lizzy?" her sister gasped from behind them. "Oh my God."

Lizzy tore herself free from Ty, glancing over her shoulder. There stood Elisa, teetering to stay upright, accompanied by *several* of their friends.

"I—"

"Don't le' ush interrupt you!" Elisa released a giggle, followed by a hiccup.

Good grief, she was in an alley, in the snow, kissing a lying, betraying cowboy stripper in bare-ass chaps, and *she'd been caught.*

two

*G*et off me!" Lizzy wrenched away, thrusting two fists into his chest. Caught off guard by her sudden change in mood, Ty teetered backward and looked over her to find several giggling women disappearing into the club with a slam of the emergency exit door.

So *that's* why she'd ended their kiss. Punched him, the little hellcat.

Devoid of the warmth she'd just wrapped him in, Ty's shoulders gave a jerk, a shiver wracking his body. His ass was freezing and his poor cock wasn't doing much better.

But cold or not, he wasn't about to throw in the towel now. Forget going inside—she could make him plenty hot with her mouth. They were nowhere near done with their kiss. Her burgundy lipstick—which he was surely now wearing as well—tasted of berries, so sweet, just like he knew she was.

And he wanted more. A lot more.

Lizzy glanced around like she was looking for a hole to hide in. "I better get back to the party."

Forcing his teeth not to chatter, Ty caught her hands and threaded her fingers in his. "Don't, Elizab—I mean, Lizzy."

Peering at him through narrowed violet eyes, she released an exasperated sigh as if he just didn't get it.

And she was right—he sure as hell didn't.

"I have to." Her words were whispered, meek almost, but her actions strong. She yanked her hands free and crossed her arms. "You have no right to be here."

"I didn't hire myself. Just following the money."

Heat blasted his face like he'd just been shot with a flamethrower. *Why* had he said that?

He might know how to score cash in his underwear, but he wasn't proud of his career. If it weren't for getting arrested and landing in juvy—

Fuck. If only he'd used his brain as a kid, instead of his dick.

Turning her back to him, she gazed up at the dark sky. "Well, Ty, go back to work." Her enough-said tone reached out and slapped him across the face. "I'm paying enough."

"Now? After I've found you? Not on my life."

A funny noise escaped her. "Kissing you was a mistake, Ty. A huge one. Now get lost."

Unable to stand even the few feet between them, he closed the distance and took her shoulder in hand. "What's your problem with me? You act like I killed your best friend."

He forced her to face him and was almost sorry he did. She stared him dead in the eye, her violet gaze as hard as amethyst. Unforgiving.

"You *did*, remember? You made me trust you. Made me believe everything would be okay. I gave you my virginity, my heart. You swore you'd take care of me. Instead, you dragged me off to L.A. and abandoned me without so much as a good-bye." Her words hitched in her throat as she unsuccessfully swallowed a sob. Mascara streaked down her face. "What I don't get is why pretend? Why the whole facade? You could have left me in Tennessee. You didn't need to make the promises you did, you . . ."

Didn't need to? That wasn't the way he remembered it.

He cupped her cheek, wiping away the black smudges, halting her rant.

Elizabeth isn't home."

Mrs. Richard's hand grasped the door, her knuckles white, her lie not.

Ty groaned in disgust. He'd heard Joe's tirade, the crash of dishes. And he was tired of it, sick to death of hearing his best friend put up with her stepfather's temper. With such a life.

Not home? Ty had seen Elizabeth through her kitchen window just ten minutes prior. She'd smiled at him, had mouthed an invite to meet that night, and he'd held up ten fingers for ten minutes before ducking under the hood to finish replacing the dry-rotted hose in the engine of his Trans Am.

"I need to see her," Ty demanded. "Damn it!"

Knowing better than to wait for the welcome mat to roll out, Ty pushed past Mrs. Richard and bolted up the creaky stairs.

"Tyler Black!" she protested, but Ty knew she wouldn't follow, wouldn't do much of anything but stand there, helpless. Elizabeth's mother never had the heart, the courage, to do anything but cower. "Ty, please!"

He ignored her protest, running down the hall of peeling wallpaper, and burst into Elizabeth's room. "Elizabeth?"

Her back to him, she sat on the edge of the bed. Her long, golden brown hair cloaked her shaking shoulders. She looked so small, so helpless, and he felt sick.

"Elizabeth?"

"Ty, are you crazy?" Standing, she glanced over her shoulder. He barely caught a glimpse of her spilt cheek, her swelling eye. But it was enough. Enough to make him want to kill. "Joe's drinking again. Get out of here," she hissed in warning. Her gaze flashed to the door and back to him, nervous.

The sight struck him so hard he could barely restrain himself. His jaw ticked, every muscle tensed. Adrenaline flooded through him, red-hot, blinding, gripping.

No! No goddamn more! At the hands of that jobless piece-of-shit alcoholic, he'd seen and heard Elizabeth deal with more than any fourteen-year-old should. Than anyone should.

And this time, this time *he wasn't going to shut up about it. Wasn't going to let it slide.*

"No, Elizabeth. I won't go. Not again, not ever again." He was done. Finished with Joe Richard, finished with his own fighting parents, finished with Shot Creek, Tennessee. He might only be seventeen, but he was man enough to put an end to all this. "Get your shit. Now!*"*

If he took her over to his house, the law would only take her home. Social Services might even take her away. The way Ty saw it, he had two choices: go get his pop's rifle and shoot the bastard guzzling beers out back or steal her away from here. Forever.

He bounded across the small room, grabbing her book bag from the corner and dumping out the contents. Papers scattered across the old rug, books plunked in a pile.

She crossed her arms, hugging her chest. Her body swayed in indecision. Insecurity. "Ty, what . . ."

21

"Pack the bag, Elizabeth. Please." He softened his request, guiding her by the shoulders. *"Trust me."*

"You're only going to cause trouble, Ty." She hiccupped. *"Just leave things be."*

"I'm done leaving things be." He stared into her eyes. *"I promise, Elizabeth, it'll be okay. I'll be eighteen real soon and I've got plenty saved up. I'll take care of you, I swear I will. Just trust me."*

And she had, right up until he'd let her down. "I never left you, Lizzy. Never. I was arrested for stealing—"

"You stupid fucker. I told you to quit taking so many risks."

"I know," he whispered, hating himself for the dumb decision long since made. "For what it's worth, I'm sorry. And I did come back for you, but you were gone."

All he wanted to do was kiss the too-dark lipstick off her lips, kiss her until they couldn't breathe, until he consumed her. He'd heard that absence made the heart grow fonder, but *fonder* couldn't begin to describe his hunger. All he could think about was throwing Lizzy down and fucking her until the detachment between them disappeared.

"From thief to stripper. I'm so impressed." She lifted her chin, blew out a harsh breath, and stepped back. "I can't have this conversation anymore. Get out of my way."

He refused to budge. "Why?"

"What?"

"*Why*, damn it? How can you kiss me like that, then act like I don't matter?"

"You don't." Sidestepping him, she stalked toward the door.

"Bullshit. You want me," he told her.

Lizzy stopped in her tracks, turning back.

Ty held out his hand, praying she would take it. "You need me."

The cocky asshole. Need? What she *needed* was to go home and break out her latest shipment of sex toys and forget all about him.

Not that the dildos had erased his memory. Not yet anyway, but she was still hopeful.

Lizzy trembled like she was freezing to death, her body quaking with the truth, though she was actually hotter than hell. She did want Ty . . . and that was a huge problem. All these years she'd spent making herself strong, putting up walls—they'd been a joke. Here, now, in the face of jeopardy, she was melting, turning to water at his words and evaporating at his touch.

She had to drive him away.

How better to do that than nasty honesty?

"Need you?" Her words were bitter, sharp, and cutting. "I have better luck with my dildos."

His dark eyes jumped in disbelief, his upper lip curling. "What is that supposed to mean?"

"You heard me. You didn't *do* it for me. I'll take a vibrator over you any day. At least I'd come."

There, let him take that. She had to push him away, even though she knew what she was saying was wrong. In reality, she couldn't blame Ty for his ineffectiveness. He hadn't had much of a chance, not compared to the practice her vibrator got. Ty had taken her virginity, and they'd had inept sex a couple of times after that. They'd been clueless, too young. But they were adults now, which made him all the more hazardous to her heart and body.

Better to drive him off before the pain got any worse, not that this moment felt particularly good.

"What are you talking about?"

Geez, take a hint already! What, did she have a sign on her back or something tonight?

At this point, taking Jayson up on his offer was looking mighty pleasant.

"I mean I never had an orgasm while I was with you," she said coldly, wiping at her cheeks and under her eyes, trying to make herself presentable. "Guess the sex just wasn't as hot for me as you thought it was."

"Bullshit."

"Oh, it's true." She let her insult sink in for effect. "You were too awkward. Clumsy. Damn fast. So, I'd say I'll see you around, but truthfully, I hope I don't."

She started her escape toward the emergency door.

"Wait a minute. You aren't getting away that easily."

Lizzy commanded herself to keep walking, but she couldn't let his comment go. "I'm not?"

"Nope." He quickly closed the distance between them. "First of all, I know you're just lying to get rid of me—"

How much more of this could she take? Why wouldn't he give up? She spun to face him, poking him in the chest. "I'm not. I didn't have an orgasm until I was twenty-two and that was at my own hand."

Uneasy silence fell between them. Reality settled in.

At least, for her.

"Regardless, you want me," he said slowly, determinedly. "You feel exactly what I feel, and if you think I'm going to let you disappear from my life again, you're crazy."

"That I am. Certifiable." This time, she was going back to the party and she wasn't stopping for a million bucks. "See ya."

That was *it*.

Possessed, Ty pursued her. He might be a lot of things, but he wasn't bad in bed and he wasn't a quitter.

Elizabeth—*Lizzy*, he corrected himself—was about to find out both.

After all this time, after all the sleepless nights, the goddamn agony of losing her, he intended to say his piece.

To kiss her. To make love to her.

He didn't care how much she protested. She was *his*, his alone, and he had to make her realize it.

She clearly desired him. He could read her like a book—Elizabeth or Lizzy, she still had feelings for him. And he was going to prove it. Prove himself.

Encircling her waist, he hefted her body against his. "You aren't going anywhere, *Elizabeth Victoria*. You're *coming* with me."

"Like hell," she protested, struggling against him. "And it's Lizzy, damn it!"

She landed one helluva kick against his knee. Pain shot up his leg, but he refused to falter. In one quick movement, he whirled her around, bent down, and tossed her over his shoulder.

Lizzy—a name he agreed was much more suitable to the wild woman she'd grown into—screamed in protest, slamming into his back with her fists and squirming with all her might, but he held fast.

Gripping her calves, he stalked in the direction of his car, which luckily he'd parked in the back, as did all the strippers, so the ladies wouldn't see them entering. He always left a spare key under the driver's seat for emergencies, and tonight was the first time he'd have to make use of it. To hell with his job, to hell with the consequences. Lizzy wasn't just ending it with him when he hadn't even had a chance to win her back.

She fought him every step of the way, but compared to his size, Lizzy was a half-pint, and he wasn't letting go, no matter how many punches she landed.

He reached his '69 Trans Am and threw open the passenger door. Ducking, he bared his ass to the world and deposited her in the seat. "Try to get out and I'll catch you, so don't even bother."

He slammed the door.

She glared daggers at him, her hand resting on the latch, prepared to flee the moment he stepped away. "This is insanity, Ty!" Her voice was muffled through the glass, but not any less spirited. "You think I'm going to just let you kidnap me?"

Thinking fast, Ty swung the door back open and pinned her down, knocking his cowboy hat off in the process. Swiftly retrieving the authentic, two-hundred-dollar Stetson that he wasn't about to pay for a second time, he plunked it down on her head.

She fumed.

Adorable . . . cute enough to keep.

Ty grabbed the old seat belt—he'd restored the engine and the exterior, but the interior was as crappy as ever—and clicked it in place. The buckle was famous for driving his passengers crazy because of the way it stuck, and he wagered he could get around the car before she could get out. To be certain, he locked the door before he shut it, then raced for the driver's side, fast as he could in the damned chaps.

"You asshole! Ty!" Squealing, she waged war with the belt. "Come on!"

Ty yanked open his door and slid into the seat just as Lizzy got the buckle undone. The seat belt zipped back, releasing his captive.

Without missing a beat, Lizzy lunged for her door, shoving it open. "Fuck off!"

"I don't think so." Ty dove across the seats, catching her upper arm and firmly forcing her back in the seat. "Shut the door. Now."

"No."

"If you don't, I'll drive off with it open. Try me."

With a hateful stare, she yanked the door shut, crossing her arms as he released her. "I know you, Ty. You won't hurt me."

"Of course not." He tenderly brushed a finger across her cheek, removing even more of the smeared makeup. Emotion jolted through him. She was hurting, *needing*, and it was up to him to make it right. *Finally*. "But I am going to make you climax until you scream. Isn't that what you want? Now buckle up."

When she didn't move to obey him, he reached across the seat and snapped the belt into place. His face an inch from hers, he smiled. "Ready?"

Behaving like a vicious cat, she snapped at him with her teeth. He snarled back and then settled in his seat. Retrieving the key, he started the engine.

It appeared he was in for one *wild* night.

three

His hat smelled, and she recognized the thick, piquant cologne in an instant. Old Spice. The fragrance had been his signature since his voice had changed, when he'd started "borrowing" his daddy's deodorant. Oh, he'd really thought he was something.

Apparently, he still did.

Ty'd changed in so many other ways, Lizzy thought he would've switched his scent by now. Instead, it seemed he'd only opted to apply it more liberally.

No way could Lizzy wear the hat. The smell was making her mind spin. Taking it off, she placed it back on its rightful place—his head. "So drive, cowboy."

She couldn't believe she'd just said that. Her stomach fluttered with excitement as Ty peeled out of the parking lot and sped down the street. Glancing back at her club, she errantly thought of the party that Ty was stealing her away from. Of the friends that had caught her kissing him.

She was almost relieved that she wouldn't have to return. She was humiliated. Mortified. She'd spent years creating her persona, assuring her friends she didn't want a man, yet in one instant, she'd been turned into a total liar. Everyone had seen her weakness, and if she went back, they'd surely notice the mascara steaks running down her face as well. She didn't want anyone—not even her sister—to know she'd been crying.

Clutching her seat belt, she braced her mind. Despite her fury, the emotional pain gripping her, excitement burned at her very soul. It tickled her belly, tingled in her nerves. Thrilled her. She felt wild, possessed; she was Jane, Ty was Tarzan. She was ready to swing from the treetops and scream at the top of her lungs.

If only that wasn't so insane!

She'd accepted long ago that you feel the way you feel, and right now, God help her, she was exhilarated, even looking forward to more sparring with Ty, not to mention oddly curious about what he might do to her, exactly how he intended to carry through with his promise to make her climax until she screamed.

He was wearing an awful lot of her lipstick and she really wanted it back.

Ridiculous! Need she remind herself—she was pissed!

How could she have forgotten that so easily? Damn it, Ty wasn't winning her over. Not her mind, not her body. Not ever.

She glared at him and, looking like a fool, his lips smudged with burgundy, he smiled back. Once again, he took his cowboy hat from his head and planted it on hers. His scent overpowered her—what'd he do, wash his hair with the shit?

She wanted to hate the fragrance, knew that any woman with a sense of taste did, but the cologne mixed with Ty's natural scent was intoxicating. Nothing else would do.

He hung a right onto a dark road leading out of town. "How about some tunes?" he asked nonchalantly, clearly attempting to break the silence. Flicking on the radio, Ty filled the car with the smooth, deep musical tones of Johnny Cash singing "I Won't Back Down." His eyes traced along her upper thigh where her short skirt had hiked up.

Lizzy quickly tugged the traitorous article of clothing down, trying to cover as much of her legs as she could. She opened her mouth to reply with a nasty retort, but nothing came out.

God, what had she gotten herself into? *Firemen!* Never again would she hire a cowboy—lesson learned!

Glancing around the familiar silver interior, she was inundated with memories, reminding her of another time he'd asked that very same question, right here in this same vehicle. *How about some tunes?*

Crud, he said it so innocently, totally concealing his true emotions.

Ty was good at that, hiding his feelings . . . she wasn't and he knew it.

"I can't believe you still have this car." Or that he'd switched from rock to country. What was with that?

And yet, it seemed the radio disc jockey had picked this song just for them. Ty, it seemed, had no intention of backing down.

"It's my baby, Eliz—*Lizzy.* I'd never let it go." He glanced at her, his gaze sharp. Piercing right through her. "Just like you."

Oh God. Her heart skipped faster, her mind went into overdrive, and it was all she could do not to crawl onto his lap and kiss him crazy. To believe his every lie.

Instead, she tossed his hat in the backseat. Good riddance.

What the hell was wrong with her? Lizzy swallowed the knot swelling in her throat and fought back more tears. Why, deep down, did this disaster feel so very good? Why wasn't she chewing him out? Threatening to call the police if he didn't take her back?

She was losing her freaking mind. She had to be.

Ty jacked up the volume and rolled down his window. Wind blew through his short, blond strands as he veered onto another road, heading farther away from Aspen—from safety.

Goose bumps erupted along her arms from both the cold and her increasing fear. The longer he drove, the farther she was from escape.

She had to stop this. Now.

Right?

"Think about what you're doing, Ty," she told him. Reaching down, she again attempted to unbuckle her seat belt, but this time, the damn thing wouldn't come free to save her life. "This is kidnapping."

He glanced at her, desperation evident on his creased forehead and drawn lips. The way he stared at her with his black-as-the-devil eyes, as if devouring her whole. As if he'd never, ever let go. It made her tremble inside.

"I don't care, Lizzy." His foot pressed harder on the pedal, sending a blast of fuel that revved the big engine. "Agree to talk to me and I'll stop."

They shot down the winding road, exceeding the speed limit.

"You mean agree to fall victim to your bullshit? Already did that once, I believe." She looked out the window at the trees whizzing by. Flurries fluttered in the air. "And last I checked, we did talk. I shot you down. End of discussion."

"That wasn't talking, Lizzy, and you know it."

"Blah-blah-blah. We both know what you really want." She gave a final, sharp tug on the seat belt latch and to her relief, the difficult thing came undone. She released the strap, letting it zip into the side panel.

Ty wanted to play hardball? Then she'd play . . . *hard.* If he wouldn't stop the car willingly, she knew exactly how to get his attention. Exactly how she'd force him to stop. Shifting to her knees, she leaned across the console and pressed her breasts against his arm. "You want *this.*"

He held steadfast to the wheel. "What the hell are you doing?"

"You want me all over you, right?" She rubbed against him, making certain he felt her nipples as her breasts mashed into his hard muscle. "Want my tits in your face?"

Because I'd sure like to put them there.

Quick, furious heat rushed to her loins, desire that had no business existing. Her inner muscles constricted and released rapidly, quickening with a surging need to climb onto his lap.

For hell's sake, she was supposed to be arousing *him.*

She'd better hurry up.

Rotating her shoulders, rolling her waist, she pushed her tightening nipples up and down his biceps. Electricity shot through her, careening down her spine.

Curling her toes, Lizzy fought the sensation. All for a good cause . . .

"Sit back before I wreck," he growled. The car jerked in agreement.

"Oh come on, baby, you want it, right?" She pressed against him harder, resolutely ignoring the fact that she was making her pussy gush.

And loving it. Wanting more.

Not to mention that she'd probably kill them both, playing such games.

Her mouth traced over his whiskery cheek and she suckled at his ear, licking along the cartilage, then down his neck, biting, kissing, devouring the salty taste of sweat on his skin.

"Lizzy . . ."

He tasted like man. Like ecstasy. She couldn't stop.

Drawing his flesh between her teeth, she suctioned hard enough to leave a mark. The more she savored him, the more her body responded, the more she got carried away in the moment, in the teasing notion of leaving reality behind. Indulging in pleasure.

"Come on, baby, you know you want it," she purred, telling herself she was only doing it to get out of his car. *Right*. Escape.

But at this point, she couldn't deny herself. She wanted to feel him *there*, to see if that had changed too.

What the hell—if that didn't get him to stop, nothing would.

Going after the bulge between his legs, she massaged his cock roughly. Ty was rock hard for her . . . and impressively large. No longer a boy.

"Ty, come on, give it to me, baby . . ." She found herself pleading, and this time, it was no ruse.

Suddenly he jerked the wheel, slamming on the brakes as he veered off the road and into the grass. The car lurched to a stop and the violent movement threw her off him.

With a cry, Lizzy fell into her seat.

She braced herself against the door, jarred back into reality. She couldn't lose herself like that again—all the more reason to *go*, as quickly as she could.

"You *are* damn crazy." Ty threw the car into park and cut the engine, turning to her.

She'd warned him, hadn't she?

His lips curled in a snarl, his forehead creased in anger. "You shouldn't have done that."

He was right—her body was raging with an almost uncontrollable, painful need to fill herself with him. But at least she'd achieved her goal.

Despite her arousal, Lizzy grappled for the door handle. This was her chance. If she was going to escape, she had to do it now. "Come on!" she cried out, more to herself than him.

His hand caught her shoulder and thrust her flush against the seat. "Don't you even think about it."

"No?" She wriggled lower, freeing herself. "What are you going to do to stop me?"

"What am I going to do?" To her shock, he dove across the console, climbing on top of her. His body smashed against hers as he pulled the lever, making her seat collapse. Pinning her, he held her arms above her head, forcing her nipples to press into his bare chest. "Finish what you started. Here. Now. No more talk. No more being reasonable."

"Reasonable? Ha!" She struggled with him, knowing good and well it was completely useless. "You're kidnapping me."

"Damn it, woman!" Reaching down, he loosened the fastenings of his chaps, yanking them away, then freed his cock from the pouch. Lifting her skirt, he pressed his thick, long cock to her cunt. The tiny scrap of underwear she wore barely protected her pussy.

"Feel that?" he asked, grinding against her.

Her whole world quaked, her resistance threatening to split in two. She looked away. "Get off me."

"No." Again he stroked his erection along her moist slit.

Lizzy rammed her lower half against his in an effort to buck him off her. Instead, her action caused their bodies to crash together. The tip of his cock pressed between her folds and nudged her clit through her panties, making the already swollen flesh pulse. An immediate, hot reaction stormed through her.

She couldn't take much more.

Correction—she could take a lot more—of him inside her. And that was the problem. "Please, Ty," she begged.

But for what?

His grasp on her wrists loosened slightly, but not enough. "We can fuck here and now, or you can agree to chill out and talk to me."

Lizzy sucked in a sharp breath. Neither choice seemed plausible to her. "Or you can take me back to the club."

"Not an option," he growled, tilting her head and nipping tenderly at her neck.

"Why?" she whimpered, lust stampeding her will. Why couldn't she control her raging emotions . . . her physical feelings? Why was her mind so very weak in the face of her desire?

Her need heightened with every loving bite. She clenched her pussy against his tempting invasion and fought for some measure of reason that just wouldn't come.

"I have some things to say to you that *will* be said. After that, fine, I'll return you to the club if that's what you want." He claimed her ear, suckling, and the head of his cock nudged aside her panties, touching her directly. Heat on heat. So close.

Oh damn . . .

Why did he have to have such a magic mouth? Such a long-ass cock?

Why did she have to want him—*this*—so badly?

"What I want is to go back to my party. *Now.*" She didn't even believe herself. Lord knew he wouldn't.

"No." He took her nerve-infused lobe and sucked hard. Tingles shot through her and her scalp prickled. "So I guess we'll just fuck."

His mouth grabbed hers, seizing her in a bruising kiss, his tongue sweeping deep. Pumping his hips, he humped her pussy lips with his cock, making her body sing. The ache in her womb expanded into a full-blown crater, an emptiness only he could fill.

"God, baby," he murmured. His torturous mouth possessed hers, drawing on her tongue as he slid his cock along her labia, creating sensuous friction. His palm pressed the side of her breast and he shifted so that he could pinch her nipple between his fingers. Tweaking the bud, he pulled on it through the thin fabric of her blouse.

Despite all her resistance, a moan poured from her.

She could so easily give in. Hell, she reasoned to herself, maybe it was better to let him fuck her than it was to talk with him. She didn't want to hear what he had to say, didn't want him to touch her heart any more than he already had.

But in the face of such danger, the risk was too great. She couldn't allow this to continue.

With every second he kissed her, every second she was forced to endure his cock rubbing along her cunt, she was losing ground. At least she could stay aloof in a discussion. Stay away from him. This . . . this was too much!

Lizzy ripped her mouth free, turning her head to the side, panting. "Fine," she exhaled on a shaky breath. "We'll go to my apartment, we'll talk, and then we're finished. For good."

But deep down, she knew it would never be over between them. She'd never forget. Forgive.

"Good girl." Ty smiled, stroking her cheek. His tongue darted out, running over his lips, tasting the raspberry-flavored lipstick she'd left behind.

"Don't delude yourself into thinking anything else will happen."

"What do you mean? Anything like this?" His lower half gyrated against hers, and his cock pressed an inch into her. Tears of furious need flooded her eyes. How easy it would be to welcome him completely inside her body. To deny her anger . . . his betrayal . . . and fuck until nothing else existed.

"Yes." Hard as it was, she angled away from him.

"Oh, too bad." He slid off her and back into his seat, returning his cock to its pouch and tightening the fastenings of his chaps. "But I think you'll change your mind."

"I won't."

To her annoyance, he laughed. With his hand, he wiped his mouth clean and winked at her.

"We'll see." He started the engine, putting on his seat belt. "We'll see . . ."

She crossed her arms, glaring out the window at the dark, ominous night surrounding them. Cutting her off from the real world, trapping her with him. "Just turn the fucking car around and drive."

four

"What's your poison?" Lizzy ducked behind a small bar that stood in the corner of her living room, rummaging. The clink of glasses and the click of a cabinet echoed in the quiet apartment. A moment later, she stood, bringing with her a bottle that rightfully should've had a skull and crossbones on it. "You name it, I have it."

It was the first thing she'd said since giving him directions to her apartment. On the fifteen-minute trip here, they'd driven in silence. She'd led him inside as if he had a gun to her back.

All Ty could do was stare. She was so damn cold, yet so fiery.

He watched her pour a generous amount of vodka into a small glass filled with ice cubes.

Her hands shook. She refused to look him in the eye.

"Don't get drunk on my account," he warned her.

Of course, she didn't pay him an ounce of attention.

"Here's to that cowboy outfit." She slammed back the drink,

clanking the empty glass on the bar. "If it weren't for your tight, exposed ass, I might not have been so easily persuaded."

She whistled.

So that was how she wanted to play? Fine. More than fine.

Spotting a candy dish, Ty crossed the room, his stride deliberately meant to draw attention. He might have his pride, but he had no qualms about using his bare butt if it would continue to *persuade* her.

Besides, he took pleasure in the thought of *her* checking him out. He was used to having female eyes devour the sight of him—a lot of woman paid for the privilege—but with Lizzy, it was a whole new feeling. Different. Not about money, not about lust, despite what she might claim.

Lizzy desired him—*him*, not just his body. And God, after all these years, that felt good.

With steadier hands, she refilled her glass. "Do you want something or not?"

That he did.

Bending slowly, Ty brandished his bare butt in her direction and plucked a cinnamon candy from the crystal dish on the coffee table. Then he stood, posing just so.

Peeling away the red wrapper, he popped the candy in his mouth, savoring the spicy-sweet flavor.

"I'm a real sucker for hard candy." He rolled the ball to the pocket of his cheek. "Cinnamon is okay, but I for one love cherry."

"Ty," Lizzy gritted out impatiently.

Ty nonchalantly pretended as if all was normal, continuing to wander about, soaking in all the details of her living room, but all the while purposely waving his ass like a red flag in order to drive her crazy.

She had a decent place, comfortable, well decorated. Oddly though, it didn't reflect her current appearance in the least. There were pictures of sunsets on the wall, lacy throw pillows, even a vase of flowers. It was tidy, smelled nice, like potpourri.

He'd expected something loud, tacky. But her apartment reminded him of the Elizabeth he used to know—sweet, soft, and feminine.

And here he was, half nude and definitely being crude.

His face flamed at the thought and he glanced at her, seeing the frustration creasing her forehead. The heartache in her violet eyes.

What was he thinking?

Enough was enough. This wasn't right.

Lord knew he could be arrogant when the occasion called for it, but had he no shame? Want Lizzy he might, want her to want him he might, but this was no time for sexual games.

He crunched down on the candy, breaking it into tiny pieces. Deciding there was a draft in the room, he took a seat on the oversized cream-colored couch and hid his exposed rear.

"Don't you dare fart," she warned him wryly.

He chose to ignore her vulgar comment. They were quite the pair, the two of them.

"I'd love a cold beer," he told her, lifting a picture frame from the end table and examining the photograph in it.

Interesting. Still young, a beach in the background, Lizzy stood with her arms wrapped around a youthful version of the woman from the party.

He couldn't resist touching the glass, his fingers lingering over her beautiful golden brown hair, wondering at the girl he'd once loved.

What in almighty had happened to her?

"Is this the bride-to-be?" he asked. "A good friend of yours? From L.A.?"

"My sister. Elisa."

Her *what*? That didn't make a lick of sense.

He'd known Lizzy and her family since elementary school, when they'd moved next door. To his knowledge, Lizzy was an only child, and thank God for that. It should be illegal for people like her parents to have kids.

Before he had a chance to question her, she disappeared from the room. Impatient, Ty returned the picture to the well-polished table and folded his hands between his knees, listening to the sound of the refrigerator open and slam shut.

A moment later, she returned with his cold beer, twisting the cap off the bottle. The alcoholic drink fizzed in the air. "Hope you like Honey Brown."

One of his favorites, but it wasn't the beer he was interested in. Just having her close to him.

When she went to hand him the bottle, he grabbed her wrist, urging her down. "Sit next to me, darlin'."

Lizzy wrinkled her nose, but didn't resist.

Taking the beer from her, Ty wrapped his arm around her shoulders and held her close. Inhaling, he drew in her sweet, fruity scent and relished the feel of her in his arms, so close, after being so far apart for so long. She was so soft and warm, so wonderfully Elizabeth.

And yet, not.

Taking a long swig of the honey-flavored beer, he twisted a finger in her crazy-colored hair, exploring its texture, the way it curled. "I don't remember you having a sister."

She was quiet a moment. "Long story, but her father adopted me." There was something in her voice, something that said there was so much more to it. "You know, after you dumped me on the streets."

Her words were a knife in his chest, killing him with the pain of it all. He hated that it had to be this way, hated that he'd let her down. But he needed her to know, if anything, he hadn't left her on purpose.

"Lizzy, I didn't *dump* you." His hands slid through her frizzy hair, framing her head, tilting it back so he could stare deeply into her eyes. Show her he wasn't lying. "I swear it."

"Oh, right. Whatever." She flipped off, brushing the topic aside. Pulling free, she sat up and twisted around, drawing her knees to her chest. "My *dad* is Lance Cross."

Wow. He didn't have to watch soaps to know the name. Ty let out a low whistle. "Made out, didn't you?"

Saying nothing, Lizzy shot him a glare, her lips pressed together in disgust. You'd think he had a forked tongue.

Ty set the half-empty bottle on the end table. He just couldn't seem to get this conversation right to save his life.

The answers he craved, the reconciliation he needed, weren't coming fast enough. Common sense told him he was pushing for too much, but he couldn't stand this, the awkwardness between them, the distance.

Leaning forward, he let his hands dangle between his legs. "And your real parents?"

He wondered if she'd ever gone home, ever confronted them. He sure hadn't had the balls to, not after running off with her like he had, then getting into trouble.

"What do I care?" She rubbed at her right eye, blinking rapidly. "My contacts are driving me crazy."

Pulling down her lower lid, she wiped the inside rim of her eye with the side of her finger and smoothed the contact from her eye. She held the violet-tinted lens atop her fingertip. "Excuse me a moment."

He'd rather not . . . he was afraid she wouldn't come back at this point.

Stopping her, Ty cupped the side of her face, turning her head so he could gaze into her sole blue eye. It was pooled with moisture, slightly tinted red. From the contacts? Or had she been about to cry?

He stared into the depths of her single baby blue, seeing truth. Seeing *pain*.

And hating himself for it.

The light purple coloring of her other eye masked so much feeling, so much of who he remembered her to be.

Ty gently wiped a tear from her cheek. "Don't put it back in," he begged her. "Take the other one out."

He'd never get used to seeing her like this, with pink hair and violet eyes. It wasn't normal, wasn't Elizabeth. And he didn't understand.

Not any more than she understood him. That was gone between them, destroyed.

"Well then, if I did that, your sweet ass would be a blur." Obviously blowing off her feelings—and his—she grinned at him sarcastically. "And I wouldn't be able to follow your beautiful lips as you spew excuses."

So she wanted to play word games?

He ran his tongue over his lower lip slowly and lifted a brow. "So, my lips are beautiful?"

This time, her smile was genuine. "And your ass is sweet."

"Sweet? So you want a taste?"

Jerk!" Lizzy wrinkled her nose in distaste. "You're a real pig, Ty."

But inside she was chuckling, almost giddy with amusement that wouldn't be suppressed.

Ty did that to her. Always had, ever since they were kids. He had this magical way of taking her words and twisting them into the corniest, sometimes grossest things. Of making her laugh even when she was mad or sad or both.

And damn him, he didn't deserve a smile from her!

But the thought only amused her further.

Resisting the urge to grin like a clown, Lizzy balanced the contact on the tip of her finger. "I'll be right back," she barely managed to say, jumping up.

Refusing to let him see he'd gotten the best of her, she rushed from the living room, down the hall, and into the bathroom, quickly shutting the door behind her.

Leaning against the safety of the solid wood, she took several deep breaths, but they did little to help. Suddenly she was laughing and crying at the same time. Losing it.

What was she going to do?

She was such a liar, so full of shit. Tough? Independent? A hater of men? What a joke!

She should have followed in her adopted dad's footsteps and become an actor, because she was damn good at pretending to be someone she wasn't.

Geez, this was bad . . . or maybe it was good. How the hell did she know?

Okay, okay . . . deep breaths, she told herself. She really had to pull it together and fast. Hiccupping, she swallowed her opposing emotions and forced herself to breathe, to steady her shaky shoulders.

Ty had something to tell her, something that would no doubt ease the pain of his disappearance.

She wasn't sure how she should feel about that . . .

But she knew how she *did* feel—shamelessly excited. Hopeful.

Horny.

Damn the bastard and those ridiculous chaps.

Going to the sink, Lizzy leaned forward and stared into the mirror. Oh God! Her lipstick was smeared, her black mascara and eyeliner smudged all over her cheeks.

She couldn't believe he'd seen her like this!

She placed her one contact in some solution. Pumping a dab of makeup remover in her hand, she turned on the water and washed her face clean, then dried it with the hand towel.

But even clean, she still looked like shit.

Heat flooded her face and she battled the urge to look away, ashamed. Not only were her eyes bloodshot, but suddenly, her hair, her outfit, looked terrible. *She* looked terrible.

And she hardly had the time for redoing her makeup.

Standing back, Lizzy gave a little tug on her skirt. If only she'd worn her little black dress tonight, something less stand out.

She didn't know exactly why she did it, but she leaned over the sink, and rather than replace the renegade contact, she removed the other one. Truth was, she could see fine. They were just for show.

Methodically, she placed the lens in the container and covered it in solution, then looked at the door. Ty was waiting for her.

Maybe she'd forgive him, maybe she'd kick him out, but somehow, she knew nothing would ever be the same from here on out. She would never be the same.

Okay, you got your wish, cowboy." Lizzy floated into the room, returning to the bar for another drink. "So spill it. I want to hear your so-called reasons."

Immediately, he noticed she'd cleaned away the ugly black makeup smeared on her face, revealing fresh, creamy skin. The natural rose coloring of her heart-shaped lips.

Pouring, she let the glass of liquid courage sit on the counter. Her eyes lifted, revealing beautiful pools of sapphire.

Ty practically fell head over heels. Oh God. *Elizabeth.*

Their gaze locked, their souls united.

Even if he'd wanted to, Ty couldn't look away. She was so beautiful, suddenly less formidable. Every bit the girl he remembered, that he'd fallen in love with, except, a woman now.

He just wanted to hold her, to squeeze her in his arms and never, ever let his Elizabeth go.

Lizzy, not Elizabeth, he reminded himself. She wanted to be called Lizzy.

Pushing on the arm of the couch, he started to rise, to go to her, but then thought twice. He couldn't. She'd seen enough of his hairy butt for one evening, and he didn't want to ruin the moment by reminding her that he was a stripper. Of everything wrong between them.

He couldn't take being pushed away again.

Ty settled back in his seat, determined to get the conversation right this time.

"Lizzy, I loved you." He couldn't think of a better place to start. "I wanted to marry you."

Her steady, almost quizzical gaze revealed no emotion. No surprise, no joy. No forgiveness. Just questions—that deserved honest answers.

"I had it in my head to get you a ring," he continued. "A nice one, worthy of being on your finger. But I couldn't have afforded a diamond if I worked three years. Let's face it, for all our big dreams, we were stuck on those streets. It would've taken a miracle for us to have made it. I just kept thinking how badly I wanted you to know how much I loved you, how I was going to do my best by you, even though things weren't great at the moment."

"Living in an abandoned building surrounded by crack heads rarely is." Her jaw twitched. The glass met her lips ever so slightly and she tasted the liquor, as if tempted, but hesitant. "So you wanted a ring and you stole one."

"Tried to. It was my only means." Turning his arm over, Ty pointed out a scar on the inside of his biceps. Years of growth and working out had stretched it, making it appear long, thin. "Got shot, arrested, and spent some time in juvy."

Lizzy swore under her breath and he couldn't help but concur—it was total *bullshit*. He'd screwed up in a bad way, had destroyed everything with one stupid decision.

And there was no wiping the slate clean, not with her, not with his parents. Not even with himself.

But he was sorry—he'd loved her, still did—and he wanted desperately for her to know that. Her forgiveness could change his whole existence.

"All I could think about was you." He put his arm down, his eyes never once wavering from hers. "If you were okay, how angry you'd be. When I got out, I looked all over for you, but you were gone. Dust on the wind."

She practically dropped her vodka on the bar, the clear liquid sloshing over the brim.

"Ty . . ." She released an exasperated breath. Her every facial expression, every movement screamed *why*? Spoke of pain he knew nothing of.

Jesus. The truth behind his story clearly wasn't good enough for her—it wasn't good enough for him. Didn't make anything right again.

And then there were his lingering questions, still unanswered, and maybe they always would be. He didn't know just what his stupid mistake had done to her, didn't know if he wanted to know. Maybe he couldn't take it.

What else was there to say?

Her lips pursed, Lizzy walked around the bar to the sofa. Quietly, she sat down next him, her arms crossed as she stared into space.

"I wouldn't have taken the ring," she said finally.

"What?"

Biting her lower lip, she glanced at him unapologetically. "I would have married you, but I wouldn't have taken the ring. It wouldn't have meant that much to me. *You* did." Anger flickered in her eyes. "And I lost you."

"I was a real idiot." Hell, he was still an idiot. He was sitting on the love of his life's couch in bare-ass chaps and he had *nothing*. All the dancing, the stripping, even college and the future he so deeply wanted—what was it really worth?

If he didn't have her . . .

"Lizzy." Ty touched her shoulder, trying to pull her rigid body close. "I'm here now. Can't we—"

She didn't budge, certainly didn't fall in his arms. Her muscles were so tense; she was so aloof.

He couldn't win, and something in him seemed to accept that as fact. It was no one's fault but his own, but still, he rebelled against the truth. Stayed determined.

And there was reason to hope, after all . . .

Lizzy certainly seemed to want him, to want his explanations, though at times, she was so damn indifferent, he didn't know her. But then, after all this time, how could he?

Nonetheless, he could smell her desire, the scent of her wafting in the air around him, her arousal from their earlier encounter still lingering.

Ty's heart wrenched. God, how he hated this!

His fingers itched to touch her. He wanted to make love to her, to make her remember him, *them*, how they *should* feel.

He was almost positive she wouldn't let him so much as touch her, didn't see himself waiting for an invitation that wouldn't come. Didn't want to consider the possibility that after all these years, maybe it really was over between them. Maybe there was no going back.

No! Angry she might be, but Lizzy *did* desire him and damn it, he refused to let her deny that. Maybe there was only one way to bridge the gap between them—hard, furious fucking. He'd tried being emotionally sensitive; now it was time to show her how he felt—completely. He *had* to, that, or let her kick him out and lose her all over again. And he thoroughly intended to spend the night in her bed.

Desperate, Ty ambushed her, pushing her back onto the couch and nestling his pouched cock up her skirt, between her legs.

She squealed in surprise, wiggling. "What are you doing?"

He grabbed her thighs, holding her there.

"What I should have done earlier," he growled, feeling like an animal. One who was about to make his territorial claim. Brand her as his mate.

Her heat greeted him, warm and inviting. Cradling her head, he lifted her lips to his, taking them. Possessing them. *Her.*

Lizzy was his. The only thing standing between them and happiness was her hardened heart. If he couldn't soften her with words, he damn well knew of another way to make her melt.

Rough and demanding, his tongue plunged into her mouth. Like a starved woman, Lizzy answered his call. She wanted him too much to fight her desire, too much to push him away.

Their lips tangled and fought, united in such a blaze that it felt like firecrackers were blasting off in her pussy. He tasted of bitter beer and bittersweet memories, of spicy cinnamon candy and even spicier love.

Needing to feel his bare flesh against hers, still needing to assure herself he was no ghost, she slid her hands down his back and over the rough leather strap of his chaps. She grabbed his ass, pressing her fingers into the flesh. Squeezing.

Ty groaned into her mouth, sliding his hand under her shoulder blades. "Where's—" He broke away, lifting her into his arms. "The bedroom?"

She squirmed in his grasp, trying to pull him back down. "No. Fuck me here."

Her body, her heart, didn't have time for this. She wanted him, wanted to *come* . . .

Like never before, her body pulsed with arousal. She was flooded with sensation, drowning in a sea of need, and she didn't know what to do, how to deal with the moisture running down her upper thighs, how to rope and ride her feelings.

She was going crazy, not that she'd ever been sane.

"No, no fucking. No hard and fast." Ty's strides from the room and down the hall were strong and determined.

She squirmed in his embrace, nestling against him as his fingers stroked her arm, slid underneath the limb to fondle her chest.

"I'm gonna do this right," he swore with a flick of her nipple. "I'm going to make you come, make love to you."

The bud responded with a zinging ache, tightening beyond pleasure. "Ty . . ."

Oh good grief. She was tempted to tell him to let her down, to get lost. She felt out of control, scared.

What if her body did something . . . weird? What if she didn't orgasm?

Worse, what if *he* didn't?

That was ridiculous. Lizzy fought the stampede of strange feelings racing through her body and mind. She was twenty-seven years old! It was high time she experienced a climax at the hands of a man.

Didn't she want this?

Of course she did! She couldn't wait to get to the bedroom.

Lizzy's hand roamed over his hard chest, exploring, enjoying the sensations the coarse hairs left on her palm. She was being silly, overly conscientious.

Oh, yeah, some real sex—orgasm included—was long past due.

"You okay?" Pushing open the door, Ty didn't bother with the light, easily navigating through the shadows. With a plop, he deposited her on the bed and began unbuckling his chaps.

"I'm horny. Hurry." Lizzy peeled off her blouse, pulled down her skirt.

Shit. Why had she worn the bra with the chocolate stain? Comfort, great support . . . sure, nothing held up her boobs like this two-year-old underwire, but for God's sake, she looked like shit tonight!

And *why* did she have to dye her hair pink? Never had she longed for her old color more than when he played with her hair. Made her feel like Elizabeth.

But she wasn't—she was Lizzy. And he still wanted her.

With a flick of her wrist, she cast her undergarments across the room, but she still couldn't gather her confidence. She was just thankful for the fact that the lights were off.

But what if he turned them on?

What if she didn't come?

Dear God, her mind was going a million miles an hour and her body had lost its mind, not that *that* made any sense.

"Ty—" She started to protest, to make some sort of excuse, but *what*?

He climbed over her, covering her naked form with his. He pressed her into the mattress, his body hot and hard.

"God, I've waited so long for this." He kissed her tenderly on the forehead, covering her face with little kisses. "My beautiful Elizabeth."

Oh God, how she wanted to be . . .

His cock nudged her cunt lips, wedged between them, throbbing and promising . . . promises it couldn't keep.

Tangling his fingers in her hair—her pink hair, damn it—he suckled and explored her neck with his mouth, moving downward along her body. Over her breasts, her belly, teasing and tantalizing. Driving her crazy.

Her body lifted against him, sang with desire.

Was he going down on her? Yes! *No!*

She grabbed his shoulders, pulling him back up. "Ty, hurry," she pleaded. God, how she wanted him. How she didn't. *"Please."*

He pressed his cock slightly into her, testing. She rammed against him, needing it to be over with. Needing to come.

Taking the not-too-subtle hint, he thrust into her, filling her to the max. A real man, a real lover, and that scared the shit out of her.

It was also the sexiest thing she'd ever felt, his hard, hot body hovering over her, the way his pubic hairs interlaced with hers, the way his breath brushed over her forehead so intimately.

God yes, she wanted this. Wanted to know what it felt like not to be in charge of her climax, to give herself up to him.

Moaning, she moved her hips against him, and he rocked into her, hard and fast.

This was nothing like a dildo. Not even comparable.

Good God, what had she been preaching to her friends all this time?

Pumping into her, increasing his pace, his drive, slamming her into the edge of sanity, his cock so filling, taking her places she'd never been . . .

Wonderful. Orgasmic.

If only . . .

Tears fell down her face, leaving hot trails as she arched higher, searching, hoping, and not finding.

She was reaching to the stars and coming up short. The disappointment was painful. She just couldn't, and she didn't need to fuck for the next hour to know that.

Nevertheless, she rode her cowboy, seeking the release she was compelled to . . .

But not finding it.

She just couldn't take it, not anymore. Not tonight, with him, like this, because deep down, she knew it wasn't him or how she felt about him, it was her. Her body was broken.

With a cry, Lizzy clenched her pussy, faking it. She panted and moaned and put on a good show. She gave up. Better that than the embarrassment.

She could feel Ty radiate, beaming with pride over her nonclimax . . . the jerk!

He drove into her one final time, his cock jerking in rapid succession, filling her with hot cum.

No condom . . .

What had she done?

five

Sunlight streamed through her blinds, creating stripes across her ceiling. Lying in bed, all too close to a gently snoring Ty, Lizzy counted the thin rays. Once, twice, three times. Twenty-three shadowy ribbons that announced the break of dawn—and she *never* woke up before noon. With her job, she usually headed to bed about this time.

No way was she falling back asleep.

No way was she awake.

How could she have slept with Ty? And on the first night he was back in her life? *Why* had she faked her orgasm? If he couldn't get her off, he at least deserved to know it!

God, she was hopeless—totally freaked out.

Lizzy whimpered. Ty's arm was slung across her torso, making her chest lift him with every breath. He was so close she could smell him, Old Spice mingled with sweat from their vigorous sexual encounter. The scent of her arousal on his skin.

She should have made him take a shower.

No. She should have kicked him out!

What in the world had she been thinking? It must have been the vodka. Most definitely. Good grief, she hadn't even remembered to make Ty use protection, and since she had no man in her life, she wasn't on the pill.

Damn it! What now?

Lizzy clutched the blanket like she was holding on for dear life. She couldn't do this, couldn't do *him*.

Yeah, last night had been life-altering, but she couldn't allow this to go any further. Couldn't bring herself to trust him, to trust anyone—even Lizzy Cross.

She'd betrayed herself, put herself in danger in more ways than one. Luckily, she'd had her period last week, so she was fairly certain pregnancy wasn't a possibility, but *what if*? She hadn't been considering the time of month while screwing him.

Life was good—she was trudging along quite nicely, without heartache, thank you. Damn Ty, showing up like he had! She felt like she'd been riding a roller coaster for the last twelve hours—and she *hated* roller coasters. She didn't need this stress, this upset. It would only screw her up.

And even if she really wanted to see him again him—which she didn't—he was a stripper. *A stripper!* She couldn't go out with a stripper.

The sun had risen and that was good enough for her. Ty really, really needed to go.

Taking the quilt in her fist, she threw it over the side of the bed, onto the floor.

"Hey!" Ty mumbled in protest, drawing his knees to his chest. "It's cold!"

"Get up." Lizzy pushed his arm off her and sat on the edge of the mattress, placing her bare feet on the plush carpet. She drew a deep breath, preparing herself. It'd be a fight, getting him out of her bed, but she was winning this one.

"It's too early," Ty grumbled, hiding his head under one of her goose-down pillows. He'd probably drooled all over it.

She sure had drooled all over hers—there was nothing like having a cock pressed to your bare skin to remind you how much you want it. All night long.

"So? I said get up!" She knocked the pillow from his face, pounded the mattress. "I want you out."

"*Out?*" He rose, his eyes narrowed to those of a predator—dark and cunning. Sexy. He moved behind her, placing a hand onto her shoulder and pulling her against him. "No, Lizzy . . ."

His well-muscled chest pressed against her back, his strong arms holding her so that his hardening cock pressed against her hips.

Trailing a finger along her collarbone, he whispered, "Let's not get out of bed today."

She shirked away, trembling inside. "Ty, please."

Lizzy bit her lower lip, tasting blood. It would be easy—too easy. But she refused to allow this to continue. She *couldn't* be with Ty. Last night proved it.

And he wasn't going to want to hear that. She knew him, knew his stubborn ass through and through. No way was he going to leave . . . or leave them be. Especially not if he thought she was dumping him.

"I have to get ready for work. I, uh—I'm not used to this. To sharing. So give me some space, okay?" She tried to sound sweet, sincere, but her entire speech came out sounding froggy. Croaked lies.

"Space." He lingered over the request, not budging, his fingers still dancing over her skin. "You want some space."

"Geez." She shuddered from his touch, tingles cascading from her neck to her pussy. "I want to shower and drink coffee and wake up, without a guy watching. Nothing personal."

"Okay . . . okay, fine." His hand dropped away and he kicked his legs over the bed, sitting. "What about lunch?"

"Lunch?"

He stood, walking around the bed to pick up his clothes. "Do you want to meet for lunch?"

"I usually work through lunch," she answered quickly.

He threw the chaps over his forearm. She had no idea how he was getting home in those.

"Dinner, then." His fingers hooked the hilarious pouch, twirling it on his finger. "And don't think I'll take no for an answer."

He strode into the bathroom buck naked and hard as sin.

Cocky son of a bitch.

After almost fifteen minutes of torturous bullcrapping and sweet nothings, she'd convinced Ty to leave her house without promising to meet him for dinner. She had a feeling she'd need to change her address—hell, her name—to get him to back off.

There was only one thing to do. Call Elisa, who'd hopefully slept it off by now.

Lizzy made a beeline straight to the phone in the kitchen and dialed her number. She listened to it ring—four, five, six times. The damn machine answered.

Lizzy could hardly wait for the beep. "Elisa, it's me. Pick up. PICK UP!"

After several minutes of her pleading and hollering for her sister to answer, the machine hung up on her. Wrapping her fingers in the cord, she hung up and redialed, walking to the pantry.

"Hello? ELISA!" she shouted into the answering machine as she pulled out her favorite, chocolate cherry–flavored coffee. "Pick up!"

Peeling back the plastic lid—she kept it in special Tupperware to seal in the freshness—she inhaled the aroma of the slightly sweet beans, then she set the container on the counter and readied the coffeemaker. "I won't go away," she warned into the machine.

Static and buzzing filled the line, followed by a wail of protest from the telephone. "This better be good," a deep male voice grumbled, clearly half asleep.

Great, Maxim. Elisa's fiancé.

"Hi!" Lizzy put on her best face, or voice rather, trying to sound chipper, like it wasn't seven a.m. and she wasn't frantic. "Can I talk to Elisa please?"

Maxim chuckled. "Uh, no. She's a little hungover. Seems someone threw her quite the bachelorette party."

Oops. "Are you angry?" Ready to break up with Elisa? Get lost once and for all?

Lizzy felt a pang of guilt. *Why* was she wishing heartache on her sister? Maxim wasn't all that bad—most of the time. Back in the day, he'd been quite the womanizer, but Elisa had seemed to tame him. For now, at least.

Lizzy just didn't have much hope for him. For them.

But it was too late now. No way around it, her sister was headed for disaster.

"Angry? Are you kidding?" Maxim answered, his tone double-edged. "Let Elisa have her fun. She came home and rocked my world last night. I'm a *very happy* man this morning."

"Ew. Enough details." Lizzy yawned. The scent of coffee wafted through the air, and she wished it would hurry up brewing. "Are you sure she can't talk?"

She needed her sister, needed her enough that she was about to go buy a foghorn and drive to Elisa's.

This was going to be a rough day.

"I'm sure," Maxim chuckled, then turned serious. "Everything okay?"

"No," she blurted. "I mean, yeah?"

Was she *asking*?

"Something *is* the matter," Maxim said. "Does it have to do with that cowboy you took off with?"

Crap. "Oh, so you heard about that?" Lizzy pressed the lid back on the coffee container, carrying it to the pantry.

"In so many drunken words. Something about you groping his bare ass in the snow? Do tell."

Scalding embarrassment rushed to her face and Lizzy swore under her breath. The coffee slid from her grasp, clattering on the tile.

How many people had Elisa told?

"What was that? Are you sure you're okay, Lizzy?"

"No, I am not okay!" she cried, crumpling to the floor alongside the coffee. "I slept with the son of a bitch! And he thinks he's taking me out to dinner!"

"And that's so terrible because . . ."

"Because I hate men!"

"Thanks."

"Sorry, nothing personal, but I've been hurt enough for one life-time." Lizzy rested her head against the pantry door and moaned.

"Hurt by who?"

"I don't want to get into it."

"You and Elisa, you two have a great dad," Maxim pointed out.

"So?"

"So you don't hate your father and you trust him, right?"

She couldn't believe she was talking with Maxim like this. Lizzy sighed, slow to answer. "Of course."

"So *all* men aren't bad."

"I can't marry my daddy." Her words were sarcastic, bitter. Even more than she hated a betraying man, she hated a correct man. It just didn't sit well with her. Why couldn't they be wrong all of the time?

"So men are just bad when sex is a possibility?"

"I swear, shut up, Maxim." Lizzy twirled her fingers around the phone cord, wrapping the coils tight around her hand.

"I'm sorry. It's just that you sound like this guy from last night really affects you."

Tighter and tighter and tighter . . . "Yeah, he does."

"And it was him who hurt you?" Maxim's voice softened. "Lizzy?"

Her fingers and thumb pulsed, the circulation cut off. "It wasn't his fault. No, it *was*. But not entirely. I don't know. He was young and dumb and we . . . I don't know."

"So you feel strongly about him," Maxim guessed. "You want to forgive him? Give him a shot?"

Lizzy didn't answer. With a flick of her wrist, she began winding in the opposite direction, freeing herself. Any more and she'd need to buy a new kitchen phone.

"Let's make a bet," Maxim suggested. "I'd wager you called Elisa this morning because you knew she'd talk some sense into you. You knew she'd encourage you to see him, to at least try to come to terms with whatever happened between you and this guy."

Lizzy snorted.

"I'd put a grand on it. You on?"

That was a bet she wasn't willing to take.

six

No! NO!

Pumping music, fog, and flashing lights created a blur of confusion as Ty played the crowd, his hips gyrating, his mind a tangled web, for once not wanting to please, having *to.*

Manicured, feminine hands were everywhere. Touching, grabbing, squeezing, their long nails raking his bare skin.

He swore he'd seen her *in the background, staring in shock, disgusted by his dirty dancing.*

"Elizabeth?" Fingers tweaked his bottom abusively as Ty tried to wrench free, only to stumble into yet another vicious woman intent on fondling him. "Elizabeth!"

Where did she go? He had to get away, find her, before she was lost again . . . lost forever.

"ELIZABETH!" Ty wrenched forward only to be yanked back in.

There she was! Right there, inches beyond his reach . . . watching him being watched, touched, by other women.

Then once again, her image faded, receding as hands grabbed at him, groped and held him hostage.

"Let me go! Elizabeth!"

Elizabeth, Elizabeth . . . His cry ricocheted, as if he were surrounded by emptiness. As if the women weren't closing in on him, suffocating him.

Like a trapped animal, twisting and turning, Ty battled a never-ending tunnel of hands and fingers, fingers and hands. Long, sharp nails that sliced into him.

"Elizabeth, come back!"

Frantic, Ty swung around. Where was the stage exit? Where had she gone?

Looking up, mirrors reflected more than he cared to see. Everything Lizzy saw him as. The choice he couldn't make, not for her, not for himself.

Mirrors, mirrors everywhere . . .

This was his punishment. He deserved no less.

In a blur of movement, the mirrors transformed into windows, see-through glass whirring around him. The hands disappeared, replaced by his mother's disapproving eyes, his father's drunken laughter. Their presence echoed around him, closed in on him.

"Elizabeth!" Ty screamed and pounded on the windows. The glass shattered beneath his fists and he ran from the tunnel, only to find himself right back in it again.

But his parents were gone. The mirrors, the windows, the hands, all vanished.

And in the pitch dark, like glowing beacons of judgment, blue eyes. Huge. Disbelieving. Accusing.

Elizabeth!

Elizabeth!" Ty jolted from his sleep. The springs of the cheap hotel mattress protested under the sudden shift, creaking loudly and driving into his back. *Shit.*

Sweat dripped from his face and Ty swiped a palm across his forehead, the dream fading and consciousness spreading through his mind.

Where the hell had that come from?

With a groan, he threw back the moth-eaten blanket and rolled to a sitting position.

So, he had a new nightmare to add to his list of troubles. His own mind had a talent for torture, reminding him of his every concern during the one time he was supposed to be peaceful.

When was the last time he'd slept soundly?

Never. And it didn't matter, because his dream was right. Hands down, his . . . *occupation* . . . was going to be a point of contention with Eliz—*Lizzy*, and he couldn't say he blamed her.

Then again, there wasn't much he could do to accommodate her. He surely didn't intend to allow her to pull away from him over something so petty.

Fast money and easy work, dancing was his means to a worthwhile end. His future.

So what if it involved taking off his clothes?

If that was his only problem, then he ought to feel damn good. At least his nightmares weren't like they used to be. Juvy wasn't a nice place, nor were the memories.

God, sometimes he still couldn't believe that had been him. It had taken years—and a lot of counseling thanks to the direction of his parole officer—to ease the guilt and pain over that time in his life, and he wasn't going back.

But no professional could fix the hole in his heart as far as Lizzy was concerned—but righting things with her could. And he would, starting today.

Having slept in some spare clothes he'd finally remembered were in his trunk—jeans and a T-shirt—he dangled his legs over the edge of the mattress and slid his sock-covered feet into his cowboy boots, not daring to place them on the carpet. This place was filthy.

It was also—quite unfortunately—a half hour outside of Aspen . . . the closest he could afford to the expensive resort city. And man did the price tag show in his room. The stench of cigarettes hung heavy in the air. Burn holes marred the rugs and small table. Rust stained the shower . . . and he wouldn't *dare* take a bath. He just thanked God he hadn't spotted any roaches.

But hell, he'd stayed in worse. Like the place where he'd left Lizzy—a decrepit, abandoned inner-city building that housed both runaways and crack addicts.

Another pang gnawed at his heart.

You'll make it up to her, he promised himself. Somehow . . .

Yeah, maybe he'd give her a free lap dance. That'd do the trick.

Frustrated, Ty wet his dry lips with his tongue, still able to taste Lizzy. At least he'd been able to give her pleasure—it felt good, knowing he'd been the first to take her there, even if he hadn't way back when. But shoot, he'd been a kid. A mighty dumb one.

And boy had he wised up—in the bedroom and out.

Suddenly eager, Ty sprang from the bed. Lizzy might not have agreed to another meeting, but he couldn't wait to see her again. And this time, he was doing it right—without his butt on display.

He'd just call his boss and—

That's when it hit him. His victimology class. GODDAMN IT! He'd missed it! Completely forgotten!

Crap!

Ty swung into empty air, wishing he had the dexterity to kick himself. Mrs. Kingsley was going to chew him up and spit him out, if he didn't take on the task himself. Which he ought to.

Ty inhaled and exhaled, accepting that time couldn't be reversed. Nevertheless, he was so damn pissed at himself, there was only one thing to do . . . only one way to soothe the pounding in his chest.

Snagging his book bag from where it rested bedside, Ty laid it carefully atop the table and unzipped the main section, pulling out his overstuffed binder and tearing a sheet of paper free from his notebook. Then he removed an envelope from the outer pocket.

These actions formed a habit that, along with his travels, had become so frequent, he'd taken to carrying supplies.

And so he did what he always did when he felt guilty about anything.

He paid his dues, so to speak. Bought himself some forgiveness.

Addressing the envelope to his mother, he retrieved fifty bucks from his wallet and folded the paper around it. He didn't dare send a penny less, despite the fact that last night had been a complete bust. Ty refused to cheapen his mother any more than his father already had.

Slowly, he licked the envelope, ritualistically telling himself all the great things Mom could do with the money. Get her hair done. Purchase extra groceries. Maybe buy some decent clothes—he'd never forget the way she'd denied herself nice things when he was younger, because he came first.

At least, he used to. After running off and getting in trouble the way he had, he didn't have the guts to contact his parents except for this little appeasing practice. Much as it pained him, he had to be realistic—they didn't want to hear from him any more than he wanted to face them, especially not as a stripper. Maybe if he had his degree, something to be proud of . . .

And he would, soon, given he made it to his next class tomorrow and there on out.

Which he would, he swore to himself, without a doubt.

His stomach rumbled loudly over his thoughts and he glanced at the digital clock on the end table. Almost one in the afternoon.

Picking up his cell phone, he dialed his boss's private number, hoping she'd be home. He knew she wouldn't be in the office this early—in their business, everything happened after five.

Julia answered on the first ring. "Jayson told me what happened last night."

"Yeah, well, don't worry about it. The woman who paid was an old friend. There won't be any complaints." Not with the orgasm I gave her, he added to himself silently.

"That's not the point, Ty." He could just imagine her steely eyes, her folded arms. She might run an exotic-entertainment company, but Julia was strict as a Catholic schoolteacher. "Fantasies has a standard to uphold, and you know how word can spread. We conduct ourselves professionally—always! You cannot . . ."

Ty barely listened to her ramble. He'd heard the lecture over and over . . . Julia gave a different version of it almost every week for almost any reason. "And whether Mrs. Cross complains or not—"

"Miss," he interrupted, again silently adding to himself, *for now.*

"Ty!"

He couldn't help but laugh. "I'm sorry. It's just I'm so very in love."

He knew she'd soften at that . . . she had to. It was his only chance at keeping his job. Julia might be a tough boss, but she had a heart of gold.

"With *Miss* Cross? You're going to ask for time off, aren't you?"

"Just a little."

"Brad's wife just gave birth—he's your only replacement. I can't lose both my blond-haired cowboys at once."

"I've already covered for him twice." If last night counted . . .

Normally, Ty would welcome the extra funds, but not even money—or guaranteed lack of—took precedence over winning Lizzy back. When it came right down to it, she was *everything*.

"And legally, federal law mandates that he receive up to twelve weeks' family leave time—"

Ty resisted a groan. "He's a stripper for God's sake!"

"Supporting his *family*," Julia stressed.

Ty shook his head at the ridiculousness of it. Brad's wife—also a stripper with Fantasies, at least formerly—had just given birth to twin boys. Call Ty crazy, but he just didn't *get* how a man could plan to raise a family on such a career. Ty refused to consider having kids until he had his real life underway and maybe not even then—*could* he be a good dad?

And what did Lizzy think of babies?

He'd have to find out—but he couldn't do that from Denver. "Please, Julia. I'm begging you."

She sighed despondently. "You aren't coming back anyway, are you?"

"Have to, eventually. I've got more bills than you do hairs on your head, but this I've got to do." Ty's toes crossed in his boots as he ventured, "It's just a week, two maybe, but if you have to fire me, I guess it can't be helped."

Not that he could afford his threat—there wasn't another company in all of Colorado that paid so well. Fantasies was the best.

"No," Julia responded quickly. "You're one of my most asked-for dancers and I'm not losing you to the competition." She sighed a second time. "But I'm going to have to hire someone. Temporarily, at least. Ty—*try to be quick*."

"I promise." Ty hung up before she could change her mind and headed to the shower, wishing he had some flip-flops to protect his feet from the filth. Oh well. He had a date to get ready for.

The sun was disappearing into the horizon, the evening air cool, sprinkled with flurries. Like the rest of the clubbers, Ty stood in line, ID and cash in hand, waiting to get inside Play.

To say Lizzy was being impossible was putting it lightly.

So much for their date. He never should have left her house this morning. He should have stayed, made love to her again.

Instead, he'd been reduced to the status of a paying customer just for the privilege of seeing her. It seemed there was no other way he was going to get inside, *if* the bouncers even let him past the red velvet rope. Damn it, they'd better.

Just as she'd claimed, Lizzy had worked through lunch. Then dinner. In fact, she hadn't left her club all day, nor had Ty been allowed inside. He'd knocked at the front door, on the delivery door, telephoned. She'd given strict instructions—if he came around or called, tell him to get lost again, and this time, *forever*.

Why? Ty didn't buy it. She'd been pushing him away and pulling him close, running hot then cold, since they'd set eyes on each other yesterday, and how could he give up on her after only twenty-four hours of mixed signals?

If he didn't know better, he'd think she was playing hard to get.

A couple of girls behind him giggled and pinched his butt.

Ty jumped in surprise. No matter how many times it happened, he never expected it. He sure didn't appreciate it . . . he wasn't some piece of meat for their groping pleasure.

Turning his head, he cast them a narrowed look. "Do you mind?"

"Not at all," the blonde giggled, while the other female whispered in her ear.

Damn kids. Probably nineteen years old with a fake ID. Certainly immature, and with all their damn cackling, their sobriety was indeed questionable.

One thing was for certain—the challenge Lizzy was making herself was at the least refreshing. After years of dancing, women that threw themselves at him—or took butt-pinching liberties—had become a turnoff to the tenth degree.

Ignoring the continued laughter behind him, he impatiently moved up in line. Just a couple more minutes and he'd be inside and seeking Lizzy out.

After he'd finally realized he wasn't getting in any other way, he'd hit up Wal-Mart for some clothes—clothes that would make him resemble a club employee . . . black jeans and a neon green shirt hidden under a jean jacket he'd remove when he got in.

Of course, his T-shirt didn't boast the club's emblem, nor did he have a badge to wrap around his neck, but he was confident he'd blend in enough that the cooking staff wouldn't question him.

If he remembered correctly from the strip gig, there was a set of stairs near the storage room behind the kitchen. His guess, they led to the second floor, where Lizzy's office most likely was.

A few more minutes passed, the line moved forward, and the bouncers let him slip by without quarrel.

He pushed his way through glass doors into the dark, crowded interior. Colors flashed everywhere, his eardrums echoed.

Ty set his eyes on the kitchen entrance, managing his way through sweaty, gyrating, half-clothed bodies. Hands seemed to come at him from all directions, swinging, groping. He should be used to it, hell, most men would like it, but he couldn't move off the dance floor fast enough.

As he walked, Ty peeled off his jacket and crumbled it in a ball. Not sure what else to do with it, he tossed it in a dark corner, out of sight. With any luck, it would still be there when he returned, but if not, hell, it'd only cost twenty bucks.

And Lizzy was worth every penny he made.

Ty stood as close to the kitchen door as possible without drawing attention and waited for an opportunity. When no other employees were in sight, and the two bartenders turned their backs, he rushed through the swinging doors, his strides quick and confident.

He hurried past rows of stoves and counters and an angry chef complaining at two waiters.

"Hey!" a male voice called after him.

Spotted already. So much for blending in.

Ty hung a right down a hall, ignoring the man and increasing his pace. His heart raced, pounded for the chance to talk to Lizzy.

He pulled open the door that led to a staircase and took the steps two at a time. At the bottom, the door creaked open. "Stop right there!" the man hollered, his command echoing in the stairwell.

Not on his life. They'd have to drag him out of here. He *would* talk to Lizzy.

"I'm calling security!" The threat echoed in the stairwell as Ty burst onto the second floor into a long, pitch-black hallway lined with offices—all were dark save one. A light glowed from underneath the last door on the left. That had to be Lizzy's.

Ty ran to it, not bothering to read the nameplate before he barged in.

"Hey! What the—" Lizzy screeched. "Ty!"

Well shit. He'd found Lizzy all right—going to the bathroom.

Her bright purple pants were around her knees, her frizzy pink hair tied at a knot atop her head, her overly made-up face stretched in shock.

Damn, he hated that burgundy lipstick she wore. But it sure tasted good.

"Ty!" she cried again. "Get out!"

What was he doing, staring at her on the toilet?

"Sorry!" Ty stumbled over the apology. "I didn't . . ."

She clasped her thighs together, glaring at him with those stony purple eyes. *"Get out!"*

"Sorry." Ty shut the door, turning and resting the back of his head against it. He listened to the flush of the toilet and the sink running as she washed her hands. Her blunt boot heels thumped across the marble floor, coming toward him. Straightening, he swung open the door once again, this time to let her out.

"What, are you applying for a job?" She didn't even look at him. Clutching a large black leather purse clad with chains, she set her focus on the elevator. "Did you not get my message?"

"Did you not hear me this morning?" He caught her arm, hauling her to a stop, wishing he could pull her into his arms. "*Dinner*. I won't take no for an answer."

Touching her was sheer torment. There was no describing the way the simple contact made him feel, the way his insides flipped over, the way his body screamed for her.

Coldly, Lizzy continued to stare in the direction of the exit. "Just because you said it—"

The elevator dinged, the doors sliding open to reveal two big goons in muscle-clinging neon green shirts and black jeans. And they didn't look happy about being bested.

"Take your hands off her," the one on the right demanded. "Step away."

"We're just talking," Ty drawled, not budging. "Everything's fine, right, *Elizabeth*?" He used her true name intentionally, wanting her to remember. To feel.

No matter how much she tried to hide from the truth, she couldn't.

"Lizzy?" The second bouncer stepped forward cautiously. "You want us to toss this joker out on his ass?"

Lizzy forced a smile. "Everything's fine."

They stared in doubt, glaring at Ty like he must have a gun to her back.

"This is an old friend of mine," she added. "We need to have a little talk. I'll be downstairs in five minutes." Her brows lifted, her voice hardened in steely warning. "And if I'm not, come after me."

Her apes obeyed reluctantly, stepping back inside the elevator. The doors closed, leaving Lizzy and Ty alone once again.

She turned to him, or rather, on him. "I don't know what you're thinking, but you're wasting your time and mine. I'm not the same person anymore, Ty. A relationship is just not for me."

Her words were like little hammers driving nails into his heart.

"Fine. Be my friend. Talk to me." Not wanting to push so hard that he pushed her away, Ty stepped back, giving her a little distance to show he was sincere. "That's all I'm asking. Be my friend."

"Your friend." Lizzy crossed her arms, looking at the floor. "That's not as easy as it sounds."

But sleeping with him was?

"What happened between last night and this morning? We—"

"I woke up. *Sobered* up." Her shoulders slumped as if in defeat, and she forced her fake smile wider. "Do yourself a favor, Ty, just give up on me. I'm not worth it."

Not worth it? That was crazy talk!

Ty wanted to pin her to the wall, to thrust into her heat and make love to her until she felt like a goddess. To worship every last inch of her beautiful body, to kiss and suckle at her until she metamorphosed back into the beautiful butterfly he remembered.

To make her scream and cry his name until she knew—or rather, accepted—what was between them. What could never be erased.

"Lizzy." He reached out, touching her face gently. "You're everything to me."

Her violet gaze, hard as jewels, refused his words. "How can you say that? We don't even know each other anymore."

"I know that you *claim* to want nothing to do with me, but your body sings a whole 'nother tune. And I can prove it."

She shirked her head away from his hand, as if fearful he'd do just that. "It's been well over a decade, Ty. Thirteen years, by my estimate. Too long. Just accept it."

"No." *No!* Like hell he'd accept that bull, especially after making love to her just last night.

Why would she have welcomed him into her body if she didn't feel something for him? Lizzy was lots of things, but she wasn't loose.

He'd prove it. Make her see she still wanted him. That she cared for him. That they had never really ended.

Taking her shoulders, he whipped her around, pinning her against the wall. Pressing his body to hers.

"Ty!" Her lips curled in disgust and she moved against him, fighting his grasp. "Let me go before I—"

His grip on her shoulders tightened.

"You what? Security is waiting five minutes," he reminded her, barely able to control himself, but determined to do just that. He wasn't trying to seduce her—not yet. "Let me make this clear. Push me away all you like, but I'm not going anywhere, not until you give us another chance."

All he wanted to do was make love to her. To make her see that no matter how much life changed, some things never change, and that included this desire between them.

They were so close, she was so soft . . .

Blood rushed to his cock, the steel shaft lodged against her pelvic area.

He didn't mean to get so turned on, to turn this into something sexual, but the reaction was involuntary.

"I already did. Last night." She stopped fighting, going limp under his pressing hold. Her body trembled and she looked away, refusing to meet his eyes. "My decision is made."

"Why are you so scared?" he whispered.

"Oh, I don't know. Maybe because you have me pinned against the wall?"

Stepping back, Ty threw up his hands and let her walk away, leaving him standing there with a raging hard-on and an aching heart.

What else could he do? Lizzy was right—he was scaring her, scaring himself, with his desire for her. He was going about this all wrong. Control was a thin thread, especially knowing she did want him, but he needed to get a grip. Needed her trust more than he needed her body.

He wouldn't give up. Wouldn't go away like she'd prefer, not unless he believed she truly wanted him to, which he didn't. Not until he'd proven to himself that the past couldn't be rekindled. Far as he was concerned, Lizzy was his, always had been, and always would be.

But before they were ever lovers, they were friends. And that's where he needed to start.

*D*o you, Maxim Cox . . . take this woman . . . to have and to hold . . . in sickness and in health . . ."

The minister had a boring voice, one that droned on and on, slowing her sister's wedding to a turtle's pace when all anyone wanted was to see the two kiss and then go party.

Lizzy, for one, was dying for a strong drink. Straight vodka would really hit the spot about now.

"I do." Maxim's reply was quick, sure.

Great. So much for hoping he'd change his mind.

I'm doing this for Elisa, Lizzy reminded herself and forced the fakest smile ever. After all, that was what family was for.

If Elisa was going to get married, she at least deserved a perfect wedding. That included Lizzy playing—and looking—the part.

The expensive brunette wig covering her head put her real hair to shame, pink or natural. Her bridesmaid dress was a cream color, simply cut, and she carried wildflowers that matched the rest of the arrangements throughout the church.

The affair was small. Elisa's father and Maxim's parents, who had flown in from Egypt, were in attendance, as well as a few of their closet friends and family members—a couple named Dylan and Sadie, who couldn't keep their hands to themselves, Aunt Sassy and Uncle Dick, who were living up to their names already.

But Lizzy could swear she was standing in front of a crowd of two hundred.

She tucked a fake strand of hair behind her ear, gnawing at the inside of her lip as she listened to Elisa voicing her vows. Vows Lizzy didn't believe any person would ever truly keep.

But opinion mattered little. Elisa was happy; Lizzy needed to be happy for her.

Not jealous.

Not *what*? Where had *that* come from?

It seemed a permanent knot had taken up residence in her abdomen, and her every thought was shadowed by Ty. He was nowhere around, but he was *everywhere*.

Bet she'd even find him in her glass of awaiting vodka. She was hopeless.

Lizzy had never felt less like herself or more out of place than she did today. She felt like Elizabeth, not Lizzy. And she didn't like it, not one bit.

It was just the wig. It had to be the wig.

She was *just fine*. She had great hair, a great life . . .

Or not.

Lizzy shifted uneasily. How much longer? God she needed to get out of here.

Every time she glanced at her adopted father and the chair next to him that held a simple rose symbolizing remembrance of his late wife, she thought of her real father, whom she'd never known. Her birth mother, who she hadn't spoken to in years. Her stepfather, who she could still easily put a bullet in.

And each instance that she caught someone looking at her, she wanted to cuss them out. To cry.

Was it the wedding? The wig? Or Ty's renewed presence in her life?

Lizzy knew one thing for certain, the sooner she got rid of him, the sooner everything went back to normal. She'd just have to keep ignoring his calls, his visits, because her heart couldn't take this constant twisting.

"You may kiss the bride," the minister announced. "And may your forever be a happy one."

Lizzy swung her head around just in time to see Maxim plant a big, long, wet one on her sister.

There was no going back now.

And God, she didn't want to. She wanted to run, run as far into the future as she could, so that her past could never catch up. Never hurt her again. It was what she'd always done, what she had to do. The only way.

seven

Lizzy had a new regular customer, one that was drawing a lot of attention. Female attention. *Her* attention.

"Apple martini," a blonde requested, sliding onto a barstool, her eyes shifting greedily to the corner of the club where Ty stood.

As always, clad in blue jeans and a T-shirt that clung to his fine-ass frame, Ty leaned against a glowing wall in his self-claimed spot under the black light.

Lizzy resisted the urge to throw the bottle of vodka at him. He had no damn right, standing there, looking so damn sexy for these . . . these sluts!

The blonde lifted her brows and crowed to her redheaded friend, "Stacy, look at *him*."

Stacy—a voluptuous woman who was oozing from her halter top—gave a little squeak. "Oh, girl, he's *fine*!"

"Don't bother." Lizzy went through the motions of making the drink, never more annoyed at the bartender who'd up and quit this week, leaving her shorthanded. If it weren't for him, she wouldn't be here, watching these bitches ogle Ty.

Not that she cared.

"Why's that?" The blonde's eyes continued to devour Ty.

"He's taken," Lizzy lied. *Sorta.* "Very committed."

She handed off the filled-to-the-brim cocktail glass and walked down the bar.

So much for running from her past. Jesus, how was she supposed to deal with this?

Ty was in every night from opening to close, never drinking anything but Coke, ironically never dancing, but always there, staring at her, waiting for a moment with her, insisting on a date. A chance.

And she was leading him on. She knew she was. Because if she truly didn't want him around, she'd ban him from the club or kick him in the ass with her combat boots—wasn't that what they were for?

But she didn't. Night after night, she allowed him to come in, allowed him to bug her. To get closer to her heart, to remind her he already *was* her heart. And no matter what she did or who she turned herself into, that would never change.

Ty. It all came down to Ty and how the very sight of him made her soul ache, her body react.

Lizzy tossed some beer bottles in the recycling bin and collected empty glasses, taking them to the tub for the busboy.

What could she do?

She glanced at Ty once again. His intent almond-shaped eyes studied her, followed her every move.

Under the gleaming beams, he seemed a strange black and white, like an old-fashioned film that kept replaying in her mind, reminding her of things long since forgotten.

Yearning for a distraction, Lizzy gathered more cocktail glasses and empty bottles.

But she couldn't shake the reality that Ty did have a point. It wasn't a matter of whether she should be his friend. She *was* his friend.

Maybe that was just an excuse, her way of reasoning herself into approaching him, but the truth was, they'd been best buds from an early age—way before anything sexual had happened—and she'd always valued their relationship.

He'd always been there for her. He had a way of making her feel like she could tackle the world, of making her laugh and smile in even the worst situations, of making her feel good and confident and *whole*.

He knew things about her, understood her, in ways no one else did. Not even Elisa.

Lizzy tried not to look at him again, attempted to distract herself by wiping down an empty portion of the counter. But her thoughts refused to turn.

A man leaned over the bar and asked for an imported beer. Taking his money, Lizzy grabbed one from under the bar, popped the cap, and slid it to him.

Then her eyes uncontrollably darted right back to Ty.

Was she really so screwed up that she couldn't reminisce with an old friend? Why shouldn't she?

No! she corrected herself. Why *would* she?

It must be her sister's recent wedding, still screwing with her mind.

She searched up and down the bar for another customer. Trash.

Dishes. Any sort of task to distract her. She found none, and unable to help herself, she glanced at Ty once again.

Did he have any idea how hard it was not to rush into his arms every time she saw him?

She had to face it. She had two choices: She could quit playing games and truly end it with him. Banish him from her life.

Or she could go on that date.

Oh, what the hell! Throwing caution to the wind, Lizzy washed and dried her hands, then walked around the bar. The night was winding to an end and the other two bartenders could take it from here.

Ty's eyes tracked her as she made her way through the crowded dance floor, coming to stand before him. She lifted her chin and stared at him directly.

"Okay," she hollered over the music. The smell of sweaty bodies, of lust and booze, permeated the air. She was used to it, but somehow, around him, it seemed so much more acute. Intoxicating. "You want to dance?"

He took her hand, lifting it, enveloping it in his and kissing its top. "I thought you'd never ask."

Her skin tingled where his lips had touched and she flashed an evil grin. "I already wish I wouldn't have."

She should have asked him to take her home. Put her toys to shame.

A tempting thought, just not a sane one. Ah well, who needed sanity anyway? Not her. What she needed was to move—faster than her feelings, her thoughts. To let go of everything.

Except Ty, that was.

Spinning on the balls of her feet, she pulled him through the crowd and onto the dance floor.

A mixer came on, fast and energetic, and Lizzy threw herself into the beat with Ty.

Hands in the air, waving their bodies like flags whipping in the wind, she and Ty lost themselves in the moment, freeing their souls to the music.

Just dancing, just having fun.

It seemed like seconds passed and all too quickly, the music skidded to an end, swiftly replaced by another fast-paced song. Lizzy didn't stop, couldn't stand the thought of this feeling between them concluding.

Harder, faster, she danced with Ty, moving in time with him, needing much more than the music could ever provide. Her mind, her world, was spinning so out of control, she could hardly breathe.

And then the DJ—earning yet another red mark in his file—skipped the song to a slower one. A romantic one—*ick!*

Lizzy's feet fell to a halt so suddenly, Ty had hardly caught on before she was dragging him from the dance floor and over to the bar.

"My DJ knows I don't like this type of bullshit in my club," she said loud enough for Ty to hear over the music.

Breathing hard, Lizzy rested against the highly polished counter littered with beer bottles and empty glasses.

Looked like her bartenders couldn't handle things without her, but oh well . . . what were some dirty dishes?

Nothing, compared to this . . . feeling. This wonderful, magical enchantment suddenly humming through her.

"Hey," Ty objected, sliding onto a stool, "don't fire the guy for being romantic."

"It's tempting." Following suit, she wiggled her butt onto the seat, arm propped against the counter and forefinger supporting her chin as she faced him.

"You know, he might have a family."

"So?"

"So don't force the man to strip." They shared a laugh, but Lizzy got the feeling it was funnier for him. He motioned for one of her employees, who rushed over like a good bartender should. "You want a martini or something?"

"I don't drink in my club."

"Guess that makes two of us. Cokes," he told the sweat-beaded Sal, who looked frantic from his inability to keep up, then turned back to her. "Why not?"

"R-E-S-P-E-C-T. If I start stumbling around, I lose it."

"Smart woman. I'm just ensuring I don't make an idiot of myself."

Well that was a lost cause.

Sal slid two opened, fizzing cans of Coke in front of them and they each picked one up, toasting.

"So," Ty inquired, "does a college degree go with this independent, knockout package?"

Flattered, Lizzy found herself glowing as she took a sip. "Of course."

Ty chugged his Coke, then crumpled the can in hand and slammed it on the counter. For a moment, he just stared at her, a twinkling in his eyes.

"And what about the hair?"

Uh-oh. A mood-murdering question.

Giving a shoulder shrug, she silently cursed the DJ. "What about it?"

With his free hand, Ty tickled the mound of curls bobbing atop her head. "Why pink?"

Not about to tell him her reasons for dying her hair—an apparently ineffective attempt at fending off the male population—Lizzy used the first excuse that came to mind.

"It's my favorite color."

Almost true, if she didn't count lime green. Which her hair might soon become. The only reason it currently wasn't was out of fear she'd look moldy.

"Mmm, darlin'." A strand caught around his pinky and he gave it a tug, then released. "I think it just became mine too."

That earned him a playful slap to the shoulder. "Knock it off! Didn't you just hear me say I don't like romance?"

At that moment, a faster song switched on.

"Huh?" Wiggling his earlobe, Ty feigned deaf. "THE MUSIC'S SO LOUD. I CAN'T HEAR YOU."

"I said—" Without saying a word, Lizzy moved her mouth to the shape of "I want you."

Ty's eyes widened in appreciation. "You want me?"

It was her turn to play dumb. "Huh?" With one last appreciating swig of Coke, she slid to her feet, grabbed his hand, and pulled him through the sea of bodies.

Moving onto the dance floor was like entering a jungle, and Lizzy fell prey to its beckoning, desperately wanting the oblivion many of the other dancers were swarming in. Knowing in her very heart she did *want* him. This "thing" between her and Ty wasn't over. It'd barely gotten started.

Just like this song.

This time, she turned her back to him, rotating her twitching bottom rapidly against his crotch area. Putting her heart, the desire she was suddenly aching to release, into her every movement.

And Lizzy danced, danced for all she was worth, couldn't stop, couldn't slow. Every beat became more intense, pounding in unison with her heart. Pounding away her doubts, racing her pulse, her mind.

Only when her legs threatened to collapse did she twist around, practically falling into Ty's catching embrace, her emotions electrified yet numbed by the adrenaline pumping through her.

Hands at the small of her back, Ty braced her against him. Their breathing was heavy, their bodies rising and falling against each other. Hot and sweaty.

"You're a good dancer," she sighed, wishing she had the stamina for one more. A hundred more.

"It pays."

No kidding.

Suddenly, she wished she'd gotten to see his entire show. Wished he'd give her—and her alone—another performance. Right now.

Ty's fingers pressed into her back, kneading muscle as if to soothe away tension.

He needn't bother. Right now, she had none. Only the deep desire to feel his naked flesh flush against hers, to escape into the excitement of the moment and never come back again.

Cue her mind—it was past time to cool off.

"Hey." Hands on his chest, she looked up at him, her fingers drumming against his strength. "You wanna get out of here?"

Do I ever." Clutching tight to her hand, Ty practically ran from the club, towing her behind him.

As long as he'd waited for the invitation, he wasn't giving this pink-haired, antiromance woman opportunity to change her mind.

Not when days had gone by, days of commuting to Denver and skipping work in order to hang out at Play, before she'd granted him as much as a "Hey, how are ya?"

Days of making no money and watching his finances dwindle—low enough that soon, he'd have to choose between staying here or staying in school. Gas wasn't cheap.

Then again, neither was their love.

As far as he knew, he had right now, this moment and possibly only this moment, to make her remember, to feel what they'd lost, what they could still have—if only she gave it a chance.

An inferno of need seared his heart as he rushed her to the nearest exit and burst into the cloudy night. Rain misted the air.

It was almost midnight. The only sound was the loud music of the club, mostly drowned out by its thick cement walls.

"I'll drive," he told her, heading across the car-packed parking lot toward his Trans Am. Reaching in the pocket of his skin-sticking, damp-from-sweat jeans, he dug out his keys.

All at once she ground him to a jerking halt.

"No, wait!"

He turned back, examining her face and seeing the way she chewed at her burgundy-colored lips, the way she looked so small in the face of a big decision. Her feet dug in despite his cajoling, she nodded her head to the left, motioning in the opposite direction of her apartment. "Come on, let's walk."

Walk? In the rain? What fun was that?

"It's cold out. Drizzling." Ty looked toward the dark, overcast sky, then to Lizzy. "And the weather report said—"

"So?" she dared him.

So? Ty grinned to himself. She wanted to walk in the rain? Fine with him . . . it only provided one more reason to wrap his arms around her. And that was worth walking through a hurricane for.

Besides, after the other night of running around bare-assed in Aspen, his skin had grown so thick he was officially immune to cold temperatures.

He stuffed his keys back in his pocket and they fell into step together, strolling through the parking lot and onto the sidewalk.

"I was beginning to think I'd become a stalker." Ty slipped his hand in hers and squeezed. "But I knew you'd come around. See the sexy man right in front of you," he joked, trying to kill the rapidly forming tension that just minutes before had vanished while they danced.

"Ty . . . Look, this isn't a date or anything." Lizzy's voice was wrought with emotion. "And I'm not having sex with you again."

Oh yes it damned well was a date, but he chose not to protest or even acknowledge her. So she might think, but either way, this wasn't about that. This was about them—a "them" that did exist, no matter how much she'd forgotten.

Better to make small talk, to take things slow. Last time things between them got too heavy, too quickly. He needed to rope in his emotions and take it easy with her . . . hard as it was, especially alone, in the dark with her like this.

Talk, he commanded himself. *Just make small talk.*

"Where are we going?" he asked.

"There's this street I like to walk along with all these old houses," she said with a shrug. "Thought I'd show you. I don't know . . ."

Trying to lighten the mood, he swung her hand high and low. "Okay, sounds neat." Her boots clumped against the sidewalk in tune with his. "Probably won't get any more snow this year." *God.* Was he really talking about the weather? All he really wanted to do was get on his hands and knees and beg her to drop the attitude. To love him. To dance with him again. But he couldn't do that. Wouldn't. Onward with the meaningless chitchat. "Spring is just around the corner."

"I don't know about that." Lizzy motioned for them to make a right, moving off the main road onto a narrow street with no sidewalk. "I've seen some heavy falls in late March."

Streetlights every twenty feet or so created a gentle glow, leading the way.

"How long have you lived here?"

"Years. I fell in love with Aspen as a teen. My adoptive dad brought us on vacation here often—he owns a cabin out in the mountains. He's very outdoorsy, loves to ski and hunt. Coming here was such a refreshing break from L.A."

"You keep referencing Lance as your father, but do you have an adoptive mother as well?"

Lizzy was quiet a moment. "She passed away."

Ty's gut wrenched. God, but heartache seemed to follow Lizzy like shadow.

"I'm sorry," he told her, squeezing her hand in his.

To his delight, she squeezed back. "I never really got a chance to get close to her. She died in a car accident almost right after they took me in as a foster child. But she was a great woman. Elisa is just like her—always wanting to save the world."

Ty latched onto the happy topic. "So when's the wedding?"

"She was hitched without a hitch, earlier this week."

"Did you take a date?" The question just slipped out. He probably shouldn't have asked, wasn't certain he wanted the answer, but it was too late now.

Her feet fell to a halt, pulling him to a stop. Above them, a streetlight radiated a yellow circle upon the street.

Slowly, she looked up, glaring at him through her mascara-veiled eyes. "*No.* No date, Ty."

Wind whipped at her pink curls. The rain began to fall heavier. Within seconds, black streaks ran down her face.

"Don't worry. I hate weddings." He winked at her and cupped her jaw in his hand, wiping away the smudges with his thumb. "So I'm not insulted that you didn't ask."

"Good." She reached up, swiping her lower lid, only making matters worse. "It's supposed to be waterproof."

"Who cares?" He let his hand fall away. "You're beautiful even with raccoon eyes."

She smiled and gave up as well, then something flickered in her gaze. "What about you, Ty? Are you seeing anyone . . . or were you?"

"No one serious."

"Never?" Her chin tilted. "Hot guy like you. *Why?*"

"Because you've always been my girl, Elizabeth. Nothing can change that." He practically growled with need, wanting nothing more than to prove his words to her. God help him, she was so unreasonably cute. Sexy and irresistible.

Screw self-control.

He took her by the shoulders and pulled her into an embrace. "I've never stopped loving you. Couldn't, not even if I wanted to."

He buried his face in her hair, inhaling her fruity scent. God, he wanted to consume her. Taste those lips—and her very essence—again.

Raindrops pounded down on them, splashing the pavement beneath their feet.

Control, he reminded himself. He had to make her remember. Make her want him.

"Have you ever danced in the rain before, Lizzy?" he asked. His jaw nuzzled her cheek and his whiskers scraped across her soft skin.

Pulling back, she crooked her head and stared at him.

Ty slid his arms under hers and took the lead. "Don't answer," he whispered. "Don't say anything."

With a quick spin, he guided her into the middle of the empty road.

Her laughter filled the air, filled his very heart as her hands circled his waist. "This is crazy!"

You like crazy." His nose brushed her ear, his voice deep and husky. "Right, Lizzy?"

She wanted to tell him no, to irrationally demand he return to calling her Elizabeth, not Lizzy. She hated Lizzy.

Instead, she laid her head on his shoulder, just feeling.

Darkness and solitude surrounded them, the rain drowning out all else. He swayed and moved his hips against her and she matched his movements, dancing with him like she'd never danced before. Slow and sultry, from the heart. She could feel his every breath, his every heartbeat.

Rain poured down, cold and stinging. Goose bumps erupted on her flesh, making every cold drop seem more intense, making his touch turn into electricity. Tilting her chin, she let the rain pound her face.

Slowly, Ty moved his fingers along her back, upward, toward her neck. Tingles followed the path up her spine, her body humming from head to toe.

Did he have any idea what his touch did to her? The way he made her feel? *Need?*

Never had she realized or wondered more at what she was missing. She wanted an orgasm, wanted one with him. Craved release even when he wasn't near, much less when he touched her like this . . . so sweetly, yet so erotically. She felt as if she would explode, and yet, she knew she couldn't. Knew it was completely beyond her.

"I'm trying so hard to behave." Ty's fingers tangled in her hair and he kissed the front of her throat, sliding his tongue toward her chin. "I could take you, right here, right now. But I want to be your friend."

His hips ground into her, his every movement becoming more pronounced, his erection growing heavy between her thighs.

Her pussy clenched at the threat, screaming *yes, yes, yes!*

A moan escaped her and her every muscle went taut in anticipation. She pressed her pelvis against his, an invitation on her lips. One she couldn't seem to speak.

"Would you like that?" he murmured, enticing her further with his tongue.

Like what—for him to fuck her or be her friend? Maybe a little of both?

Lizzy swore she could feel everything—the tiny bumps of his taste buds as he licked her, his breath blowing against her like a hot wind.

"Ty," she heard herself whimper, but didn't accept it. Didn't want to believe he was truly seducing her in the street, practically making love to her face with his mouth, sliding his hands up her shirt. Or that she was letting him, enjoying it.

No, this was a fantasy. A dream.

And in her dreams, she could screw the love of her life in the middle of the road in the rain. She could *come*. God, she needed . . .

His palms cupped her breasts through her bra, massaging. Steel against her pussy, his cock nudged the fabric of her slacks. He moved his lower body along hers, driving her mad, pushing her to the edge.

Lizzy rode his cock, amazed at how she felt. "Ty, make love to—"

Beep, beep! A car horn screamed at them, tearing them apart. Lizzy whipped free and turned around, staring at the taxi.

Beep! The car horn sounded again, but she was too stunned to move.

"Come on." Ty took her by the arm, urging her.

Shaking her head no, she tasted her lips where he had kissed her. Her whole body quivered from his touch.

Lost in herself, she continued to stare into the blinding headlights. For the first time she could see herself clearly . . . too clearly.

A tiny sound emitted from her throat. *Oh God.*

She was broken, as damaged as they came. Avoiding men, avoiding *Ty*, wasn't doing her a damn bit of good because underneath it all, her life was what it was. She was what she was.

And she was tired. Tired of dildos, tired of being bitchy, tired of pushing people away. It was true: She wanted Ty, wanted all a relationship with him had to offer. And she was finished battling that.

eight

"I'll make class next week, I promise." Not wanting to take no for an answer, Ty pushed the pad of paper he was drawing doodles on aside and stood, clutching the cell phone. "I swear the work is done—I just need an extension for turning it in."

If he went to Denver today, he'd miss his and Lizzy's first date. No way could he let that happen.

Why the hell hadn't he made their date for tomorrow? Because he was anxious. Hopeful.

Not thinking intelligently and pretty pissed at himself for it.

Mrs. Kingsley was a great victimology professor—but she was also a tough one. Divorced and bitter too, definitely not the type to sympathize with romance. He should have known better than to hope she'd work with him.

"Ty, the paper was due today." Her severe tone forbade further argument. "E-mail it as an attachment if you must, but I have to warn you, skipping class today isn't smart. The semester ends in three weeks and you'll miss important notes pertinent to the final exam."

"I'll zip the file to you right away." Clearing his throat, Ty paced his hotel room, annoyed at the reality that he was taking a huge gamble. He'd already been struggling with this class—if he failed the final, he was tossing a big chunk of money and a whole lot of effort out the window. "I'll get the notes from Doug."

What else could he do? Reschedule with Lizzy? This "date" was already on her terms, which included her driving. And paying.

It wasn't perfect, but it only proved he was right—Lizzy did want to be with him. She was just intimidated. And if he let another day pass, who was to say she wouldn't change her mind entirely?

Way he saw it, he needed to get her to lighten up around him, have a little fun. Get comfortable and then *he* could be comfortable. And he knew just the thing . . .

Best of all, his plans for tonight wouldn't require her to open her purse—or get behind the wheel.

"Ty," Mrs. Kingsley interrupted his thoughts, bringing him back to the conversation, and issue, at hand. His love for Lizzy was like a real-life fantasy, but school and his need to complete this semester were hard reality. "Unlike Doug, you're one of my more devoted students—and so close to your associate's degree. Once is too much, so don't let this happen again."

She was right. "I promise, this is it," he swore—to himself as well as his professor. A ragged breath of mental exhaustion escaped Ty and he drummed his fingers against the hard plastic of the phone, quickly stopping when it echoed a *thap-thap* in his ears. "Thank you."

"I better see you next week. Good-bye, Ty." Mrs. Kingsley hung up and Ty glanced at his watch. Three thirty. Lizzy would be here any moment—thank God she hadn't arrived during his phone call. The last thing he wanted was for her to know that he was letting school slide, even if it was just this once. Twice, actually—he had to count last week, even if he hadn't planned that screwup.

He knew it was wrong, stupid, and if it were any other woman, he wouldn't give it a thought. But this was *Elizabeth* . . . and he just had to. The class could be made up. Life with her couldn't.

Bending over the bed, he took a moment to e-mail his paper, then shut down his laptop and folded it shut, sliding it into his backpack. A knock sounded at the door, and his heart kicked with excitement. *Lizzy.*

The doors and walls of Ty's hotel were paper thin and Lizzy had overheard Ty's phone call. He'd been asking for a reprieve, but for what?

What was he up to?

Lizzy dropped her hand away from the door, waiting for him to answer and cursing herself for knocking. She shouldn't even be here. She was so nervous her brain was about to go into shock.

And yet how she looked forward to seeing him again. To the glorious feel of his touch, the way his deep voice rumbled through her. Made her remember what it felt like to love.

Crazy. She was crazy to have agreed to this date, to even consider trusting him an iota. He was probably still a thief. Or some sort of criminal. Who knew?

"Come on in," Ty called. "It's unlocked."

Mustering balls she didn't have, Lizzy pushed the door open and stepped inside, standing with folded arms. "Hey."

"You look sexy." With quick strides, Ty crossed the room and hugged her sweetly. Squeezing her in his arms, he kissed her gently on the cheek. His hands brushed along the knee-length skirt of her easygoing sweater dress. "You've always looked great in blue."

"Thanks." *Ribbit, ribbit.* She sounded like a damn frog. Clearing her throat, she croaked, "And you've always looked great in your jeans."

Oh Lordy, didn't he? He seemed to have an ass designed for Levi's . . . and making a woman drool.

"I'm almost ready. Have a seat," he offered. He left her standing there, her heart pounding from the casual greeting—as if they were boyfriend and girlfriend.

Like this was all so normal. And maybe it was, but she wasn't.

Stepping across the tiny, rather dilapidated room, she slid into the chair and crossed her legs. Ty returned to his task at hand, packing a bag full of textbooks and folders of paper.

"What are you doing?"

"This hotel is such a hole, I don't trust it. Whenever I go out, these come with. I'll keep them in your trunk."

"Are those . . ."

"My books and laptop. I'm attending Colorado Tech."

Wow. Her criminal theory flew out the window.

"Really?" Lizzy tried to hide her surprise, but surprised she was. He hadn't mentioned he was attending school . . . or that he'd ever gone back for his GED. With the way he'd been hanging around town, she'd just assumed stripping was his life.

"Really," he confirmed. He glanced at her, his eyes dancing with amusement. "You're quite surprised. You didn't think I was taking my clothes off purely for the fun of it, did you?"

"Of course not." But boy was she ever glad to hear him confirm it. "What are you studying?" she asked, completely intrigued by this new side of Ty.

"Criminal justice. I'm a year away from my associate's then I can get a real job. But I'm aiming for a bachelor's degree, eventually." Sitting on the edge of the bed, he pulled on his boots. "I want to be a juvenile probation officer."

Double wow.

"A probation officer . . . *really*?"

Talk about pegging him incorrectly. He couldn't *be* a criminal and want to fight them, now could he?

"I know—every convict's worst enemy—after the judge and the prosecution." Ty stood and walked to the table where she sat, gathering his wallet and comb and sliding them in his back pocket. "When I got out of juvy, no one helped me more. My PO was a great guy. He really cared about what he was doing. He was my friend."

"From what I've garnered from television, not all POs are like that."

"But I'm going to be." Picking up his Stetson, he plopped it on his head, and offered his hand. "Ready?"

She accepted it. Accepted more than he had any idea of. More than she thought she was capable of.

Him, her, possibly together. The moment. Hope.

"So, where are we going?"

"Roller-skating."

"Roller-skating? Are you serious?" She opened her mouth in disbelief as he hauled her to her feet. "But I don't think there are even any rinks around here."

"Good thing I bought some then."

Lizzy's heart skipped a beat . . . or two or three. He'd bought *roller-skates?*

It was goofy. Ridiculous. Still winter.

And it sounded like a ton of fun. Maybe he was just her type of guy after all.

Leave 'em," Ty urged Lizzy, coming up behind her as she scraped stuck-on cheese from their plates into the garbage disposal.

Molding her body with his, he reached around her with both arms and claimed the dish, setting it in the metal basin under running water.

"Hey!" Lizzy promptly snatched the dish back, bucking her ass against his groin in an unsuccessful attempt at driving him away. "Easier for you to say—it's not your kitchen."

"You cooked—" Mozzarella sticks and extra gooey cheeseburgers, without a single mention of how fattening the meal was. So unlike a woman, but when it came to amazing him—and turning him on—Lizzy never skipped a beat. Admittedly though, both of them had burned plenty of calories on their roller-skating "date" today. "And after such a great meal, I owe you, so I'll clean up."

"Mmmm. Must admit, I like the sound of that."

And yet she deposited the dishwasher-ready plate on the empty side of the sink and picked up another. Stubborn woman . . . didn't she know a good offer when she heard one?

Perhaps she wasn't paying him enough attention, but that could be easily remedied. He knew just how to capture her interest.

"I think . . ." Brushing aside frizzy hair, Ty leaned into the crook of her neck, seizing smooth, pale skin between his teeth and suck-ling. Amidst love bites, he managed to murmur, "Mmmm . . . can't let my manners lack." His tongue darted out and wet the area. "Bet-ter show my appreciation for such a good cook."

And then he took a hearty nip.

Her surprised cry filled the air and Lizzy dropped the dish with a clank.

"Ty!" But despite her complaint, she went weak against him and he suckled her neck, drawing a whimper from her. "Bastard! Now you *are* doing the dishes."

"Exactly what I wanted to hear." Taking her by the upper arm, he swung her around and pinned her back against the breakfast bar.

"Ty!"

Trying to get past him, she drove at his chest with pathetic little shoves, but he would have none of it, holding her in place with his presence alone.

"The water! You can't—"

"Let it run."

"But—"

"Let. It. Run."

Now that he had her cornered, he wasn't letting her go. Not un-til he'd had his way.

All day he'd wanted this, wanted her, through roller-skating and the drive to her place, watching her cook and eating the mouthwa-tering dinner she'd made. He was mesmerized by the new woman she'd become, despite the little bits of Elizabeth he saw shining through her colorful surface.

Since they'd reunited, one thing he'd quickly learned about Lizzy was that when it came to being intimate—the hated *romantic*—she had a talent for inventing hundreds of silly little distractions. But right now, he wanted her, wanted her bad, and he was *taking* her.

So forget the dishes, the running water even. He'd clean up whatever mess he might make—and do all the dishes to boot. When they were done.

"Really, Ty—"

There she went again.

"Shhh . . ." Not saying another word, he shoved her sweater dress up over her head and cast the garment aside, then tore down her tights, lifting each leg as he ripped them free, leaving her standing before him in a black bra and panties trimmed with pink lace.

A dessert more delicious than any he'd ever set eyes on.

"Don't move," he told her, knowing he was venturing a little far when he added, "or else."

He could see it in her eyes—she was debating whether or not to make a dive for the sink. And he wasn't letting her get away with it.

Her deep inhale hitched as he tugged the satin straps of her bra over her shoulders and down her arms, pulling the undergarment along her body, not bothering with the hooks.

Hated those damn things anyway . . . they never came free fast enough.

And this was so much more fun, seeing her holding her breath to the finish, the way her flesh gave way to the soft fabric. Her naked beauty, slowly revealed to his hungry gaze.

Her luscious breasts popped free, and still he pulled the lace undergarment south, over her waist, her hips, her thighs, until it dropped around her ankles.

Then he followed suit with her panties, hooking his fingers beneath black satin, his thumbs caressing the lace as he yanked them past the curve of her ass, her thighs, letting them fall atop her bra where it rested at her feet.

Abandoning them there, Ty rose, his clothed body parallel to her naked form. Ever so gently brushing along her breasts, like a sensual whisper, he kissed her, this woman he was coming to know, the girl he'd once adored.

Kissed her with all his need, wishing he could erase the distance between them as easily as he managed his way into her body.

With a moan of encouragement, Lizzy mirrored his passion, her tongue flicking in his mouth, plunging against his. Swirling and dancing and evoking his need.

His balls lifted, tightening in unison with his cock as his hands went to her breasts, cradling their weight. The running water hissed in the background, accompanied by a strange sort of dripping.

"Really, Ty—" Lizzy came up for air, angling her chest into his palms even as she persisted at her escape attempt. "There's a slow—"

He still didn't give a hoot.

Before she could protest again, he pinched her beaded nipples between forefinger and thumb, squeezing, rolling. Pulling her desire forth.

Her chest arched higher against his hands and she threw her head back, welcoming his rough touch, which only served to provoke him further. Ty twisted the buds, coaxed little whimpers from her and all at once, he couldn't wait, not a moment longer. Not that he was being very patient in general this evening.

Oh, but he had been. All damn day long.

Taking her by the shoulders, he spun her around and pushed her facedown against the breakfast bar, lifting her slightly, so that her body rested on the marble top, her ankles trapped by her bra and panties, her lush behind displayed . . .

Displayed and bruised.

Ty's fingers traced the outline of the injury earned roller-skating—she'd taken them both down more than once. He didn't even want to know what *his* ass looked like.

Placing his mouth on the purple and blue flesh, Ty licked over it, wishing he could lick away her pain, erase the damage. Erase what wasn't perfect between them.

Maybe he couldn't, but he could bring her pleasure, and a whole lot of it. Exactly his intention.

Reaching into his back pocket, he dug out his wallet and plucked a condom from the money slot. Casting cash and credit cards to the floor, he opened his jeans, freed his cock, and then tore the wrapper, sliding the rubber on.

"Ty, hurry," she pleaded. "HURRY!"

Stop, go, hurry, slow down—how was a man supposed to please her?

He'd have to follow his instincts. Perhaps throw in a good smack to the rear here and there.

With a swift slap to her unbruised cheek, he reveled in her cry and situated her body so that her wriggling little butt hung far enough over the counter that his cock could reach between her legs, and he nudged between her folds, locating her entrance.

Hovering there, he searched out her clit with his fingers, massaging the knot. Coaxing it from its hood, feeling it thrum against his touch.

When he entered her, he wanted her screaming his name, begging. Wanted her writhing and wild. Wanted her never to forget who brought her ecstasy first, who she belonged to, heart and soul.

"Hurry," Lizzy pleaded, "the water!"

Not what he wanted to hear.

Deeper he rolled her clit, tweaking the bud, deliberately adding a little pinch of pain to his pleasure attack.

Working that bundle of nerves for all it was worth.

Then for good measure, he spanked that ass again. Twice, in quick succession, because he had a feeling he was taking liberties he'd pay for later.

"T-Ty! Knock it off!"

But he felt her quivering beneath him, heard the way his name caught in her throat, and he knew she was teetering on the edge.

Knew she was exactly where he wanted her.

Unable to restrain himself a moment longer, Ty drove home, filling her tight cunt with his eager cock and immediately thrusting away, fast and hard as he could take her.

Lifting her legs, he drove into her body until she was pealing with an orgasm, until he was as well. Until he completely lost himself inside her, jerking with a completion so intense, so dick-throbbing, mind-reelingly incredible, the room around him went fuzzy. Sound faded, reality blurred, and if it weren't for the desire to do it all over again, he could've stayed like that forever, lingering over her, lost in bliss. Lost in Elizabeth.

"Hey, cowboy?" She wiggled, pushing her butt against him. "TY!"

"Huh?" He shook off his near delirium, his fingers flexing on her ass cheeks. "That was fantastic."

"Know what would be even more fantastic?"

"Hmmm?"

"Get off me and clean up the damn mess you've made—the sink overflowed!"

"Shit." Ty eased free, releasing her legs as she slid to her feet. Cock hard and hanging free, he observed the kitchen turned swamp. "Double shit."

"No kidding!"

Slopping through the ever-growing puddle of water around his boots, Ty crossed the space between the breakfast bar and the sink, shutting off the flow. He looked around with a sigh.

What a way to end great sex.

She crossed her arms, flashing him an I-told-you-so glare. "I tried to tell you. I've got a slow clog and I rescheduled the maintenance man in order to be with *you* today."

Well then, every drop of wasted water was worth it. "Where's the mop?"

"In the pantry. I'll get it."

"No"—catching her arm, he hauled her to him—"You go get a shower and wait for me in bed."

Her upper lip curled, the glimmer in her violet eyes sparking with a response he knew he wouldn't appreciate even before she let it pour from her lips. "Not a chance, cowboy. You're going back to the hotel."

"What? You're banishing me?" After what they'd just done? Besides, it'd take half the night to clean the kitchen up! "Come on, baby. Don't be cold."

On cue, she flashed him a smile chiseled from ice. "I never let a man spend the night on the first date."

"Third," he corrected. "By my count."

"*First.*" Her mischievous gaze settled on the sink. "And if you want another . . ."

Ty threw up his hands, but didn't throw in the towel—he'd need that for the mess he'd made. "I'm cleaning; I'm cleaning!"

"Fix the clog too," she tossed over her shoulder, sauntering from the room.

Denied more sex and given chores to boot—and they weren't even engaged.

Yet.

Who could that be?

Mouth foaming with toothpaste, Lizzy glanced up at the clock on her bathroom wall, still brushing away as the buzzer rang a second time throughout her apartment.

Three in the afternoon—she was supposed to arrive at Ty's hotel by four. He'd been in Denver for a few days, attending school, time apart that had given her ample opportunity to realize how greatly she wanted to see him again. *Try* for an orgasm. For the third time.

On a plus, she was getting very good at faking it.

But it better not be him at the door, darn it. Miss him she may have, but she'd made herself clear—she was driving. Paying too. That little bit of independence was all she had, her only means of staying true to herself as her world spun out of control.

Seeing him again . . . it was so much, so fast. Ty was like a whirlwind wiping out her defenses, unraveling the firm grasp she had on her life.

Sometimes she wanted to let her reins slip free, perhaps hand them over to him. Other times, she wanted to hold on tight and run as fast as she could, as far as she could.

The buzzer rang again, three times in quick succession. Ah, persistence.

It *had* to be Ty. Damn his hide.

At least he wasn't so early that she was still running around in her bathrobe.

Lizzy spat and continued scrubbing away at her molars, meandering from the bathroom, down the hall, hoping maybe he, or whoever it was, would go away. But knowing better.

Saying nothing, she pushed the button for the intercom.

"Hey, Liz, it's me," Ty's voice crackled over the speaker. "Buzz me up."

She knew it! He was lucky she was anxious to see him.

Twisting the bolt lock, Lizzy buzzed him up and walked into the kitchen. She was rinsing her mouth when he let himself in, sauntering in like he owned the place.

Just like a man. He fixed one sluggish sink and he thought he'd been granted farting rights.

Not in her apartment, not ever.

"Hey, babe." Walking up behind her at the sink, he kissed her cheek and rested his chin on her shoulder, pressing his front along her back, igniting memories of their last date.

The unfulfilled ache between her legs.

"Hey, babe," she mocked, twisting around and pointing at him with the toothbrush. "What are you doing here?"

"Saving you the trouble of driving half an hour out of your way." Using the corner of his sleeve, he swiped a spot of foam from the edge of her mouth. "Besides, I couldn't wait to see you."

"Which means, conveniently, I'll have to bring you home tonight."

He took that as his cue to step back. Smart man. *Sometimes.*

When he wasn't behaving like some romantic fool. Or overstepping himself.

Lizzy slipped past him, setting her toothbrush on the breakfast bar. Again a rush of images besieged her mind—Ty, ripping down her bra and panties; Ty, fucking her from behind; Ty . . .

Lizzy snatched her toothbrush back up, spinning around only to find her face in his chest.

"So where's my hug after all this time?"

"I'm still driving," she muttered, even as his arms enveloped her, wrapping her tight and smashing her face to his pectoral muscles.

His rather well-developed pectoral muscles.

"I know." He gave her a good squeeze, followed by a kiss to the head. "But this way I can leave on my own time. You know, in the morning. It is our fourth date."

"Second!" And that earned a smack to the chest. "You devil! There went your invitation inside!"

He simply winked at her. "No worries. I'll earn it back."

Yeah, yeah." Pulling away from him, Lizzy crossed the kitchen and swung the fridge open, digging around with a swish of her tight butt. "So, where're you taking me?"

God, he loved that ass.

Not wanting to get caught drooling, Ty stared into empty space and focused on the conversation at hand. "The mall. Thought we'd grab some pizza."

Any other time, he'd be embarrassed to even make the suggestion. The mall? Pizza? Today's date had cheap and cheesy stamped all over it.

But Ty had his motives, and they were good ones.

"Cool. Sounds great."

Somehow, he'd known she'd like it. Lizzy was different from other women. Fun and free, comfortable to be with.

And at the same time, hard to get. A challenge.

But given the number of women that threw themselves at him regularly, for Ty, a challenge was stimulating. Refreshing even.

Standing up from her refrigerator rummage, Lizzy held two clear, rectangular florist boxes that she must've had buried behind her food. "I have something for us."

One glance and a giant, glowing question mark pulsated in his mind.

"Uh . . ."

Lizzy smiled at him as if the boxes she held in her hands were perfectly ordinary.

"So, you don't know this," she told him, "but by the time my foster parents took me in, I was so behind in school, it would've taken me years to catch up. Instead, I had a tutor and was schooled from home, passing the equivalency test right on schedule." Taking the boxes to the breakfast bar he'd screwed her on days before—now that roused some memories *and* his cock—she popped open the box and pulled out the arrangement. A solitary purple rose amidst tiny ferns and greenery. "So anyway, neither of us went to prom. We should've gone together."

"In a perfect world," he agreed, feeling his mood darken, his interest in the breakfast bar plummet. "I would've treated you like a princess."

Instead, he'd been stuck in juvy, a damn criminal amongst criminals, again and again returning to illegal behavior just to keep his rep up and his hide intact.

"So tonight's our prom," she announced, spinning on her heels. Ever so carefully, she pinned the boutonniere to his T-shirt, then stood on tiptoe, her lips brushing his as she spoke. "Look, Ty. A lot of bad things happened to us and when I think about . . ." She swallowed and forced a big, wide smile, dropping back onto her heels and giving the boutonniere one final adjustment. "I want my prom with you."

It was the closest to forgiveness, to wanting to make things right, he'd ever felt her venture.

Needing desperately for it to be so, Ty wrapped his arms around her, drawing her against him. Not wanting to let the moment—the closeness between them—vanish. "Maybe we should adjust our plans," he suggested. "I'll take you somewhere nice. Romantic."

She looked at him like he was the weird one. "Why?"

Had she not heard him say he intended to take her to the mall? For pizza?

Of course she had—she was just being Lizzy. If it weren't for the black jeans and T-shirt hugging her body, he'd have grounds to be concerned she expected a fancier date.

But this was just another quirky, original Lizzy idea. She was a pro at being innovative, a part of her that intrigued him like nothing else.

Now if only she'd invest her creative spark in the bedroom. His cock twitched in agreement, as if shaking its head *yes, yes, yes!*

Oh . . . the interesting, *original*, and *innovative* things she might come up with.

And suddenly, his mood was light all over again, his determination to give her what she wanted strong. "Go get changed." He smacked her ass playfully. "We'll go dancing."

"No way." She shook the idea off and returned to the counter, picking up the other box and handing it to him. "Tonight, we're seventeen again, and pizza it is. Besides, I hate romance, remember? Now pin this sucker on me."

You've got sauce on your—"

Completing missing, Lizzy wiped at her cheek, and Ty set his slice of pizza down on the paper plate it came on and leaned over the wobbly table they'd found in the food court.

"Let me." He swiped the red blob from the corner of Lizzy's mouth, his fingers lingering on her lower lip. "There."

"Thank you." Her tongue darted out, licking the tips of his fingers, slowly, sensually teasing him. More accurately, torturing him with hints of erotic delights . . . and not delivering. "But I can't eat with your hands on my mouth."

His forefinger edged back and forth, reluctant to abandon those glistening maroon lips assuredly seasoned with an Italian flavor.

"Sorry. Just so irresistible." Nonetheless, Ty retreated. There'd be plenty of time for touching later, when they got back to her apartment. He could hardly wait—and this time, he'd no intention of making any messes that might get him kicked out. "So, what'd you do while I was out of town?" he asked.

Lizzy wrinkled her nose, shrugging. "Boring me? Just the norm. Worked, watched television."

"Awaited my return?" he suggested.

In the almost three days since their last date, he'd returned to Denver to attend a couple of classes and drain his bank account some more.

And every second of waiting to see her again had been agony.

"Cocky." Lizzy rolled her eyes in that adorable way only she could manage and took a tiny bite of her pizza, creeping along a crust she obviously wouldn't finish. "But maybe."

"Give it to me." Ty took the burnt end of the mall pizza, trading her for his almost finished slice. "Waste not, want not."

Lizzy took a nibble of hot, gooey cheese, studying him. "What about you? How was school?"

"Female classmates weren't too happy to hear I'm officially taken."

Her brows shot to the ceiling. "Who says it's official?"

"After four dates?" Ty pointed to his boutonniere in reminder. "And don't argue with your prom date."

"Why shouldn't I?"

"Because you're supposed to be all doe-eyed and shyly hoping I've booked a cheap hotel room."

"Oh please. I would've never been *that* girl."

"Better take off your corsage then."

"Why's that?"

"You're not doing a very good job at playing the part. My prom date would get all quivery when I touch her. She'd hang off my every word. Pet my muscles and—"

"You're about to get a soda dumped over your head." Lizzy took another bite—likely to keep her from biting her tongue against sharper words—and chewed silently.

Ty reached in his lap, retrieving his cowboy hat, and plopped it on his head. "Don't mess with the hair."

That earned him a grin and another roll of those shimmering violet eyes.

After a few moments of noisy silence—the food court wasn't exactly the most intimate of places for a date, but it was one he didn't have to feel too guilty about her paying for—she swallowed and re-laxed into her smile. "Seriously, Ty. I'm really proud that you've gone back for your degree. I know you're sacrificing a lot though, driving back and forth like you are."

"No worries. You're worth it."

"Maybe next week I can meet you in Denver instead."

"And let you drive again? I wouldn't hear of it."

Besides, he was avoiding Denver as much as possible. He might be attending school, but he was still playing hooky from work. Just didn't sit well with him, the idea of making love to Lizzy, then head-ing off to strip for strangers.

But eventually, he'd have to. Waiting tables wasn't going to pay his rent and tuition, as well as the cost of commuting to Aspen. It was just a darn good thing he'd been so steadfast about saving and could get by for now.

"Don't count on driving," Lizzy reminded him. "We agreed to my terms."

Terms he had no taste for. A woman should never pay, or drive, on a date. It was emasculating, not to mention that all he wanted in the world was to prove to her that he could take care of her this time around.

Rather than argue the point, he took a sip of Coke and shrugged the conversation off. "We'll see."

"So," Lizzy asked, returning the leftover crust of his pizza. She adjusted her corsage, which kept twisting to one side on the stretchy fabric of her T-shirt. "We've enjoyed delicious mall pizza, what's next?"

"Why, milady, I've aspirations to whisk you off to the arcade. What say you?" Stuffing the entire crust in his mouth, he stood and scooted his chair out of the way, patting his pocket as he chewed and swallowed. It jingled. "I've lots of change for us to blow."

Her gentleman, determined as ever to pay.

What say she? Was he serious? The *arcade?*

"Lead the way." Rinsing the pizza down with one last sip of soda, she stood and took his hand. "In case you've forgotten, I can beat you at pinball any day."

This was the best prom a twenty-seven-year-old woman could have!

"Ah, but I've been practicing," he warned as they walked through the mall, hands swinging in rhythm to their pace. "Don't be so certain."

Lizzy could barely contain the tingles of excitement bubbling through her, making her smile from the inside out.

If he was trying to remind her of what it felt like to be a teenager, he was succeeding.

If he was trying to appeal to her quirky side, he was succeeding.

And if he was trying to get her to loosen up? Again, succeeding.

She'd had the time of her life roller-skating with him on their last date—even though she'd taken a spill or two that'd left her butt bruised and his ego inflated from getting to play the hero. Even if he had virtually destroyed her kitchen and left her hot and horny.

And now they were at the mall, acting like a couple of kids. Ty apparently knew exactly what he was doing when it came to wooing her.

But one thing was concrete—he wouldn't beat her at pinball. No man could, just like no man could . . .

Ah, orgasms. Not what she wanted to be thinking about right now.

Lizzy swung their hands higher. "You really think you got a shot? Wanna bet?"

"Hmmmm." With a sly smile, he slipped his fingers free and wrapped his arm around her shoulders, pulling her close enough that their hips connected and their legs brushed. "Depends. What're we wagering?"

His suave voice conveyed exactly what was on his mind . . . sex.

"Not *that*."

Although . . .

"Okay, okay," he withdrew, too quickly for her taste. "A kiss then."

"A kiss?"

"A long, slow, *wet* kiss." His hand slipped south and tweaked her bruised butt suggestively. "And next date, I drive. And pay."

"You're on, cowboy. And if I win—which I will—I come to Denver and I drive." Lizzy swatted his rear end and pulled free, skipping ahead. "Now giddyup—I'm anxious to win."

Because either way, she was getting that kiss and milking it for all it was worth. Being around Ty had her hormones hopping, her libido shooting through the roof, and she was looking forward to another round in the bedroom. Couldn't fake it forever, after all, and with the way Ty made her feel . . .

She ought to be *running* to the arcade. The sooner she won, the sooner he kissed her. And then some.

"Wait a sec." Ty caught her forearm, drawing her back to him. "We have to seal the deal."

And before she could protest, not that she would've, his lips swept down upon hers and he kissed her deep—*long, slow, and wet*—his tongue plunging into her mouth, making her knees shudder with weakness, her desire spike to the surface.

Forget pinball . . . but heck, maybe they *should* bet on sex. Then they'd both win.

Lizzy kissed him with everything in her, reaching up and cradling the back of his head, never wanting to let go as her fingers threaded in his short hair.

She really had no idea how she'd gone from her vow that they be "just friends" to this, but one thing she did know—it felt great. Fun and exciting and freeing.

Nodding her chin, she lifted her tongue, running it over his top lip, inviting him to suck her lower one. Just the thought made her nerves spark, her body quake.

Ty's teeth grazed nerve-infused flesh, promising delight as he cupped her face and broke that very promise, pulling free. "People are staring."

"So?"

So wasn't she the woman who'd all but freaked out when her friends saw her with him?

But who cared? Not her, not at the moment. The only thing on her mind was winning at pinball.

And the reality that maybe Ty was winning back her heart after all. Maybe.

I WIN!" Thirty minutes later, Ty was doing the happy dance around Lizzy. "*Booya! Shazam!* I win, I win, I win!"

The dinging and beeping of video games filled the air, the flashing numbers on the board above displaying his high score—a whopping hundred points over hers.

He'd won by a thread, but he'd still won.

"You—" Before she could protest—that, or tell him what a sore winner he was—Ty claimed his victorious kiss, taking a lush little tidbit of raspberry flesh between his teeth and sucking hard. Lifting her, so that her legs wrapped around his waist as he dove into her mouth and released her lower lip, invading her mouth with his tongue, carrying her from the arcade.

Watching her play pinball—the way her tight body, molded in black jeans and an even snugger black top, moved against the game, consoled by the way she hadn't lost her expert skill in all these years—had him wondering if he'd make it to her car, much less her apartment.

He wanted her. Wanted her so much, more than he ever had, that if it weren't for certain rejection, he'd propose here and now.

"What's . . . your . . ." he murmured between tongue plunges, flinging open glass doors and rushing into the sunshine. "Favorite restaurant?"

She shook her head, her mouth sliding over his desperately. "It's . . . too . . . expensive."

"Don't . . . care." His feet pounded over pavement, his tongue pounded her mouth. His cock rose to full attention between her legs, pounding as well, with a desire so overwhelming, if it weren't for the circling security guard, he'd take her in the car.

"Just . . ." His finger and thumb found her nipple, and she moaned in his mouth, thrusting back, her tongue circling his, dancing faster and harder than she had that night in the club. Furiously driving him wild. "Get us back to my place."

nine

Lizzy leaned her head against the cold window of Ty's Trans Am, staring out at the whizzing trees and pounding raindrops as he drove her home from their latest date.

Tonight it wasn't kids' play, arcades, or roller-skating. He'd upped the romanticism, the emotional intimacy—and ergo, the tension—by taking her to a fancy restaurant, despite her protests and insistence on paying for the meal, denying her every argument otherwise, and reminding her that he'd won the pinball bet. But she was certain throwing around money like that was beyond his means.

Come to think of it, this past week or so, he'd traveled back and forth to attend college, but she hadn't heard a lick about work from him. Lizzy wasn't sure whether that should impress her or concern her, but she wasn't about to protest his presence.

For all her stressing, she had to admit—it was fun seeing him again. Their past couple of dates, she'd felt like a kid again . . . she hadn't laughed so much in years. Maybe ever.

And yet, once they'd stepped inside her apartment, she'd been anything but relaxed. She *couldn't* seem to come, knew tonight would be no different. For a while, she'd held up hope, but hope had crashed around her after the last nonrelease.

Letting out a sigh, Lizzy glanced at Ty. What was she going to do?

"Tired?" He reached across the console, resting his palm on her knee. He squeezed. "You look down."

Lizzy shrugged, not sure what to tell him. "Just . . . confused."

"About us?"

She didn't answer. Couldn't—she didn't want him to get the wrong idea.

Loving and hating the way his gaze turned dark at the prospect of her being anything but perfectly happy, she stared into his eyes. He was so protective, so demanding of her heart. And sometimes . . .

Sometimes she had nothing to give.

God, why'd it have to be like this? Ty made love to her wonderfully—the man had foreplay down to an art. Had a way of getting her so damn horny, she could hardly breathe.

Yet it still wasn't enough for her disturbed body. It kept playing games with her, screaming for pleasure, then refusing it.

Lizzy closed her eyes, wishing she could shut out the pain. Tonight she couldn't have sex with him, couldn't pretend. Not again. Each time was like the first—she came close, but no release. It was agony.

She was really trying. She really wanted to be with Ty, to love him like she used to.

But how could it really be love if she couldn't fully enjoy their lovemaking?

Ty pulled into her apartment complex, sliding into one of the few open spaces in the rear of the parking lot. Shutting off the engine, he took the keys in his hand and cleared his throat. "I'd like to walk you up, if that's okay."

Despite his overstepping ways, he was always the gentleman, asking for permission, even though they both knew no wasn't an answer he accepted easily from her.

Probably because he was worried she'd pull away again. And he was right. She probably would.

"Sure." Lizzy cleared her throat. "Um . . ."

How could she tell him she didn't want him to stay? That he didn't do it for her? That she wasn't sure this could work between them? That maybe all she had was her dildos and a hopeless, loveless future?

Frustrated, Lizzy tugged at her seat belt, and he leaned over, helping her free the tricky latch.

"There." His face met hers and he searched deep in her eyes. "Everything okay, Lizzy?"

You've no idea. Lowering her gaze, she swallowed the knot forming in her throat.

Frantically, she hopped out into the bad weather. Rain poured down upon her, soaking her silk dress. The soft fabric clung to her, became a second skin, and her heels squished, threatening to dump her out.

Thunder cracked above, lightning lit up the sky. Ty met her halfway, wrapping his arms around her, trying to protect her from the storm.

"No." She didn't want to be shielded, didn't want to cower. To hide, to pretend.

She needed to do something, anything, other than that.

Frantic, she pushed him, driving his ass against the hood of his car. His keys dropped to the pavement with a clang.

"Whoa," he protested, steadying himself. "Lizzy?"

What was she doing, beating him up?

Her tongue flicked out over her lower lip as she made a split-second decision. She needed to get a grip. *On his cock.*

Yes, there was only one thing to do. She had to take control of this situation. Of him.

"Lizzy," he chuckled as she crouched, attacking his fly. "What's gotten into you, hon?"

His fingers tangled in her hair, wrapping around the strands, exploring her scalp. Tugging her up, as if he wanted her to stop. But she knew better.

"The other night, in the rain." Breathless, she sputtered for some sort of explanation. Thank God for April showers. "I think that evening deserves to have its ending rewritten."

"Damn." He sucked in a sharp breath then groaned as her fingers slid inside his jeans. Shoving the pants out of the way, she grasped his cock through his boxers. "Liz, I think you better stop."

She rubbed over the soft fabric, stroking his length. "You don't really want that, now do you?"

Not any more than she did.

Somehow, if she wanted to be with him, she had to find a way to fully enjoy sex. It wasn't Ty or his ability, God no; it was her that needed to be fixed. Tonight though, she knew she wouldn't be able to come, but she wanted Ty to. She'd give him an orgasm—and save herself the torture—for now.

She dropped to her knees, landing in a cold puddle. Her panty hose soaked up the moisture rapidly, drawing cool wetness to her hot cunt. A shiver ran through her, straight up her legs, under her skirt. Her pussy constricted and rippled at the thought of being filled.

Well, shit.

Light flashed across the parking lot as a car drove past, and her heart pounded furiously.

Ty cupped her head. "Lizzy, get up."

He tried to pull her to her feet, but she refused. She pushed his boxers down to his knees and circled his cock with her fingers.

"Lizzy, they could see—"

His protest faltered as she took his cock in her mouth, slowly enveloping him. She stroked her lips over the buttery-soft skin covering his shaft, loving the way it moved under her attentions. Loving how hard he was for her and knowing that she could make him come, could control his pleasure.

Besides using toys, it was the only power she had over her sexuality, the only thing she could *make* happen.

With one hand she held his cock and with the other, she grabbed onto his rear, bracing him. She opened wide, inviting him to fuck her mouth, sliding him in and out, taking all of him.

"God, Lizzy, you're nuts," he growled, his grasp tightening on her head, pulling on her scalp. "Hurry."

He thrust into her, his movements rapid, demanding as his cock plunged into her throat, stroked her tongue.

Teasing him, she flicked the back of his head and frenched his dick from top to bottom, doing everything she could to make him so horny, he hurt.

At least *he'd* have the privilege of releasing his pain, of experiencing a climax. If only he could do so for both of them.

Heaven help her, she was dying from desire all over again. Sure, later, when he left, she could break out her toys, get off, but something about that didn't sit right with her. The notion just made her feel guilty. Hopeless.

Despite her intentions, her loins pulsed with heat, flooded with desire. Every raindrop that hit her skin sent shivers through her. He was so big, so long and thick, and she loved every inch. Wanted him deep inside her. Wanted the release she could never seem to find.

Her fingers pressed into his skin, clenched for dear life. His movements slowed, then increased, alternating. She gave him whatever he wanted.

Letting out a holler, he spasmed rapidly and filled her mouth with cum. His hands slid free of her hair, down around her face to her jaw. Softly, he held her head.

Lizzy closed her eyes and swallowed, appreciating the way he touched her, the way he tasted, even the fact that he was back in her life. She wouldn't change any of it, but she would change her body if she could. If only.

Every night had its dawn, and Lizzy woke with a realization: Her life was a sad song, one she was tired of singing. Rolling out of bed, she threw her legs over the edge of the mattress and let them dangle. It was early, too early for even the sun.

A shiver wracked through her and she grabbed the quilt, pulling it over her lap with a sigh.

She'd put Ty off last night with a blow job, but she couldn't keep using the same tactics. Eventually, he'd figure her out. Realize she was lying each and every time they had sex.

And heaven help her, she didn't want to continue being known as the "Dildo Queen," didn't want to go through the rest of her life never experiencing great sex with a real man. Or love.

Ty's return to her life had made her realize that if *he* couldn't get her to come, something was seriously wrong with her and she needed to fix it. Since her adulthood had been relatively happy, the only thing to do was look to the past—and it was littered with skeletons.

Maybe she couldn't rewrite her childhood, but she needed to face it, open her closet and free the dusty bones trapped within it.

She was going to go home, face her parents. Try to get past her pain and move into the present. Doing so was long overdue, but maybe if she healed old wounds, she'd have a shot at having a normal relationship with Ty.

But first, she was calling her sister. So what if it was Elisa and Maxim's honeymoon? Maxim had whisked her sister off to Egypt of all places and didn't intend to return her. Lizzy needed support, and wasn't that what families were for? She'd worn a wig, so Elisa owed her this. If Elisa couldn't—or rather, *wouldn't*—talk her out of all this craziness, the least she could do was listen. Help her figure out what to do.

Lizzy dialed the numbers, waiting for it to ring. Finally, the international call went through.

"Hello?" Immediately, Lizzy could tell her sister was busy. *Happily* busy.

Lizzy started to smile, but stopped herself. She refused to get too optimistic about her sister's relationship . . . ever.

"You're contagious," Lizzy blurted loudly, not sure what to say. How to say it.

She wasn't used to admitting how she felt—at least not in a *nice* way. And she sure wasn't used to the notion of admitting to anyone that she was wrapped up around some guy.

Not just some guy, her inner voice reminded her. *Ty.*

Shouldn't she get, like, a free pass or something on him? He *was* different. After all, he had been a part of her life longer than the dildos had.

"*What?*" Elisa asked, laughing at her. "What'd you catch?"

Real funny. Soon she'd be the butt of all her friends' jokes.

"You gave me the love bug," Lizzy wailed. Had she just said *love bug*? "Or just the craving for *real* sex. But either way—"

"Uh, double *what*?"

She might as well just confess instead of all these word games.

"I'm sorta sleeping with someone," Lizzy admitted. "A lot."

The strangest feeling invaded her—red-hot, chest constricting. Lizzy didn't know what to say, didn't want to say anything more. She bit down on her lower lip. *Damn.* She'd always felt like she could talk to Elisa about anything, but suddenly she was so nervous she was behaving like a fruitcake.

Shoving the blanket to the floor, Lizzy stood and started pacing. She wanted to ask Elisa what to do. To beg her to come home and hold her hand. But she could do none of those things. Suddenly, Lizzy realized she was on her own, that she *needed* to be on her own for this.

"You're sleeping with someone?" Elisa couldn't have sounded more pleased. "That's fantastic!"

Lizzy bit at her thumbnail. "Uh, not really, but do me a fave?"

"Anything!"

"Kick Maxim." Lizzy didn't mean to sound so serious. Didn't mean to *mean* it. "If that bastard can turn good, it's got me thinking even the worst of the worst can and I'm terrified."

"I don't know about kicking him. We were right in the middle of—"

"Okay. Ew."

"Call back later and we'll chat."

"Can't." Lizzy sighed and flopped on the bed. "I'll be on a date, but I'll call and let you know all the awful details."

"Bye, sweetie, and have fun!" Elisa cooed.

Fun. Lizzy didn't know about that, but suddenly she knew what she had to do. Maybe she'd known it all along.

Her call to Elisa had been anything but soothing, but it felt good to hear her sister cheering her on. Their quick conversation had been like drinking courage juice. Right now, she needed all the guts she could muster.

Lizzy pulled herself out of bed and headed into the kitchen to find the phonebook. She had a date to cancel and arrangements to make—she was going *home*.

ten

*H*e couldn't survive like this much longer. Not and have anything left to show for it, except, hopefully, Lizzy.

And she was all that mattered, right?

All Ty knew was that he had to try. Couldn't quit trying and wouldn't now, not when Lizzy was finally starting to come around.

Sitting in the wobbly chair at the burn-mottled table that had been used by one too many crackheads, Ty slowly breathed in the musty air of his cheap hotel room. He hated it here.

His eyes flashed to his stack of textbooks, to his newly balanced checkbook and bank statement. He wanted to throw them out of this damn shithole in a fit of rage. Burn them until they were gone, not eating away at him any longer.

Life wasn't fair. Some people had things handed to them on a silver platter, but he—

Ty let out a long sigh. He'd long since accepted that he had no one to blame for his misfortunes but himself. Not even his worthless parents could shoulder his decision to rob that damn jewelry store.

Don't get him wrong. He was all too happy to earn his way, to fight to have a future. That was what stripping and going to college were all about.

But sometimes it plain pissed him off.

He couldn't even date Lizzy like she deserved. One nice meal and he was in the red. She was used to finer things now, and he wanted to give them to her—not have her pay her own way.

Sooner or later, he hoped they'd get serious again, but how could he ever give her the kind of life she already had? He didn't want her money, didn't want her to *need* her money. He should be taking care of her.

He was in a no-win situation. The longer he stayed in Aspen, the closer he got to her but the further he pulled away from his own life. Everything he had going for him was going to shit. He was pretty sure his boss was about to fire him, and he was dancing for the best outfit in Colorado. Not to mention how hard keeping up with college had become or that he was spending all his extra cash. As it was, he was going to have to dip into his school savings.

And why had Lizzy canceled their date? The last time they'd gone out, despite their bet, she'd put up a fit about paying her own way. Was she angry that he hadn't let her?

Money ruined everything.

Torn, Ty struggled with what to do. He cracked his knuckles, clenched his teeth. Stay or go? *Stay or go?*

His cell cut through the silence. *Lizzy?* His hand zipped across the table, snatching up the phone and flipping it open. "Ty here."

"Hi, Ty," Lizzy said despondently. "Bad news. I've got a flat."

He stood, toppling his chair over and rushing to throw his belongings in his book bag. "Where are you?"

She didn't know why she'd called Ty and not a tow truck. Or AAA. Or a local gas station.

Instinct? Of course. She knew she could depend on Ty. That or she missed him already.

God, she had it bad.

A breeze whipped at her hair, gentle and cool. She sat on the tailgate of her cherry red GMC Canyon, hugging herself. God, it seemed like it'd been forever since she'd called him, but she knew he would get there.

Two hours out of Aspen, she'd hit something, blowing a tire. She'd barely managed to pull off the curvy road without wrecking. Was it a forewarning?

Perhaps she shouldn't go on this trip. Perhaps she was doomed to start with.

And yet, even with that prospect nagging at her, she knew she still had to go. If she didn't, she'd implode. Once she'd started thinking about it, her mind began going crazy with questions, at the things she'd say to her parents, making her realize how very unresolved her past was. It was no wonder she had issues.

For years, she'd been hiding from herself, under pink hair and crazy clothes, pretending like she was tough, not hurting. But Ty's presence brought it all to the surface. Every time she looked at him, it was like holding a mirror to herself, that part of her she'd tried to bury in that box of sex toys. She'd never gotten over her past, and if she wanted to be with Ty, hell, if she wanted to give herself a chance at having any type of intimate relationship, even with a dog, she needed to deal with her issues and quit covering them up.

She heard the roar of Ty's engine before she saw him. His black Trans Am whipped around the curve, slowing to a stop behind her.

Clad in his usual knock-a-woman-breathless, molded-on jeans and T-shirt, along with his cowboy boots and hat, Ty stepped out of the vehicle, slamming the door behind him. "You mean you own this beautiful truck and can't even change a tire?"

She smiled and shrugged. "Isn't that what men are for?"

She'd selected it for the four-wheel drive, but only drove it when necessary. Living in Aspen didn't give you a lot of vehicle options, so it was the car around town, in good weather, but otherwise, this truck. Besides, something about the vehicle made her feel in charge of the road, strong, and she needed that on this trip.

"Good thing you had yourself a man to call." Ty grinned like fool as he walked over to her.

"Don't go getting cocky."

"And why haven't I seen this beautiful truck on our dates?" He shoved his keys in his pocket, glancing at her flat.

"Didn't want to make you jealous." She slid off the truck, and his hands settled on her hips, pulling her closer.

"Me? Nah, you seen my car?" He nodded at the Trans Am. "Enough said."

"Old," Lizzy teased, wrinkling her nose.

"A classic," he debated.

"Just like you." Their pelvises met, pressing flush against each other, and she could feel the tempting bulge between his legs. She gazed up at him with narrowed eyes and gave his belt loops a tug. "Just fix my truck, cowboy."

"Please?" he demanded, his face shadowed under the rim of his hat.

She let out an exaggerated sigh. "Please."

His hands moved up her back, trailing from her hips to her spine in a gentle, tingling caress. "First you tell me where you were headed. And why you canceled our date."

"Home," she told him. She rested her face against his chest and gave herself permission to appreciate his touch, wishing to God she could enjoy it more. "To Tennessee."

She felt him go tense. "You should have told me. I would have taken you."

That's what she'd been afraid of. Weeks on the road with Ty? And no orgasms? Pure torture.

No, this was something she had to do on her own. Her demons, her fight. She wanted her privacy. Some of the issues she was dealing with mentally and emotionally were pretty embarrassing—like the Dildo Queen issue.

What's more, dragging Ty back to Tennessee if he didn't really want to go wouldn't be fair. Not to mention he had school and his own priorities.

She pulled away, crossing her arms. "I need to make the trip alone."

Now that wasn't going to fly with him. No way was he letting her make that trip by herself. Neither of them had seen her parents in years and back then, her stepfather had been nothing but a woman-and-child-beating alcoholic. Ty sincerely doubted the fiend had gotten nicer. Or found a job. Hell, with any luck, the bastard had drunk himself to death.

And even if her parents were great, which they weren't, Lizzy had no business being on the road solo. There were nasty truckers, bad drivers, his lonely heart . . . a thousand reasons why he couldn't let her go without him.

Alone his ass.

"You're too independent, Lizzy." Clenching his jaw against what else he wanted to say, Ty took off his hat and handed it to her, then walked around the side of the truck. "Let's just see about that spare."

And how I can get rid of it.

Kneeling, he pretended to look at the damaged tire, then he laid down and slid under the bed. Rough pavement scratched and pulled at his T-shirt.

The spare hung above him, never touched.

"How's it going under there?" Lizzy called.

"Well . . ." Digging in his pocket, Ty pulled out his knife and unfolded the blade, pointing it at the tire.

What was he doing? Was he seriously about to sabotage his girl-friend's truck? And how could he go on this trip—what about college? His finals this upcoming week?

"Hey, Liz," he called from under the truck, "why don't you wait until next week and let me take you to Tennessee?"

"I'm going myself, Ty."

Stubborn woman. What choice did he have?

With a hard thrust, he stabbed it into the rubber. *Oops.* "Hate to say it, but looks like your spare is flat too."

"What? It can't be! It's brand-new!" Lizzy protested. The heels of her boots clacked on the pavement. "How does a tire go flat hanging under the bed of a truck?"

Ty folded his knife and shoved it in his back pocket, then pushed himself out from under the bed. "Could have been faulty. Flying debris maybe. Not really sure."

His heart was pounding, his face flaming hot. He sucked at lying. Standing back, he grunted and stuffed his hands in his pocket. "Well, Lizzy . . ."

Damn, he hoped she couldn't see right through him.

"Shit," she swore under her breath, her eyes turning on his car. "What about yours?"

"Suddenly you want me to drive you?"

"No, silly, your tire."

He took his hat back, placing it on his head. "*My* spare? You crazy? You can't put a car tire on a truck."

"Great." She groaned in despair, tossing up her hands. "What am I going to do?"

"Looks like you're going home after all." Ty pulled his cell from his back pocket where it was nestled alongside the treacherous knife. He flipped it open, dialing information. "I'll call for a tow."

A few minutes later, help was on the way.

"It's a little windy on this mountain. You want to wait in my car?" he suggested.

"Sure." She shrugged quietly and groaned again. "I can't believe this. I finally worked up the nerve to face my parents and this happens? It must be a sign."

Ty preceded her, opening the passenger door. "So go next week. I'll take you."

"I'll be chicken shit by then and you know it." After she'd pulled her legs in, he gently shut the door and went around to his side, sliding into the bucket seat.

Ty tossed his phone on the dashboard, his mind reeling with thoughts of her going to Tennessee alone. His stomach in knots.

He *had* to get her to change her mind.

"Darlin', you sure you won't reconsider? Let me take you to Tennessee." Reaching out, he tickled a piece of hair that curled around her ear. Ran his finger along the lobe. "Listen to me—"

"No." She shuddered at his touch, looking up at him with frantic eyes. "I really don't think that's a good idea."

She had this deer-in-the-headlights look. Like she was trapped, scared. From what? His touch? Or the prospect of going home?

Ty dropped his hand to her knee. "Okay then. It's late afternoon, and I'd wager the local garage won't have your truck fixed until tomorrow at best and Aspen's two hours back. Let me get us a room. We'll uncancel our date."

He was pretty sure he saw her gulp before she answered. "Sure."

Lizzy stared at the hotel bed in disbelief. She couldn't believe she was so easy. So *stupid*.

How had he managed to talk her into this? Oh wait. He hadn't. He'd simply asked, and the only thing she'd managed to muster was "sure."

Behind her, Ty carried their belongings into the room. "Everything okay?"

And that damned tire. Why had she called him, anyway?

She placed her hand on the mattress, pressing down. Well, at least the bed looked comfy, not that she wouldn't be suffering in it all night long.

Why did sex have to be so difficult for her? After almost two weeks of being tortured by his presence, she felt ready to blow. But she couldn't and she knew that. The pressure was unbearable.

"Hey." Ty tossed his hat on the thick floral comforter. He circled her waist, pulling her against him. "You good?"

"Fine." She forced herself to be nice, commanded her body to relax against him. His hard torso felt so nice pressed to hers. Comforting. Enthralling.

Lizzy closed her eyes, relishing his presence. Secretly—unwilling to admit it even to herself—glad both her tire and her spare were flat.

"Want to take a shower?" With his lush, world-rocking lips, Ty kissed at her ear. His nose nuzzled the lobe and his tongue darted out, flicking and wetting the nerve-infused skin. "I'll wash you. Thoroughly."

A bolt struck through her, hard and fast. Demanding release.

"Mmmm." Unable to help herself, she twisted in his arms, turning so that her breasts brushed against his chest. Her nipples tightened, ached as they made contact with his well-muscled body. "That sounds nice."

Taking the thin fabric of his T-shirt between her fingertips, Lizzy tugged him as close as he could come, so that their bodies were flush. Their hearts beating in unison.

His hands snaked down her back, copping a feel.

"Maybe we can try some new things while we're in there." His voice was deep, husky. And his suggestion? Ever so tempting.

New things . . . like actually having an orgasm with Ty? Yeah, perhaps it would take some inventive play, some dirtier teasing, to get her there.

At the thought, she felt herself growing wetter, her nipples harder. God, she wanted him. Wanted what he offered.

"Even nicer," she agreed, standing on tiptoe. She kissed his chin,

suckled at his bottom lip. She was so tempted to tell him her problem, to ask him to do something, to help her . . .

But she could do this. By herself. Like any other normal woman.

She so urgently wanted to know what fully enjoying real sex felt
like and he was offering . . . No matter how discouraged she was,
she was compelled to try again. And again. And again.

New things. That would do the trick. What else was left?

eleven

$\mathcal{New}$ things?" Her curly neon hair falling haphazardly from its ponytail, Lizzy gazed up at him with violet eyes. She stood on tiptoe, tugging on the front of his shirt with playful fingers, teasing his mouth with her tongue. "Let your imagination run wild."

Hot *damn*. Did she have any idea how freakin' sexy-cute she was? Downright fuckable?

"My pleasure." Ty brushed a pink strand from her face, hardly able to maintain control. "Hard and slow and kinky, how's that sound?"

"Mmmm." Her burgundy-colored lips suckled his and her tongue darted out, laving the flesh.

Ty's mouth watered. He held in a groan, restraining the urge to throw her on the bed and take her *very* hard and *very* fast.

But not this time.

He yanked at her ponytail, pulling the band off. The black elastic shot from his fingers, flying across the room, and he fluffed her hair, letting it free.

Tonight, Ty intended to rock her world. To make her scream his name. *Beg.*

Since the first time they'd made love, something hadn't been right between them. They weren't clicking . . . especially in the bedroom. Lizzy said nothing, certainly made no complaints, but he could sense it, feel it from his heart right down to his toes.

Lizzy was the love of his life—*love*making should come easy, be automatically sizzling hot. But it wasn't, and Ty hated that things weren't more intense between them.

A problem he intended to remedy. Right now.

A growl formed in his chest, the urgency to come into her so great it was killing him, but he tamped it down. Forget his pleasure. He intended to put the tension and doubt to an end, to prove to her that no amount of time could change that they were one, heart and soul. To brand her with his passion and her own—something he should have done long ago.

Hands on her shoulders, he turned her around. His lips claimed her neck, nipping and suckling. Exploring her with his hands, he pulled open the button of her jeans. Sliding the zipper down, he pressed beneath the coarse fabric, dipping his fingers in her hot pussy. Testing.

"You're wet," he murmured in her ear.

"Naturally."

Ty drew back his hand and brought it to her lips. The scent of her filled the air around them, thick, pungent. *Delicious.*

"Taste how you feel." He could barely contain himself, his cock threatening to explode from his pants as he traced his fingers along her upper lip. But she didn't let him in. Instead, she crooked her head away from him.

Here he was sharing and she silently denied him?

Her mouth remained clamped shut as he swept the silk of her desire along the length of her lips, drawing her against his shoulder. Her head lolled and she closed her eyes, resisting.

"Open your mouth, Lizzy." There was a hard edge to his voice, one he hardly recognized. He wanted Lizzy to listen, to cooperate for damn once.

She made a small sound as he forced his fingers in her mouth. They butted against her teeth.

She turned away, closed her eyes.

"I won't stop," he warned her. "Not until you taste yourself."

Giving him a glare, she took his fingers into her mouth, drawing on them hard, almost painfully. *Obeying.*

A rush bolted through Ty, heat from his head to his toes. His arm tingled, little shivers dancing from where her mouth suctioned his fingers, straight to his shoulder. Down his spine.

"Darlin'." He retrieved his hand and stripped down her pants, letting them fall around her ankles. "So beautiful."

He explored her soft curves, the way her thong hugged her hips, slid between her ass. Following the thin strip of fabric, he dove deep between her cheeks, rubbing her anus. "And *all* mine."

She trembled against him and he pressed harder, threatening to plunge into the tight bud.

"Tell me. Say you're all mine."

Her only response was to whimper.

Fine, she didn't need to say it, but he damn well was going to prove it. He fisted her thong, yanking it with all his might. The fabric gave and he tore it in two, yet she still remained silent.

Tossing the thong aside, he swatted her bottom. Again, harder. Finally, she cried out. "Ty!"

"You're enjoying this, aren't you?" he hugged her against him, so that her bottom rode his cock through his jeans. "Soft is too sweet for Lizzy."

"But not Elizabeth," she whispered. Her ass moved against his shaft, rubbing the rough fabric along the thin skin, torturing.

"So which is it?" he inquired, his hands fondling her breasts roughly through her shirt. "Lizzy or Elizabeth?"

"Elizabeth doesn't exist anymore."

For now, Lizzy was in his arms. At his mercy.

And he intended to take her.

Ty lifted her shirt, pulling it over her head, then he unfastened her bra, casting the garments aside. She stood naked against him. Beautiful.

Again, he smacked her rear, this time like he meant it. "In the bathroom. Now."

She squealed, jumping as his hand connected with her bottom once again. Casting him a sensual smile over her shoulder, she hurried into the bathroom. He was hot on her trail.

Shaking, hornier than ever, Lizzy practically ran into the bathroom, going straight to the sink. She looked in the mirror, hating and loving who she saw.

She was so screwed up and all she wanted was a taste of normalcy. To know what it felt like to be loved, pleasured.

Ty stood a few feet behind her, peeling his tight-fitting clothes from his hard body. She watched his slow and sure movements in the glass, feeling anything but slow and sure herself.

Not that it was the first time, but she'd lied to Ty. Elizabeth wasn't gone. She was alive inside of her, begging to be released.

And some deep, well-hidden part of her needed to be Elizabeth when she made love to Ty. At least in part.

Leaning over the vanity, she slid her contacts from her eyes, letting them drop in the porcelain sink basin. She turned on the sink, washing them away.

"Good-bye," she said under her breath.

"Ready?" His cock sheathed in a condom, Ty walked up behind her, sealing his hips to her ass. His erection rode her butt cheeks, sliding between them and nestling along her anus.

"I was born ready." *But with an unwilling body.*

With an animalistic groan, he lifted her against him and whirled her around. He set her inside the shower, cranking on the hot water.

It blasted out cold, and she screamed, trying to jump out. "Ty!"

"That'll wake you up." He kept her pinned inside, moving under the cold water himself.

Goose bumps erupted along her skin and she shivered, sensitized from her hair to her pinky toes. "I'm already awake!"

Ty pressed her against the rear wall, grabbing the soap. Lifting her leg, he propped it on the edge of the tub and ran the soap over her body as the water turned hot, streaming down on her prickled skin, melting her.

"You know what I'm doing, Lizzy?" His hands slid between her breasts, over her nipples, down her belly.

"You're washing me?"

Over her mons, between her legs. Deeper.

The bar slid over her body, leaving cool, bubbly trails. Some sort of green deodorant soap. And the water kept getting hotter. Sauna hot.

Lizzy struggled to breathe in the steamy air and relax. If she could just close her eyes, escape under his touch . . .

"Washing you, yes, but so much more." Ty circled her belly and his pinky dove into her navel then retreated. Her stomach muscles clenched. "Let your pain, let your anger at me, slide away with the soap. Let it go down the drain." He looked up at her with dark eyes. "Please."

Her knees were shaking. Her feet felt as if they'd slip out from under her. "What if I can't?" *What if I never can?*

Oh damn, she needed something to hold on to. Her fingers clawed at the tile furiously and she pushed the small of her back into the hard wall as he tormented her with the bar of soap, running it over intimate areas, deep in her crevices.

His fingers spread her, forming a *V* as they held open her pussy lips.

"You can." The bar pushed at her clit, washed the tiny bud. "Just feel. Experience. That's all you have to do, darlin'. And I'll be here, making you feel good."

Damn, she wanted to. Arching her back, welcoming him into her, Lizzy closed her eyes and gave herself up to the hope that he *could* wash away her pain and anger. That she *could* forgive and forget. Move beyond her past and into a future. *Orgasm.*

Ty shifted to his knees, placing his head between her legs. The soap and his fingers slid deeper inside her, until he was washing her ass. Teasing her anus. Back and forth he explored, driving her crazy.

His hands took her by the hips and he guided her directly under the hot rush of water. The skin-singeing stream made her give a little cry. The suds covering her washed away, disappeared down the drain.

Something inside her shifted. Lightened.

Her pain? She couldn't make sense of how she felt. She was so on fire, numb to all other feeling. All she wanted was release, release from her desire, from all her pent-up emotions. She knew Ty could give her that.

If she could just let him.

"Lizzy." Ty buried his face between her legs, hugging her thighs. He ate her cunt, his nose nuzzling her clit as his tongue plunged inside, swept up and down.

Her fingers wound in his hair. Her need climbed even higher.

His tongue danced in her pussy, did the salsa with her clit. She wasn't sure she could take much more, but he just wouldn't quit. He kept licking and loving, teasing and torturing.

It was all too much.

Suddenly Lizzy wanted to pull free. To ask him to stop.

It felt so good, but . . .

Too good.

She cried out as his hands snaked around her hips and grabbed her ass. One of his fingers plunged between the cheeks, pressing.

Oh damn. All of her muscles went tense. The feeling was so scary, too intense. Lizzy tried to angle away, but he chose that moment to turn her around.

"Ty . . ." She braced her hands on the shower wall. He kissed her bottom, rising. His rubber-sheathed cock nudged her pussy. Grasping his shaft, he rubbed the head against her clit.

"Tell me how you feel," he asked her. "I want to hear you tell me."

Lizzy pressed her eyes shut, tears coming. "I can't."

And she couldn't. Couldn't enjoy fucking. Couldn't come.

He stilled behind her. "Don't I make you feel good?"

She hesitated. "Yes."

That was the correct answer, right? She couldn't tell Ty how scared she was. How terrifying the concept of letting him back into her life, into her body, was.

He'd already taken so much . . . How could she give more?

"Lizzy." Her name was filled with disappointment. "What—"

God, she needed this to be over. "Fuck me, Ty!" she cried, practically pleaded. "Hurry!"

His cock, positioned at her slit, drove inside her in one forceful thrust. He buried deep, holding her hips firmly so she couldn't move away.

"Now, tell me how you feel," he demanded.

There was no escape, not from the pleasure, not from the pain. She was stuck in this feeling. Cornered.

She bucked against him, trying to get him to move. To fuck her.

"Ty, please, I need you . . ." Her fingernails were breaking off from clawing at the walls. "I don't know what to do."

"Oh, Lizzy. Darlin'." Ty swore under his breath, pulling back and driving into her. "Don't bother faking it."

Ty wanted her too bad not to come. His cock was raging, pulsing, and so damn erect he could lift weights with it.

He took her hard and fast, trying to outrace his disappointment. He needed to come, to clear his head. He'd need that strength to deal with Lizzy.

Because he'd be damned if he'd just let this go.

Her whole body lurched as he took her, driving home his desire. His cock exploded in the sheathed confines of her hot pussy and the condom. Convulsing, he braced himself over her and rode out the orgasm until every last drop of cum had been expelled from his body.

His breathing was heavy, ragged. Slowly, he peeled himself off of her and stood. He gathered her into his arms, drawing their wet bodies together.

Stroking her hair, he held her as she cried. Sobbed.

For a moment, he said nothing. He just let her cry, comforted her.

"I don't know what's wrong with me," she wailed. "I just . . . I can't."

"I know, darlin'."

"I've been lying to you this whole time. I can't orgasm. I just . . ."

"It's okay." But it wasn't—not to him. He hated that she'd been faking it. That he couldn't give her pleasure. Talk about cutting a man off at the knees.

But what good was getting angry over it going to do?

He caressed her hair, nuzzling her ear. "Promise me, Liz. Promise you'll never fake it again."

"Are you serious?" she sniffled. "But—"

"No. I need to know that. You need to tell me."

"It's embarrassing."

"Please, Lizzy, let me help you. Be here for you." He pulled her head back, cupping her face and looking her in the eyes. "We can work on it together. I'll get you to come, I promise."

He was pretty sure it was the most ridiculous promise he'd made in his life, but also the most serious. Shallow as it seemed, his fate hinged upon whether or not he could give her an orgasm.

The tension between them was too much, and no relationship could survive such strain. He would always feel inadequate, she would always wonder if some other guy could do better.

"Okay," she answered, making him exhale with relief.

He guaranteed this—he'd get an *A* for effort.

"How about we practice together on the way to Tennessee? We'll take my car, leave tomorrow morning."

"But what about—"

"No worries, darlin'. I'll talk to my teachers, work something out."

"You can do that?"

"Sure I can."

He was lying through his teeth. Maybe, *maybe* his English teacher would let him e-mail his final paper, an even bigger maybe that his juvenile justice professor would do the same. But as for victimology? And college math?

Oh, he'd still put up a fight, but potentially, by making this trip, he'd be blowing a whole semester just at its end. By far, the stupidest thing he'd ever done.

But when he thought about Lizzy going to Tennessee by herself, when he thought about the prospect of making a road trip with her, the closeness it could bring them, the progress they'd already made together the past couple of weeks, Ty knew that every wasted penny and ounce of effort was worth it. He knew, in his heart of hearts, that this time he had to make the right decision, for just as he'd once chosen his hopes for the future over their relationship, he was now choosing their relationship over his future.

She pulled away, wiping at her eyes. Slowly, she nodded. "Okay. We'll go together."

twelve

Only thirteen hundred miles to Tennessee." Taking a sip of the bitter coffee from the gas station they'd just stopped at, Ty veered onto the highway. Gunning it, he slid into traffic past a rumbling eighteen-wheeler hauling wrecked cars. "No turning back now."

He didn't know why he said it . . . to reassure himself maybe? But on their way they were—he'd even stopped off at a twenty-four-hour Wal-Mart, stocking up on clothes for the trip since all his were back at the hotel. At least he'd thought to bring his books and laptop with him.

He just couldn't believe they were really doing this. The last place he thought Lizzy needed to go was to visit her parents.

She had an understandable need for closure—who in her situation wouldn't? He just didn't think she was going to find it in Tennessee, not after all this time. She needed to look for it in her heart, as he had. He'd long since accepted his relationship with his parents for what it was—over. There was no changing that.

Ty took another sip of coffee, almost spitting it out. He forced himself to swallow. The shit was terrible, but after tossing and turning all night, thinking about school and facing home, he needed the caffeine. Besides, the offensive taste offered a much-needed distraction from the nagging reality of what had happened yesterday in the shower. He'd never felt like less of a man.

"Thirteen hundred miles? *Shit*," Lizzy swore under her breath. She leaned forward, messing with the radio. "Not a chance are we listening to this the whole way."

She flicked the dial, changing the station to some dance music. Hip-hop tunes filled the car's interior, bass so deep, it made his heart thud.

"Hey!" he barked in protest. "You can't seriously expect me to listen to this. The sun's barely up. Turn it back."

She didn't budge and he didn't bother to change the channel himself. Funny, he ought to, but he didn't mind all that much. There was something exciting about her music. Appropriate.

"I remember when country was all you listened to."

Lizzy shot him a look of defiance, rolling her eyes.

"My woman left me; my dog is dead. Cue the crying!" she burst out in a twangy wail, making fun of the song he'd been listening to. "And my house just blew up. Yee haw! Where's my beer?"

Unable to prevent his grin, Ty veered into the fast lane. "Hey, country isn't that awful."

He might have to put up with bad music, but at least he knew this trip wouldn't be boring—he had the most interesting woman on the earth in the passenger seat of his Trans Am.

Just look at her. She wore her crazy hair pushed back in a neon green bandana. Her nails were orange. Her pink, clinging T-shirt—blinding pink that was—matched her black tights with pink polka dots.

Ty's fingers curled against the wheel as she sat back, smoothing her short, pleated black skirt underneath her. Her legs stretched out, incredibly long and tempting for someone so tiny.

Damn, he wanted them wrapped around him, that pussy squeezing his dick as she came.

Heat rushed to his loins, filling his cock. Stretching it. All he could think about was kissing every damn one of those polka dots. Ripping open the crotch of her tights. Feasting.

His cock hardened, straining in his blue jeans.

Ty held in a groan, trying to concentrate on the road—he was close to pulling over to the shoulder to plead for a blow job.

A lot of guys might've been turned off by her uniquely colorful choices. Maybe he even had been a little at first. But now? Something about her wild ways set off sparks in him.

He just wished he could set off sparks in *her*.

"Country's not all that bad? Are you kidding?" Lizzy shuddered in dramatic distaste. "It's depressing. I mean, get over it."

"Some of us never get over it." He flashed a meaningful look, sliding his hand onto her knee and squeezing. "I could *never* get over you."

She shook her head like she was shaking him off. "Don't get all serious on me, cowboy. This gal's just lookin' for a good time."

His hand slid higher, moving along the muscles of her inner

thigh, under the flimsy skirt. Every time his palm encountered the change in texture where a polka dot was, his fingers flexed. "Hmmm. A good time, eh?"

The polka dots disappeared, soft fabric covering her cunt. He cupped the mound, ready to stop traffic and show her just how good a time this cowboy could provide.

If she'd let him.

Beep, beep! Behind them, a car horn blasted out a complaint. *Beeeeeeeeeeeeep!*

"Shit." Lizzy glanced over her shoulder then at the odometer. "You know, you're going forty-five."

"Oh." Ty glanced in the rearview mirror. *Oh.* He'd gotten so distracted, he'd practically stopped driving. There was a mile of pissed-off traffic to his rear and he was putting along with a ten-inch tent in his pants.

Better let them by. Speeding up a little, Ty flicked on his turn signal and waited for an opening.

But the dumb jerks wouldn't let him over. And his cock wouldn't relax.

Beeeeeeeeeeeeep! The tailgater blasted his horn again. *Beeeeeep! Beep!*

"Assholes!" Lizzy tugged at her seat belt. "Back off!"

After several experiences with the difficult latch, she'd learned to unfasten it easily. Turning in her seat, she gave the car behind them the finger.

Beeeep!

A little giggle came from her. She lifted her shirt, flashing them.

"Jesus!" Ty cried. "What are you doing?"

His cock pressed harder against the zipper, demanding release.

And why the hell wouldn't anyone let him over? The cars seemed to close in around him, sandwiching him. *Beep! Beep!*

"Giving them something to honk about." Lizzy gave a little shake, wobbling her boobs for all to see. "Whoo!"

Not her boobs, *his*, damn it! Lizzy was *his* and he damn well didn't need all of Colorado getting a peek.

"Elizabeth Cross! Sit down!" Blood and adrenaline pumped through his veins so hard he wasn't sure if he was turned on or angry. Gripping the wheel, he cut off a car, steering across the slow lane despite the fact that no one was letting him by.

Brakes screeched, wheels squealed, horns honked.

Cars zoomed past, and he turned the wheel sharply once again, taking an exit.

"Party pooper!" Lizzy pushed her shirt into place as she twisted back into her seat. "We could have teased them all the way across the state."

What? Ty couldn't speak. Couldn't think straight. He was shaking and hard and so damn excited he was about to lose his mind over her.

Speeding off the exit, he pulled into the first store parking lot he came across.

"Jesus, Lizzy." Breathing heavily, he shut off the engine. He rested his head against the wheel. "You could have gotten us killed."

She laughed, shoving open the car door. "Damn, Ty, did I turn you on or what?"

"Huh?" Ty looked up, straight into a glowing yellow XXX. An adult bookstore? God, of all the luck.

Lizzy reached back in the car, grabbing her yellow vinyl purse. "You coming?"

Not yet, he wasn't. But if this was how she was going to play, soon, *she* would be. He guaranteed it.

Lizzy, you sure you want to go in there?" Ty walked up behind her, catching her hand and slowing her down. He wrapped his arm around her like she needed to be sheltered. "It's not exactly a place for ladies."

What, like she hadn't been in sleazy adult bookstores before? She loved these places. She always found something new to play with.

Ohhhh. But Ty didn't know that, now did he? She may have expressed her inability to orgasm with him, but she'd never expounded on her collection of sex toys. Or her nickname, "The Dildo Queen." Not really, and she wasn't sure she wanted him to know that about her.

Then again, what if he couldn't get her off . . . *ever*? What if sex toys were her only way?

Lizzy stopped in her tracks, standing under a blinking neon sign that read VIDEOS. Gazing up at him, she basked in the protectiveness that shone in his eyes. The concern. Ty evidently still thought her innocent and naive.

She could set him straight, clear up matters.

But something about the way he looked at her made her feel good, like she was unscathed, that her problems were a million miles away. She longed to curl into his arms and pretend it was so. To hide.

And yet, to do that was to be Elizabeth.

"Lizzy?" Ty asked again. "Let's get back in the car."

Hell, maybe she'd find something new to try in the store and tonight she'd actually orgasm. Maybe it was time she introduced Ty to her "tastes." Let loose and had a little fun with him—her style.

Yeah, that was exactly what their sex life needed—vibrators, dildos, you name it!

At the idea, sweat beaded on her brow, desire surged in her pussy. Oh yes, the more she thought on it . . . Ty wielding a vibrator? Hot, hot, hot! Actually coming tonight? Irresistible!

Clearing her throat, Lizzy shrugged off his apprehension and urged him toward the door. "I'm fine. Don't be silly. Come on."

"Okay." He hugged her closer to his side. "If you insist."

Threading her arm between them, she clung to his waist, so that they were arm in arm. "I do."

Together, they walked around the corner of the concrete building to a glass alcove covered in posters advertising porn.

Ty pulled the door open for her. "This place is a dump."

"So?" Lizzy walked in, Ty right on her tail.

Dry heat and the stench of cigarettes blasted her in the face. Barely looking up from his tiny television, the man behind the counter nodded a hello.

Ty shot an "I told you so" look at her and Lizzy turned away, focusing on a rack of dildos.

"Wow." Still not sure how to go about her plan, she feigned shock.

Or maybe *she* was shocked—that they could get thirty bucks for such a shorty. She'd seen bigger—a lot bigger—on men even.

"You want one?" Ty shifted and his hand tugged at her upper arm, pulling her away. "Or, um . . ."

His words were left hanging.

"What?" She looked up at his unmoving lips. Oh gosh. Ty didn't know what to say, much less suggest! *He* was nervous!

Funny, in a place like this, she was comfortable and he wasn't. Yet when it came to actual sex . . .

God, she wanted to avoid that thought at all costs.

"Whoa, look at that." Trying to distract both of them, she guided Ty down a narrow aisle, past shelves of butt plugs and various anal lubricants to the back corner, until they couldn't be any further vested in the place.

So what now?

Turning, she stared at the selection at her fingertips. Dildos, vibrators, videos, and games. Toys for anal play. Bondage. Whips and chains.

"We should have picked up a basket," she joked. "So, what do you want? Whips and chains?"

No sooner than she heard herself say it, her heart gave a kick, jump-starting in her chest. Pounding in her ears. *Why* had she asked that? Given him control of this situation? What if he *was* into whips and chains?

Lizzy sucked her lower lip between her teeth. Now she really was nervous. For all she knew, Ty was secretly into something really kinky, just like her. Except, who knew what he might ask of her . . . and he'd asked a lot already.

Could she take being any *more* intimate with him? No. It was her turn to do the asking, before her knees gave out or her face turned yet another shade of crimson—which didn't look good with her hair.

"Um . . . never mind. Don't answer." Lizzy told him, relieved he hadn't already. "Because I'm not. I mean, I can't believe I even said that and . . . you're not, are you? Wait! Don't answer that either . . ."

She was rambling.

Ty gave a little laugh, obviously over his hesitation. "Let's take it easy on your first shopping trip," he suggested, his voice smooth as velvet, firm for someone who was as tongue-tied as he was when he'd walked in.

Oh, she got it. Now that she was shaking in her shoes, *he* was the big man?

To her relief, Ty pointed to the shelf left of them. "How about a board game we can play together?"

Easy enough.

"Which do you like?" Lizzy walked to the shelf, examining her choices, and Ty positioned himself close behind her, so close she could feel his breath on her neck.

There were more romantic-looking games, sex dice, and the naughtier. Some were even designed for more than a couple. *Fun.*

But she had no idea which was right for them. Her specialty was toys, not games.

Browsing, she chose a box covered in roses entitled "Enchantment." The game looked easy enough to play, and the last thing she needed was to put herself out there.

"How about this?" She handed it to him.

Ty took the box, turning it to read the back. His eyes roamed over the instructions and pictures, then settled on her. "Sweet. But if I remember correctly, you're not sweet, are you, Lizzy?"

She looked away, stumbling over her response. "I don't know."

Damn it, who did he think he was, hanging on her every word like that? So she'd claimed she wasn't sweet . . . maybe she'd changed her darn mind! Maybe *Ty* made her feel sweet . . . and even a little shy about sex.

Craziness.

"You don't know? You've only reminded me a hundred times." With a chuckle, he hauled her against him and pressed his hips against her behind, making her aware of his erection.

And damn, his hard cock felt tempting . . . but it wasn't enough, she knew that.

Hadn't she, just five minutes ago, decided to introduce Ty to her bedroom preferences? And now she was choosing games with roses on the box?

Enchantment her ass.

"This is driving me crazy," Ty whispered.

That made two of them.

His cock pressed between her ass cheeks, letting her know just how *crazy* he was feeling. "If this is the game we're playing, I think we need to up the ante."

Up it? Little did Ty know, he was already in over his head! "Who's betting?"

"I am." He pulled her even closer, his fingers snaking around her hips to rest on her upper thigh, precariously close to pushing up her skirt an inch too far and coming into contact with her heating pussy. "That I make you climax tonight."

She closed her eyes, wishing he would—and not tonight, *now*. She wanted him to touch her, to make her explode. Banish this ache.

His fingers danced over her skin, teasing her unmercifully, his lips brushing along her neck.

Lizzy found herself clenching her pussy muscles, wanting to beg

Ty to take her right here, this minute, against a rack of worthless sex toys just so she could show the junk she didn't need it. Prove herself.

But need it she did.

"Betting? I thought you were *helping*," she countered, defensive against the way she suddenly felt, the reality she had to face. Against his attitude about her problem. Like not being sexually normal was no big deal . . . jerk. "Am I a game to you?"

"No, but what's wrong with having a little fun in the bedroom?" he drawled. "Lovemaking doesn't have to be so serious. Or so intense. Let's just have some fun."

Fun. He was right. *So* right.

He picked up a dangerous-looking black box with flaming red lettering that read "Confessions and Explorations."

Staring at the game, a torrent of desire to do just that—*explore*—left her tingling and ready to investigate . . . this store, Ty's determination to get her off. "What do you have to do?"

"It's kind of like Truth or Dare. Except dirtier."

Dirtier. Just what she needed.

"Okay." She pushed herself from his embrace and walked casually into the next aisle. Selecting a huge vibrator—the Wallbanger—she held it up. "This too." *Just in case.*

Ty gave a little laugh. "Are you serious?"

"It's not for me."

His eyes widened and his smile fell. "Put that damn thing back."

Not on her life.

"Don't be such a party pooper." Because she wasn't going to be either—not anymore. She was done stressing over what she couldn't achieve and ready to show Ty exactly what she needed. In fact, a few more items were necessary. Lizzy returned to shopping.

And that's when she saw it. The Rockin' Rooster.

"Oh wow." Lizzy grabbed the package from the rack. She'd seen the Rooster online, had wanted to try it *so* bad. Six months she'd been admiring this unique vibrator, but could never justify purchasing it. Without a man, this toy was useless.

And now, she had a man.

Oh, yes, yes, yes! She couldn't believe her luck.

"The Rockin' Rooster!" Turning the package, she held it up for Ty. "It's a cock sheath *and* a vibrator."

"A sheath? I wear it?"

"Of course, silly."

"Never heard of that before." His brows furrowed as he peered over the rack of sex toys between them. "Read the back to me."

"The Rockin' Rooster is four inches long," she quoted from the meant-to-sell description, "made of bright red, rubberlike material meant to hug a man's cock and hang on for a wild ride, ridges intended to stimulate a woman senseless, and a rooster head at the base, for 'pecking' a woman's choice of clit or anus . . ."

"Holy crap."

"Wanna know the best part?"

"Dare I?"

"It has three speeds. Remote operated." Lizzy tucked the Rooster under her arm, along with the other vibrator. "I'm getting it."

She was pretty sure she'd stunned Ty speechless, but the important part was that he wasn't protesting. Oh baby, tonight her world was getting rocked by the Rooster.

Excited, her self-consciousness completely forgotten, Lizzy walked down the aisle, along the way grabbing a pretty pink strap-on clit simulator—the Hopper, she had it at home already—which wore like underwear, with a bullet encased in a pink, gel-like thing designed to ride a woman's clit and of course with remote-control operation.

"Having fun?" Ty met her at the end of the aisle, carrying their game and a box of condoms. Multicolored and glow in the dark—so, for a guy, he had some taste after all!

Taking the products from him, Lizzy marched to the front, grabbing some lubricant on the way. Yeah, she was having fun!

thirteen

"Lizzy, Lizzy." Ty couldn't contain the humming satisfaction that vibrated from his chest as he backed out of the parking space in front of the adult bookstore. He couldn't believe her. Yeah, any woman liked to shop, but she'd racked up a two-hundred-dollar bill on sex toys! No shame, little hesitation, only the silent, sultry promise of tonight.

Forget tonight, he wanted *now*.

He was so damn excited and aroused, his face hurt from smiling. His toes were curled. His dick? The little guy was jumping to Lizzy's tune like this was a game of Simon Says and he didn't have a clue how to follow the rules.

God, Lizzy had a way about her. Her every little action sparked something in him, drove him near crazy with want, and he couldn't stop grinning like a fool. Everything she did, said, he felt more *alive*, like all this time, he hadn't been living, just going through the motions and now, he was, twofold. He knew he'd made the right decision, abandoning school to take her to Tennessee. She was worth it.

"You never cease to amaze me."

Heading the opposite direction of the highway ramp, Ty pulled onto a city street into slow traffic. He had no idea where he was driving, didn't care, so long as it involved a bed. Fishing in his ash-tray, where he kept a stash, he retrieved a hard candy and unwrapped it, popping it in his mouth.

"I amaze you? Why's that?" She crooked a brow, cooing sweetly, naively. Ty didn't buy the act, not for a spilt second. He crunched down on the cherry-flavored candy.

Lizzy certainly wasn't innocent, but just how guilty was she?

"I expected you to be uncomfortable in a place like that."

"And I didn't expect you to be." With a snort of amusement, she rested her head back and glanced out the window. "Ty, where are we going? The on-ramp is the other way."

He ignored her question, still stuck on her first statement.

"Uncomfortable?" More like shocked. And turned on. "No. You read me wrong."

Hanging a left, Ty drove down a busy street, deeper into the city. He glanced at the bag of sexual goodies that rested between her feet on the floorboard.

Forget getting back on the highway. They needed a motel for the afternoon—and night.

At this rate, they were going to get nowhere fast on this trip. Except maybe to Orgasmville, if he—and those toys in her bag—had anything to say about it.

She laughed. "Read you wrong? I don't think so. You were tongue-tied! Your cheeks were redder than a radish."

"Yeah right," Ty dismissed the notion, clearing his throat. He turned down another road, searching. Damn, weren't there any decent places to stay on this stinkin' street? He'd passed one or two shitholes, but he'd never take Lizzy to a roach motel. "And anyway, the point is, you walked through that store like you'd been there before."

She shrugged. "Not that one."

"Huh?" What was that supposed to mean? And how on earth did she go from looking and sounding so cute one moment to behaving like such a vixen the next? "What are you saying?"

She'd been in a store like that before? With who? Why?

"Oh, nothing." She lifted her feet, folding them under her thighs and causing her skirt to hike up. "There's lots you don't know about me, Ty."

"There is?" His eyes were drawn to her legs, so long and covered in those silly polka dots, and higher—who knew what sort of panties she wore? *So damn sexy.* "I mean, I know we have a lot of catching up to do, but what does that have to do with adult bookstores?"

Lizzy cried out, bracing herself. "Ty!"

He jerked his gaze back to the road. *Oh shit.* A red light.

Slamming on the brakes, he barely stopped in time.

"Sorry," he told her, clenching the steering wheel. First the highway, now this? Jeez, she was a dangerous passenger to have on board. A major distraction. Half a day on the road and he'd almost wrecked several times already.

All the more reason to find a motel. Fast.

"Watch where you're going. Not me." Grasping the door handle, she returned to their conversation. "That night we first found each other—I told you I had better luck with my dildos. Remember?"

It stung every time he did. "Yeah, and you'd take a vibrator over me any day. Real funny."

"I wasn't kidding."

"Wasn't? Don't you mean *was*?"

She chewed at the crimson color covering her lips. "I own more sex toys than I do appliances. Actually, vibrators are my most used appliance."

Well, shit. Forget his ass—she might as well have kicked him in the heart.

She enjoyed a toy more than him? What did that make him?

Ty held in a groan, trying to concentrate on the road.

He wasn't the jealous type. Not usually. So why did he suddenly feel so damn possessive about her . . . and resentful over the hunks of plastic and batteries by her feet?

Because she preferred them. Because they did it for her and he apparently didn't.

He'd assumed since she couldn't come with him, she never had, but she had to be getting something out of playing with the damn things, right?

"You still haven't told me where you're taking me."

Ty spotted an Econo Lodge. He nodded toward it, making a right into the parking lot.

Thank God he'd found a place. It was high time he claimed his rightful spot—as her *sole* pleasurer.

"Take it back." His hand darted across the seats and he tickled her side, showing no mercy. "And I mean it. Take it back!" His fingers danced over her skin, poking and teasing.

"Stop!" She squirmed, howling pleas and giggles. "Take what back?"

"That you prefer a damn toy over me." He pulled into a parking space, his fingers still going crazy against her ribs. She twisted, trying to escape, laughing so hard she was crying.

He tickled faster, determined.

"Okay, okay," she wailed, breathless. Their eyes connected as he shut off the engine. "*Until* you, I preferred toys. But I still like them!"

"Now that, that I can deal with." Reaching up, Ty lifted his cowboy hat from his head then replaced it. "Just so long as I'm number one—in the bedroom and out."

"Hmmm. You want that position?" Her eyes sparkled. "Why don't you convince me?"

"It would be my pleasure, ma'am."

But would it be hers?

Lizzy's chest tensed at the thought of another sexual encounter with Ty. Not just sexual, she reminded herself, loaded with toys. Toys that could do the trick!

The muscles of her pussy contracted, her loins quickened.

The prospect was so alluring and yet . . . overwhelming. She'd trained herself to climax with plastic assistance, to lose herself in the orgasms vibrators and dildos could provide her, but would human involvement, in the form of Ty, kill that buzz?

Perhaps she just needed to train him to use her toys. It was all in the wrists, right? Not that Ty was the type of man to bring to heel. Or that she wanted to.

No, right now, the only thing she *wanted* was to end the ache between her legs, the unfulfilled arousal that had plagued her since he'd showed up in those damn chaps.

Flushed, growing wetter by the second, she watched Ty get out of the car and come around to her side. He was so damn sexy, strutting like a wild animal on the prowl. And she was his prey, soon to be writhing and at his mercy.

Shit. She wasn't sure if that was good or bad.

Maybe she should have let him tickle her until she wet her tights. That would've been less embarrassing than if she failed to orgasm—yet again and with toys involved.

No. All was good, she decided. She had the answer in the plastic bag resting at her feet. Lizzy picked up the merchandise, wrapping the handle around her fingers.

This had to be it. *Had to.* She couldn't have sex with him one more time and not climax, could she? No. She wanted it too badly. Needed it . . . needed him.

Ty opened her door and, brushing his body along hers, reached across her lap to undo her seat belt. Heat infused her as he quickly unlatched the buckle and offered his hand, helping her out.

Clutching her merchandise, Lizzy rose and stepped into his embrace, right where she belonged. "So, tell me, cowboy, ever used toys in sex before?"

"You tell me . . . afterward." He cupped the back of her head, bringing her mouth to his. "We'll see if you can guess correctly."

"So I'm supposed to gauge your experience?"

"You," he murmured against her mouth, his hot, cherry breath blowing into her, "are to orgasm, whatever you need me to do. Way I see it, I owe you—five to none."

She could taste every word he spoke and oh, how she wanted a *taste* of what he offered. "I've got some catching up to do."

"That you do. And will." With that guarantee, Ty kissed her, his tongue diving into the moist recesses of her mouth, swiping along hers. Taking control of that deep, wild part of her that needed him and the release he offered so very much, she'd do anything. *Anything*.

Melting in his arms, Lizzy clutched the bag tighter and unleashed her passion, her tongue driving against his, exploring spicy promises.

Almost two weeks. Two weeks of continuous sexual torture and no release. Her cunt was an inferno, her nipples like magnets in her chest, drawing her to him, making her rub against his torso, seeking more as the buds tightened, encompassed with sensation.

How was she supposed to cope? A woman could only take so much, be so strong. And Ty . . . Ty was making her weak. The way he sucked her lower lip, drawing blood to the sensitized area, the way he held her like she belonged to him . . .

She'd come in the damn parking lot with her panties still on if he kept kissing her like this. And why not? She had five orgasms to blow! One here, one in the lobby, one in the elevator . . . that still left two for the room!

All sensibility lost, she encouraged him to go further, flicking her tongue against his, loving the way they danced in each other's mouths as she pressed against him in slow, sultry movements.

Wrapping her arms around his neck, she climbed his legs with her feet. Ty lifted her, and she wrapped her thighs around his waist, hugging her cunt against his lower abdomen. His jean-covered erection pressed against her lower buttock as his hands claimed the flesh, holding her tightly.

"God, I need to get you inside." Kissing her and stumbling as he walked, Ty carried her across the parking lot.

Couldn't he walk any faster?

Lizzy temporarily broke free of his mouth, claiming his ear. "I'm ready now," she whispered, licking the lobe.

"That so?" One of his arms pinned her securely to his torso and she rested her weight against him as his fingers darted up her skirt, his touch wickedly diving between her legs.

"You're wet," he whispered in her ear, pressing the pads of two fingers into her tights, against her clit, his thumb hovering at her entrance, making her pussy constrict with the need to grab hold of him, to have him. "I bet I could make you come—"

"Here and now. In the parking lot," Lizzy finished for him. "In front of everyone."

Everyone? Holy—

What was she saying? Thinking?

Only that she had a bomb between her legs and if he kept toying with it, pushing her buttons . . . boom!

Instinctively, Lizzy humped his hand, nipped at his lower lip, and thought about telling him to toss her bottom-up over the hood of the nearest car and do her there.

So maybe she ought to stop him, but then, she was never very good at doing things the right way. Behaving.

And maybe that's what had her so very turned on, the prospect of breaking the rules, the kick she got out of getting hot and heavy in a parking lot, the thrill of knowing Ty was carrying a bag of toys, and willing to use them . . . eager to, as was she.

Just the thought of Ty wielding a dildo—or maybe two—was hot, hot as her pussy.

"Ty," she whimpered, not even sure what for.

"Hold that thought." Gently, his fingers skimmed down her thighs, leaving a hot trail of need in their wake as he set her on her feet. "We can't go in there like this."

Well, why the hell not?

Of course, even as her chest lifted and fell with excitement, her pussy dripped with need, she knew he was right . . . but booking their room better go fast. Real fast.

She was *ready* and didn't want to lose it.

She flashed him a seductive smile, smoothing her skirt into place, and giving her hair a little shake. Hand in hand, they walked inside looking normal as ever—a cowboy and his horny punk rocker.

*T*en minutes later, Lizzy all but barreled down the door to their hotel room. Hugging her bag of goodies, she flopped on the bed and began wiggling out of her tights.

"I've never seen you so excited about sex." Flashing a hungry look, Ty claimed the bag and peered inside. "So, want to play our game?"

Play the game . . . or play with Ty and her new Rooster? Hard choice.

She imagined that realistic cock sheathed around his, vibrating away inside of her, and nearly went wild. Her pussy muscles constricted around empty space, demanding.

She tossed her tights at him and they landed on his shoulder, dangling haphazardly. "No way. Save that for a rainy day."

Ty lifted her tights, hanging them on his forefinger and lifting them to his nose. "I'd say it's raining plenty—between your legs."

That it was. She was more than wet enough to take the width of the Rockin' Rooster. Cock-a-doodle-doo!

"And I'd say don't waste water."

"Who me?" Ty feigned innocence, like he wasn't the one who'd flooded her kitchen. "Never!"

"Yes, you!" Off flew her clothes—directly at him. "I'm all about conservation. Now hurry, save my orgasm!"

A crooked, amused smile lifted his whiskered cheeks as she approached him naked, seized the buttons of his jeans, and tore them open.

"One cock to your rescue." Throwing the bag on the bed, Ty disposed of his T-shirt as she tore down his pants. He stepped from his bunched-up jeans, kicking them aside with a chuckle. "I've never seen you so keyed up, and for you, that's saying something."

"Are you kidding? I've got the Rockin' Rooster! It's like . . . like I'll be doing a robot or something! Half man, half vibrator!" Jumping on the bouncy bed, Lizzy fished in the bag and pulled out the Rooster, fighting the plastic package for her little guy's freedom.

Keyed up? She was excited as all get-out. The more she thought of it, the more she realized, this was *it*. Maybe, just maybe, if her body just once could do her a favor, this would be the end to her orgasmic trouble.

She was on the dawn of a new her—after all, before Ty, trying something like this had been out of the question. Now, with him and the Rooster, she could have her cake and eat it too—sex with Ty, with the plus of actually being able to climax. Toys and man, coming together to form the Liz-bot, a match made in heaven, by a female God of course.

"Here, let me." Wielding his pocketknife, Ty took the package from her.

Lizzy watched him, watched the blade, as it sliced through the top of the clear plastic and he tore open the package.

The trash fell to the ground and Ty took the Rooster, twirling it on his finger.

Oh, it was too cool! She had to touch it, feel it. "Give it to me!"

"No way." He winked. "Hope it fits."

Pushing her back, he straddled her chest, so that his cock was directly in her face, so close she could smell him, that fleshy, salty scent of arousal and man, then the new-car smell of the rubber sheath as he enveloped his cock.

It was so much bigger in person, adding unrealistic inches and width to Ty.

Holding the remote in hand, Ty clicked the button, turning it on. A low hum filled the air as he leaned forward, rubbing the quivering cock along her lips.

All the blood in her body rushed to her mouth—the effect, dizzying. "Oh my . . ."

Ty pulled back slightly. "Where do you want me to go with this?"

"*Go?*" The question brought about a million possibilities, like the way her lips tingled, her mouth watered. What would it feel like to suck a vibrator? To have it humming down her throat, thrusting past her lips, in and out, bringing Ty pleasure?

What's more, the possibilities were endless. Her mouth wasn't the only spot he could use the Rooster on, now was it?

Holding it at the base, he waggled the Rooster in front of her. "Well?"

Her tongue darted out, licking the wide head of the Rooster.

"Ty," she whispered, drawing a deep breath that jostled the

hovering Rooster in her face. "Make me crow. Take that damn toy and use it until I beg you to stop."

"Beg me to stop?" He chuckled as he slid down her body, letting the toy hum along her length. "Now why would you want me to do that?"

Sitting between her legs, Ty lifted her feet to his shoulders, and set to work like a man on a mission—a mission of orgasmic proportions—and Lizzy focused on one thing and only one thing. *Feeling.* Feeling the way only he could make her feel—he and the acclaimed Rooster—as he held the cock against her clit, riding the nerve-infused bud in quivering circles, sliding up and down the length of her pussy, venturing almost too far south, into un-tried territory with the Rooster's turned-down beak, then back up, riding her cunt so thoroughly, so wonderfully, that he left Lizzy panting. Hot and ready, wet and willing, for whatever he might do with that thing.

And *do,* he did, pressing the Rooster flat against her mons, draw-ing her legs downward, so that her thighs clamped him securely as he switched the speed even higher and rode her without entering her.

The beak pecked at her anus and her body arched, meeting his strokes, riding tidal waves of tingling ecstasy. She was high and fly-ing higher—the way he wielded that thing, she could *never* make herself feel this way. Never *had* felt this way.

But that wouldn't stop her from aiding his efforts. God, yes, she needed this, needed to be touched everywhere, needed to fill the hole growing wider and wider in her. To complete herself . . . *them.*

Cupping her breasts, she molded the soft mounds in her palms, tweaked her nipples with her forefinger and thumb, drawing and rolling pleasure to the tightening peaks, climbing higher as she rode his every stroke.

He hadn't even entered her yet, but she could feel it, the climax rising in her, the release to come.

And that's when he plunged into her, driving her home with the wide, curved, and bumpy cock that reached so high, the pressure on her G-spot was almost unbearable.

She knew that part of her cunt well, had praised it many times, but she'd never known this, this . . . whole body experience. The way her toes curled and her mind whirled.

Dear God, it almost felt too good. She couldn't contain herself as he nestled deep and circled those hips.

"Ty!" She screamed out, feeling his name as it whooshed past her lips just as she released, gripping her breasts, squeezing and humping against him as Ty continued to drive into her over and over, completely and totally turning her world inside out.

Not slowing, certainly not stopping, not even as the orgasm faded, replaced by an even fiercer drive for more—*more, more, more!* Lizzy pinched her nipples hard. Twirled them in demanding circles as she lifted her hips and Ty reached beneath her, stroking her anus with soft and sweet touches, praising the quivering bud in a way that threatened her sanity.

"Come again," he commanded as he thrust his hips and pummeled that special spot deep within her, shook her very core, fucked her plain silly.

And climax she did—Lizzy came like the mother lode. Her pussy convulsing, her thighs quivering, she gasped for composure and thrashed on the bed, her mind fading in and out in blurry waves as Ty milked every last cry from her and she was so spent, all she could do was close her eyes and lie there as he pulled free, rolled on a condom, and slid back inside of her, finishing himself off in a few sure strokes, then collapsing on top of her.

Six to two. Ty had his pride—puffed up as it currently was—and now that he knew how to handle Lizzy, he intended to catch her up on her orgasms, make up for lost time, so to say.

Sprawled on the bed, Lizzy slept soundly, exhausted from their lovemaking a couple of hours ago. But ever since watching her come the way she had, Ty couldn't rest to save his life. After cleaning up her and the toys, he'd tried and, for distraction, had ended up calling all four of his professors. His first analysis had been correct—two courses saved, two lost—but rather than working on his final papers, anxiety and anticipation had Ty pacing the tiny hotel room. All he could think about was the things he'd do to her next time . . .

And "next time" was now. She'd had plenty of sleep.

Rummaging through their bag of goodies from the adult bookstore, Ty pulled out the second item she'd purchased. Admittedly, he hadn't a clue what the thing was, but it was pink, and Lizzy liked pink.

Standing at the edge of the bed, he inspected the picture of the woman wearing strappy underwear that held some sort of bulb over her clit, then he read the directions. A clit stimulator.

Thinking of the Rooster that he'd positioned to tease that little behind of hers, Ty smiled to himself. He removed the Wallbanger from the bag and held it up, grinning even wider. If last time had been a thrill, just wait. He planned to pummel every erotic spot on her body with these sex toys.

He tore open wrappers, tossing the toys on the bed next to her,

then he sheathed himself in the Rooster—he kinda liked the thing.
It held his cock so tightly and the ridges and vibrating . . . blew his
mind, his cock. The Rooster was quite the experience—for a male
or female—that was for sure. Heck, he could really get into this sex
toy thing. Right now, though, the only thing he wanted to *get into*
was Lizzy.

Lizzy awoke to the sensation of being lifted. Her hips were angled in the air, masculine fingers tingling along her back and behind. And straps . . . the feeling of being belted in. She had to be
dreaming still.

Something cool and gel-like, with a hard center, rested against
her clit.

Huh?

"Ty?" she murmured, winking the sleep from her eyes, yawning.
"What time is it?"

"Six to two. Time to catch you up." Ty's deep voice, his sugges-
tive connotation, washed over her. Fuzzy awareness set in, followed
by immediate memories of the love they'd made—Rooster included.
And the orgasms . . . oh the orgasms!

Damn, she must've passed out—and it was no wonder!

Buzz . . .

Her hips jerked, glorious shivers bolting through her pussy.

Holy smokes! "Okay, I'm awake!" Fully opening her eyes, Lizzy
jerked up to half sitting, propped on her elbows, and discovered Ty
had put the Hopper on her . . . and the little torture device was just
humming away.

What's more, he was wearing the Rooster again—and wielding
the Wallbanger!

Six to two? Boy, he was really serious about keeping score. Did he actually expect to give her *four* more orgasms? God, she hoped so—this stimulator was stimulating the crap out of her!

Blood flooded her loins, her cunt clasped at empty air as he positioned himself between her vibrating legs. Lizzy immediately lifted her hips, needing that Rooster inside her.

Instead, Ty switched on the Wallbanger, bringing it to her mouth. "You can't imagine how you look right now."

Slowly, he traced the quivering fake prick over her lower lip. Tingles shot through her and he lifted a piece of her hair, twirling it in his grasp. Below, the Hopper was still thumping away at her clit, to the point where she'd clenched every muscle tight, almost painfully.

"How do I look?" she managed to ask, wanting to scream at him to get on with it already. Who cared how she looked; she knew how she felt. She was damn close to coming . . . It was almost embarrassing how very fast her body wanted release, after so long of holding out.

The corner of his lips lifted wryly. "Like you're ready to come already." He tugged on her hair and slid the Wallbanger over her top lip, then past it, forcing her to open for the vibrator as he explored the depths of her mouth, over her tongue. "And beautiful. My little pink-haired sex vixen."

Who knew having a piece of rubber in your mouth could feel so very ecstatic? Turned on to no end, Lizzy clamped her mouth around the shaft, sucking as Ty moved it in and out.

The sound that came from him was animalistic, *hungry*, and he withdrew, sliding the Wallbanger over her chin, down her throat, leaving a wet trail of saliva as he made his way to her breasts. He circled each nipple, drawing them into peaks that he then tormented with vibrations, teasing the tips, flicking them back and forth, rubbing them without mercy.

Instinctively, her hips lifted, and the climax that she spun into was so unexpected, she was slammed into an uncontrollable whirl, sky-high, out of her mind. Screaming, she clutched the bedsheets, then tossed that effort to the side, clutching at his shoulders, trying to pull him down. "Fuck me, Ty!"

Her pussy muscles flexed rapidly, grasping at emptiness, begging to be filled as her cum trickled from her in a rush and the orgasm faded, leaving her body on fire in its wake.

Only then did Ty move down her, positioning himself between her legs. Not once did he let the Wallbanger stray from her breasts, continuing to pleasure her nipples alternatively. With his free hand, he turned the Rooster head down once again, so that its beak met her anus.

"Oh, God," she hiccupped. It was all so much, and more was to come. She knew what this was going to do to her, almost feared the way he was about to make her feel . . . *never* had she experienced so very much at once. But Ty, Ty wielded these toys with a talented hand. *Very* talented.

He entered her an inch with the Rooster, switching the toy on as he did. Her cunt jump-started, her body filled with so much humming, she was shaken to the very core as he drove into her, slamming the Rooster's beak into her rectum.

He rode her hard, demanding, fucking her like he was out to prove something, and if it was making her come, he achieved it again. And again. In a rage of ecstasy, her mind a blur, Lizzy's body shattered into little bits every time he plunged against her G-spot, only to shatter again, until she could shatter no more.

"Ty." She felt herself losing consciousness, little pieces of her mind fading in and out as he drove home, nestling deep within her and dropping the Wallbanger from her breasts to the mattress beside her. Sliding his hand under her head, he rested above her, his hot body melded against hers as he held her. Just held her.

And in that moment, Lizzy couldn't imagine a more perfect existence. Indeed, she'd found a man who understood her, who loved her for her. She didn't need to fight any longer, to be ashamed. She just needed to lie here, in his arms, enjoying all he had to offer.

fourteen

Don't get out of bed."

Now she couldn't argue with that, could she? Who'd want to? And what a way to wake up! Lizzy had no idea how long she'd slept, but she was roused now, and feeling totally refreshed. Currently, the world's most happiest of women.

"What a nap. What time is it?"

"Tomorrow, almost afternoon. You really slept hard." Ty strutted across their hotel room toward her, naked as the day he was born and looking like a Greek god as his cock wagged between his legs. "Guess someone wore you out."

Desire hitched in her throat. God, he was so fine. So strong and manly, tan. It was no wonder he got paid to take his clothes off.

Lizzy gave a little cough. "I can't believe I slept that long."

No wonder her stomach was growling, but the hunger pains in

her belly were fast forgotten as he bent over and grabbed spring water from the minifridge.

He had the finest ass in all of Colorado. *Damn, damn, damn . . .*

"Do you work out?" she asked him, practically drooling as he handed her the bottle and she cracked the seal, taking a sip of cool, refreshing water.

"No time, what with school."

Just watching him strut around made her loins burn. Her nipples became instantly hard and she was ready all over again. "I can't remember . . . how many more orgasms do you owe me now?"

Eyes glittering, Ty climbed into bed, set her water aside, and pulled her into his arms. "Just one, by my account."

She'd come five times yesterday? *Five?* What's more, she wanted to come again?

Indeed, she did. Who wouldn't? She rested a hand on his chest, directly below one of his tiny, masculine nipples, pulling gently at the curling hairs around it. "Pity."

"Think you have it in you?" Practically growling, his arm tightened around her.

"What? An orgasm?" She laughed. "I've plenty. Want to try me?"

"That I do."

"Go get the Rooster."

"No." Ty's fingers traced over her bare arm, leaving a trail of shivers. "No toys this time. I want to make love to you, just us."

Lizzy resisted the urge to squeak in fear. Just them? No toys?

I can do this, she promised herself, *no toys*. She didn't need them; she needed him!

Rolling over, he rummaged through the box of condoms sitting on the end table, pulling out his choice. "Pretty pink, just for you."

And ribbed, for her pleasure, right? His dark eyes steady on her, Ty slid the rubber on, turning her free of his embrace and flat onto the mattress. "Stay on your stomach."

The tone of his voice made her toes curl in anticipation.

Her abdomen clenching, Lizzy moved to obey him, spreading herself facedown on the soft mattress. The heavy scent of floral-perfumed fabric softener intermingled with their previous love-making, and she tried to concentrate on the smell and not the trepidation suddenly crawling through her.

Lying on her back was one thing, her belly, another. Something about the position made her feel vulnerable. Exposed, as she was about to be, if she couldn't come.

But of course she would. Doubting herself was silly.

He moved over her, propping his elbows next to her head. His body was warm, hard, smothering hers and keeping her pinned flat.

Trapped and at his mercy. "Ty?"

"Shhh . . ." He whispered in her ear, his lips sucking at the lobe. Nibbling the sensitized cartilage, he pushed her head to the side.

Thick and spicy, his cologne overwhelmed all else, arousing her senses. His cock rode her ass cheeks, so solid, so *close*.

"You're beautiful, baby." Kissing, sucking, biting, his mouth traveled all over her face and neck. A mixture of pleasure and pain. Of teasing and tempting.

He thrust his hips, plunging his erection between her ass cheeks, moving the hard shaft along the soft crevice, over her anus.

He didn't enter her, just rubbed over the twitching bud, back and forth, his hands gathering her rear and smashing the globes together, sheathing himself between her buttocks.

Lizzy found herself holding her breath and clutching the blankets. Her every nerve sang in ecstasy. She'd never experienced foreplay like this before—curious, unique, mind-blowing hot. Hell, who needed the Rooster anyway?

Her pussy contracted and released, demanding fulfillment as he raised onto his knees, moving his mouth lower, along her spine. Tangling his hands in her hair, he massaged her prickling, tingly scalp.

"Lizzy," Ty murmured. His hands and mouth flowed over her, smoothing, touching, discovering. "Tell me what you'd like from *me*. What feels good."

Closing her eyes, she bit her lip to prevent herself from demanding the toys. "Everything."

For once, she *could* do without them. The feelings rampaging through her body proved it.

Sliding his hands under her, Ty lifted her chest and palmed her breasts, squeezing her nipples between his thumb and forefinger. Rolling. Massaging.

"And this? How does this feel?"

"Tingly. Hot. Like a rubber band. Stretching and stretching . . ." A lightning bolt hit her, sending shocks through her cunt. He pinched harder and she arched her back, pushed to the edge. "Oh God, Ty . . ."

"I'm going to snap that rubber band for you."

Like yesterday. Over and over. God, yes, that was what she needed. Craved.

And what she could have, as long as she didn't think about it.

Lizzy grasped the sheets, forcing her mind away, allowing herself just to feel. All that existed was his cock strokes between her bottom, increasing, becoming swift, furious and the sudden shudder as he came, groaning loudly and resting his cock against her lower spine, the cum filling his condom branding her skin with heat.

Score—now he owed her two more orgasms!

"Don't move." Sliding from her body, he backed off the bed and stood. From the corner of her eye, she watched as he changed condoms.

Remaining at the edge of the bed, Ty slid his fingers under her hips and lifted her onto her knees. His thumbs caressed her ass cheeks, smoothing the skin.

"So baby soft," he murmured. "And your pussy's so wet."

He bent, kissing her bottom, nuzzling his face in her cunt. She felt him inhale, taking in her scent.

He ran his tongue downward, slowly, until he discovered her clit. Taking the tiny bud between his teeth, he drew on it, applying pressure, then he bit down slightly, pulling harder.

Lizzy cried out at the sharp, wonderful feeling. Pressing her face in the mattress, she pushed her pussy into him, trying to alleviate the intenseness.

She clenched her teeth, prayed for relief. It was too much, just like with her toys, yet different, intimately different. "Ty . . ."

"Shh . . ." he hushed her once again, releasing her clit. Lapping, he plunged several fingers inside her. "Just enjoy it."

Her whole world lurched as he dipped the fingers deeper, knocking her off balance. The feeling was sharp, almost overwhelming.

"Oh God. I can't." The words, the reality, poured from her before she could stop them.

"Don't be silly." Ty's hot breath blew into her cunt, whispering over the inflamed skin and tormenting her. "I've already made you come numerous times."

"I really can't. It's, it's . . ."

"What you need. Let *me* love you." He slid another finger deep within her, filling her. His hand pumped in and out vigorously, his tongue darting to and fro, licking and loving her.

Let me love you . . . How she wanted to. Every muscle in Lizzy's body wound taut, her mind tauter. His every touch felt so wonderful, even better than the toys, driving her higher and higher, to a pinnacle that scared her to death.

And all she wanted was to come—to *do* it and never doubt herself again.

So why . . . *Why* . . .

She needed him inside her. That had to be it. "Ty, I'm ready."

"Are you sure?"

"Finish it," she pleaded. "Please!"

Ty straightened, pulling her to the edge of the bed. His cock nudged her pussy, stilling at the entrance, and her cunt twitched, waiting, hungry to draw him in, end it.

All at once, he plunged into her, piercing through her deep ache and leaving her with a strange sort of feeling. Something inside her just shut down. Turned off.

Oh, she was still hornier than the devil, but she knew she wouldn't climax. It just wasn't in her. She could almost hate herself, hate her body. But that would be giving up.

She thrust her bottom against him, determined to try. Determined not to throw in the towel. She couldn't do that, not yet.

Holding on to her hips, he thrust into her rapidly, grinding himself deep. She pushed against him, took all of him.

They fucked like rabbits, bouncing against the mattress and

each other's bodies. Trying and trying until Ty was cursing under his breath, begging her to come.

And she couldn't.

Shit, babe. *Please.*"

Ty's cock convulsed, filling his condom as he was blindsided by another powerful orgasm. The world went white then slowly came back into view as waves of pleasure rolled through him.

Disappointed, he slowly slid from her body and sat on the edge of the bed.

"Sorry," he muttered.

He'd tried to hold off. Hell, he'd even purposefully come before entering her so he could last longer. But a man could only take so much and he was spent. Too exhausted. Losing his erection.

And shoot, a little angry.

What the hell was wrong with him? Why couldn't he get her off? Things had worked just fine when he was wearing that damned Rooster. So what, was it him? Didn't *he* do it for her?

That was silly of course. If he didn't arouse her, she wouldn't be sleeping with him.

So what was the deal? What would it take to get through to Lizzy?

Ty just didn't know what to do.

"Ty?" Lizzy turned over. Her mouth was flat, her eyes, desperate.

"I don't know." He shrugged, exhaled in frustration. "Lizzy . . ."

He hated seeing her like this. Hated knowing that she just might prefer plastic to flesh. Hated that he'd made her a promise he wasn't sure he could keep.

He'd said he'd help her get past this, that he'd make her

come—and when he'd said it, he hadn't meant with toys. She could do that on her own.

Maybe he'd bitten off more than he could chew. Maybe he, their past love, wasn't enough.

No! Damn it, no!

None of this was right! Maybe if she didn't play with toys, she'd be more responsive to men.

Tortured by rampant emotions, he walked around the bed to the end table and picked up the Wallbanger he'd used yesterday on her breasts. He had to know.

"Ty?" Crooking her head, Lizzy gawked at him like he'd lost his mind, uncertain, perhaps even pissed. But no doubt still as horny as ever. "Ty, what are you doing?"

Giving her what she wanted. He flicked on the switch and a low hum filled the room as he tossed the toy on the bed next to her. "You prefer it; you deserve it. And I'm gonna watch. Have at it."

*T*he nerve of him! Ty was supposed to be her friend. To be "helping" her. And he, he . . .

Damn him! Damn *all* men!

What right did he have to be mad at her? To make her feel so damn inadequate? It wasn't her fault. After all, she'd *tried*.

Lizzy snatched the vibrator from where it lay on the innocent white sheets, grasping it firmly. She spread her legs and lifted her knees.

His eyes bored into her, drank in the sight of her pussy. Waited.

Suddenly, more than ever before, Lizzy needed to prove herself. Needed to make all her claims true—that toys were better than men. That battery-operated fun was the best.

That she didn't need Ty, didn't need his so-called help at all.

Here she was, horny and wet, and he wasn't getting her off, so why shouldn't she let the Wallbanger do the job?

Crying out, she rammed the buzzing vibrator into her pussy as far as it would go. It filled her with a gentle vibration, a fullness no man could provide.

But it was so cold, so unnaturally hard.

Not loving, not warm. Not Ty. There was no touching, no kisses, only his eyes, studying her every move.

He watched her intently, his gaze unreadable. Resisting tears, Lizzy bucked her hips, performing for him. He wanted to see it, and she damn well intended to show him. To come.

She pressed deep, pulled out slowly, grinding the toy against the magic spots that made her body sing and draw tense.

Her mind reeled. Her body flushed with desire. She swam in feeling, fought to stay afloat amidst drowning sensations.

But why just stay afloat? Why not soar?

This was the Wallbanger! And she had something prove!

Lizzy pushed the switch, turning the vibrator to the highest setting. The toy hammered into her, making her back slide against the bedding as she slammed her hips into it.

He wanted to see her come, well damn it, she'd come! She'd have the orgasm of a lifetime.

She tilted the head, and it pressed against the marvelous part deep within her. She couldn't breathe. Her thoughts disappeared. Only Ty's eyes existed—so dark, so demanding—and the vibrator rapidly firing into her. Stretching her, filling her. Driving her wild.

Something was happening. She felt so damn high, driven impulsively. She couldn't stop even if she wanted to.

Her pleasure became so intense, so inescapable, yet all she

could do was search for more, whimper and cry his name, hoping, yearning . . .

Her pussy muscles contracted in short rhythm, convulsing around the toy. Her every muscle constricted, drawn taut in resistance to the explosions occurring in her. It was like rapid fire inside her loins, exploding, repeating . . . so glorious.

And all at once, it was over.

Lizzy fell against the mattress, the vibrator still plunging into her, shaking her very core. But she couldn't move, didn't have the strength. Closing her eyes, she took in a deep breath and immediately wished she hadn't done that.

Disappointment crept into her heart and she lifted her eyelashes, peering at him.

She still wasn't satisfied, didn't feel like any kind of woman. And that's when she realized—coming wasn't enough. It never had been.

It was about love. With toys, her heart could stay aloof, with him, she couldn't.

What do you need me for?" Reaching down, Ty pulled the vibrator from her body. He switched it off, tossing the piece of junk down. "I sure can't compare to this."

Ty's emotions were so rash, his feelings so raw, he couldn't decide if he was mad or sad. Let down or impressed.

God. He was such a wreck. He had to get away from her, before he said something else he'd regret.

Without another word, he dressed then stalked from the room, slamming the door behind him. Much as he loved her, he couldn't deal with this. His pride couldn't take it.

Lizzy obviously didn't feel the same way about him that he felt about her. Maybe she hated him.

No, that didn't make sense. But why the hell couldn't he make her come and that damn vibrator could?

He'd never felt so helpless, so very worthless and inadequate.

Fuck! His fist lashed out into open air, coming damn close to punching a hole in the wall.

The knots in him drew tighter, winding and pulling, and he knew he had to chill, and fast. Set his mind straight.

He stepped out into the sunshine. Tilting his hat so it shielded his eyes, he looked down the street. What he needed was something strong to drink, a dark corner to hide in.

And lucky him, it looked like there was a rowdy bar within walking distance.

fifteen

The scent of her desire saturated the air in the hotel room, choking her. *Bittersweet.*

Trying not to breathe, Lizzy lay there, cursing herself. It was like being hungover after drinking. Eating chocolate on a diet.

Coming had been so damn wonderful while she was riding that vibrator, but now she just felt like crap.

Her release slid down her inner thighs, sticky and uncomfortable. She needed to get up and wash, but she was too damn preoccupied. Angry at herself, confused over Ty. Nothing was right.

Flopping over, Lizzy buried her face in a pillow and groaned, pounding the mattress with her fist.

She hadn't satisfied herself, hadn't erased the ache. The only thing she'd managed to do was make a jerk of herself.

Despite her inability to climax with him, it was Ty she wanted, the feeling of being loved. They way he held her, the way she could talk to him about anything. The way he made her laugh, the way he made her so darn mad at moments. The way he flopped that cowboy hat on her head time and again, the way her stomach fluttered when they took off together in his car, and how she could never resist staring at his fine ass—clothed or not.

Those were feelings some damn piece of junk couldn't provide. With a vibrator, there was no emotion, no soft touch. No matter how fast it could go, it ran on batteries, not heart.

And she wasn't running on heart—despite how Ty made her tremble with the need to. But she wanted to, very much, and that was what scared her the most—made her hold back.

None of this was Ty's fault. In fact, he had to be given props. He knew how to handle her body, toys or not.

God, why'd she have to go and get off in front of him like that? What was her problem? Okay, Ty hadn't exactly been sweet, but really, what man would have been? Until this, he'd been so patient, so understanding with her, and what did she do? She took a baseball bat to his pride. *Bam, bam, bam!*

Might as well have whacked his dick off while she was at it. *Bam! Bam!*

Wasn't it enough that she was dragging Ty across the country, probably causing him to lose his job (which she admittedly would like to happen)?

She really owed him an apology.

Pushing up from the bed, Lizzy stood on shaky legs, almost weak from having expounded so much energy. Her body still tingled with the aftereffects of the orgasm, only heightening her desire for Ty.

She hurried into the bathroom. She had no idea where she'd find him, but she couldn't just sit here and wait.

Not when she wanted so very much to be with him, the right way.

Smoke clouded the air in the crowded bar, but it was a stench he was used to after all his years dancing. Ty hid at a table in the back corner, trying to avoid repeated requests to dance.

Seemed he could have lots of women, but never the one he wanted.

Sitting back in his chair, he clenched a cold glass of brandy on the rocks. He swirled the drink, staring at the clanking ice and waving liquid, listening to a country song that played in the background, barely audible amidst loud talking and laughing,

Lizzy wouldn't like the music.

But Lizzy wasn't here. He was alone, again, like he'd been half of his adult life.

The thought caused his chest to grow tight.

Jesus, he didn't want to give up on Lizzy, didn't want to be frustrated with her. And damn his pride! He'd only made things worse with his sore comments.

Taking a swig of the smooth liquor he held, he relished the burn in his throat. Might as well finish it off and get another. He dumped back the remaining brandy and motioned to the waitress for a second round, then relaxed in his chair, closed his eyes, and tried to clear his mind of thoughts of her. To relax and enjoy his buzz.

"Do you always sleep in bars?" A trademark sassy female voice asked the question.

Well, shit.

"Lizzy?" Ty opened his eyes, not quite sure how he felt to find her standing there, an extra-large glass of wine in hand.

So much for clearing his mind.

His eyes swept over her. She must have gotten her luggage from his car, because she'd changed into a casual outfit of jeans and a black T-shirt. The denim hugged her hips, accented the way her bottom curved and the length of her legs.

Ty's mouth went dry. His cock twitched in interest.

Shit. Here he was lusting for her again . . .

And she was probably there to remind him how much she didn't need him. How great her damn toys were.

"I'm sorry." She bit her lower lip, chewing it hesitantly as she always did when nervous. "Can we talk?"

Sorry? Well that was a surprise, especially coming from her. She was always so damn self-righteous.

Needing to hear what she had to say, he nodded. "Sure."

"Thanks." Pulling out the wooden chair, she sat down and folded her hands on the table. She glanced at him through mascara-veiled eyes. "Ty, for what it's worth, none of this has anything to do with you. You're great in bed."

So great she couldn't come. Ty made a small sound in the back of his throat, but remained silent.

"I, uh . . . I have some issues, okay? The old, 'it's me, not you,' line." Her voice wavered slightly as she spoke and she plucked a napkin from the dispenser, tearing it in two, then three. "And you know something, when I used that vibrator on myself, it was nothing compared to the way you make me feel, toys or not. You're very dexterous."

He'd take that as a compliment. "But you still came with it and not with me."

"But it was empty. You see, the way you touch me, it's not that you don't arouse me, it's that you arouse me too much."

Interesting.

Ty leaned forward. "How so?"

"I mean, it's hard to explain, but let's just say you're hard to handle."

"And you're hard to get."

"I have to get used to all this . . . you and me . . . and I don't mean in bed. That's just a ripple effect." She gave up shredding the thin paper for the moment. Shrugging, she leaned in. "Know something? Even after I came, I still wanted you. Needed you. Still do."

The confession warmed him. Stroked his ego.

She *needed* him. Now that was what he wanted to hear. Lord knew he'd waited long enough for her to drop down her guard. To admit she felt anything at all for him.

He covered her hands with his. "Lizzy, I know life's been rough on you, but you keep pushing me away. Don't you remember how much we used to love each other? Don't you wish it could be like that again?"

Her hands turned underneath his and she laced her fingers between his.

"I do, Ty. I promise. You mean a lot to me." Suddenly she smiled—too much. "And by the way, you asked—I'll answer. If I had to guess, I'd say you have had your fair share of experience with sex toys."

"Never touched one before you."

"Really? Well, it doesn't matter, from now on, the vibrator only gets used on you. I promise."

The rather slow waitress chose *that* moment to arrive with his drink.

"Here you go. Brandy on the rocks," she said in a barely controlled tone, clearly trying to pretend like she hadn't heard a thing. But there was no smothering her grin, hiding the way her shoulders shook as she walked away.

"Oh God." Lizzy snickered, then burst into peels of laughter. "Sorry, Ty."

He swore under his breath. "I hope you know those damn things are going in the trash." But he couldn't help a few chuckles himself. He'd be lucky if he didn't get sued for making that woman choke on her own laughter.

He took a deep drink, watching Lizzy down half her glass. Thirsty, was she?

"Don't get drunk," he warned. "I expect we have some making up to do tonight."

"Who me?" She feigned innocence with a bat of her eyelashes, pulling her hands from his. "I just want to cut loose tonight, Ty. Have some fun. Talk."

Sitting back, she surveyed the bar.

"I can do that." Hell, he was glad to hear it. Maybe if Lizzy relaxed more around him *out* of the bedroom, she could have more fun with him in it. Sure sounded like it.

"So . . ." Her gaze returned. "What about school, Ty? Did you work something out for the classes you're missing?"

"Yeah, pretty much," he lied, not wanting her to know about the courses he'd chosen to fail for her. "I've got two more papers to turn in and then it's Spring Break."

"Two papers? I thought you had four classes this semester?"

"Yeah . . ." Waste of money, waste of time. A lot of it. He was so close to graduation yet stalling it straight into '09. Just what he needed—another year of dirty dancing for hard cash. Lizzy would love that.

Talk about being stuck between a rock and a hard place. But right or wrong, he'd made his decision, and there was nothing he could do now but move on. Even if he regretted the choice, he couldn't make it back in time for his finals now—not that he was prepared for them either.

"So?" Lizzy pressed.

"Doesn't matter, Lizzy. It's just money and time." He stared at her hard, letting her know he meant it. He'd learned a harsh lesson about love versus material things once, wouldn't make the same mistake twice. "You, you're everything."

Ty!" Lizzy protested, both angry and touched at once, feeling ever so guilty as a smile threatened her lips. "You shouldn't have done that. School's important."

"So are you."

Jesus. Ty should *not* be screwing up school to be with her. And what about work? She didn't like him dancing, but didn't he need to earn a living?

She ought to walk out, disappear on him. Give him no choice but to return to his life in Denver.

But the selfish, ugly truth was, hearing him say she was everything made her feel like she was the only woman in the world. It made her believe she could trust him again.

Once upon a time, Ty had been so wrapped up in money and things, she'd come in a sad second place. Being first ... it was nice. Real nice. Heartwarming.

And also concerning.

"So, what about—" She started to ask him about what Fantasies thought of his disappearance, but fate brought the touchy subject of his occupation up for her.

A blond knockout in high heels and a black miniskirt half stumbled, half strutted to the table, talking loud enough for Lizzy's sister honeymooning in Egypt to hear. "Oh my God. It's Ty! Cowboy Ty!"

He knew this bimbo?

Lizzy looked at Ty, seeing pain on his face. Embarrassment.

"Shit," he muttered under his breath and cast the woman a steely glare. "Not tonight."

"Oh my God, are you escorting now?" Clapping her hands, the woman cried gleefully. She turned to Lizzy with a glowing smile. "This is the finest stripper in Colorado. Have you seen his ass? His chaps? Mmmm."

Lizzy wanted to sarcastically tell her to drink another, but she bit her tongue, not wanting to be a hypocrite. This was likely to be her later—unable to stand without teetering and fawning all over Ty.

"Not a good time. I'm with someone," Ty said firmly. "I'm sorry, but *please*, excuse us."

The woman looked like she'd been slapped, then she laughed Ty off, like he couldn't possibly be serious. "Oh, come on, baby. I just got paid." Grasping her purse, she gave it a little waggle.

Toying with his drink, spinning it around nervously, Ty looked to Lizzy. His eyes were filled with apologies and regret. Shame.

Lizzy didn't care if he took his clothes off for money—no one was disrespecting him like this!

"Uh, *no* . . ." Trying not to overreact, Lizzy rocked her forehead in her hand. What did she say? Thanks, but no thanks, for the compliment? No, you're mistaken, this stripper is my lover? This situation sucked! "You are going to need to leave us—"

The bitch giggled.

Lizzy looked up, not happy with what she saw. The woman had her hands on Ty's arm! Her fingers were tracing over his bared biceps, diving under the sleeve of his T-shirt to test his shoulders.

And he was letting her.

Ty stared at Lizzy, as if waiting. Waiting! Well, he was going to get it!

"Get your hands off my man," Lizzy ground out. "Now."

"Whoa. Possessive, aren't you?" The woman stepped back. "Well, I guess you paid for your time . . ."

The slut! Where did she get off? She acted like Ty was some man-whore. Some piece of meat to perform sexually and—

God. Suddenly Lizzy she felt like she was looking in the mirror.

Hadn't she been using him all along, never worried about what he was giving, how he felt?

She was so damn selfish.

Lizzy cast a glance at Ty and pushed herself up to standing. Selfish enough that she sure wasn't sharing him.

"Get. Lost. *Now.* Before I put my steel toes to use." She waited for the woman to walk away. With a snort, she turned on her heels, strutting and swinging her ass straight to the dance floor.

Lizzy turned her gaze on Ty and tossed up her hands. "Were you going to just *let* her fondle you?"

"Just wanted to see how you'd react."

"Well, are you satisfied?"

"Quite." He looked ornery enough to spank. "It's nice to know I'm your man. Makes me a little less jealous of your vibrator."

Lizzy plunked back in her seat, taking another sip of her wine.

She pushed around the napkin pieces she'd shredded. "Ty, how long are you going to keep dancing?"

"Honestly?"

"No, lie to me."

"Lizzy, you think I like taking my clothes off for cash? Sure, it's easy money, but it's not a thing a man can be proud of—not with the people that count in his life." She could hear the pain and dissatisfaction in his voice. "I want to make money in a respectable way. But my goals are important to me and until I graduate—"

"Whatever it takes," she finished for him. At least she knew where he stood. He could easily bullshit her. "I can tell becoming a PO means a lot to you."

"It does. If I can do half the job mine did, I know I can make a difference in some kids' lives."

Just talking about it changed the look in his eyes, made him beam.

She was really proud of him and had no doubt the career choice would make him happy, despite how hard it was to picture him in such an authoritarian role. In her mind, he'd always be a bad boy.

And God help him if some punk teenager caught wind of his former employment. The only thing Ty would be doing was helping the kid laugh.

"Oh God." She sucked back a chuckle, but couldn't help her amusement. "A stripper turned probation officer. What will your new bosses think?"

She didn't mean to make fun, but it was pretty hard to picture without a grin.

Ty raised his brows. "They'll never know."

"I do."

"Oh yeah?" Under the table, his feet hooked hers, wrapping and holding her legs. "And I know you orgasm with vibrators and not men. Guess we're even."

Oh, he wanted to spar, did he? "Everyone knows that already." *Now* they were even.

Things got quiet between them. Ty's boot stroked her calf through her jeans.

"Lizzy," he said after a moment. "Let's forget all this life talk. You want to cut loose tonight, remember?" Standing he offered her his hand. "Dance with me."

Lizzy cast a glance at the worn wooden floor where the blond bimbo was gyrating against an older cowboy. "Yeah, I'll show that whore—"

"Now, now . . ." Ty tsked with a wink. "Behave."

"Never!" she swore as she stood.

He led her to the dance floor. Taking her in his arms, Ty held her close, gliding his hips along hers to the pace of the bluegrass song.

"Ty?" She laid her head against his chest, her fingers hooked in the back of his jeans.

His chin rested against her forehead. "Yeah?"

"I may not like what you do, but I respect what you're doing. I'm proud of you."

His hands slid from her waist, higher, until he was holding her at her shoulders. Lovingly, he kissed the top of her head. "Thank you. That means a lot to me."

Lizzy couldn't shake the sound of that bimbo's voice. The way the slut's hands had touched her man. The jealously she'd felt.

The fact that soon they'd return to the hotel together and have sex.

And this time, certainly she could get off. After all, she'd pin-pointed her problem, what was holding her back emotionally . . . and she sure was feeling anything but aloof from Ty right now.

No, she wanted him, from her head to her toes. Easy peezy, right?

The music blared around them, easily heard now that the bar was emptying out. Sitting at their table, she leaned back in her chair and stared at Ty. *Her man.* Her eyes soaked in the sight of his arms, the way crossing them made his biceps curl, so well-defined and sexy.

And that damn woman had touched him. Jesus, how many had touched him? Lord knew enough had seen him baring it all.

Why was she still thinking about it? *She* got to take him home. Keep him.

Lizzy ought to be excited. No, she was excited—too excited. Too nervous. Too overwhelmed by the prospect of Ty being her man—of sealing their connection tonight—with an orgasm.

She felt like a damn schoolgirl. Like coming with him was so permanent.

And there wasn't enough booze in the world to calm her. About an hour ago, she'd switched to martinis, had already knocked back two, and had a killer buzz to show for it.

But unfortunately, she was still thinking reasonably, and tonight she just wanted to quiet her mind, to kill all the stampeding thoughts and worries that wouldn't leave her alone.

She reached for her third drink, stealing the olive from it. This one would do her in, she knew that, and she wanted it.

"You okay?" Ty asked, leaning forward. "You look preoccupied."

She took a sip. "Jus' thirshty."

"Maybe you should slow down." His brows furrowed in concern, his lips turned down. "You've already had a lot to drink."

"So? Are you now the alchol p'lice?" Oh shit. She was slurring. Big-time!

Well, slur on! At least she didn't have to think. Lizzy took a big swig, raising her glass in the air. "Le's toast."

Ty lifted his empty glass, the ice cubes clanking. He'd stopped drinking when she'd switched to martinis.

Lizzy was pretty sure he thought he was protecting her and also pretty sure she thought it was adorable.

"A toast to what?" he asked.

"To us," she purred with a wink. "To tonight."

His eyes glowed with appreciation. "I'll toast to that." Their glasses clinked together. He returned his to the table and pushed his chair back. "Now let's get out of here."

"I'm all yours, cowboy." But first, she was finishing her drink. Lifting her cherished martini, she downed the rest in one full swig.

sixteen

$\mathscr{A}$ gentleman wouldn't take advantage of his drunken girlfriend.

But this minute, there was nothing gentle about him. Supporting her at the waist, Ty guided her down the hotel hallway. Lizzy staggered and giggled, having no idea what she was in for.

He felt like a jerk—a horny, *determined* jerk with an opportunity not to be taken lightly.

Lizzy was feeling wild and ready. He had an opportunity.

Sure, he didn't need her to be inebriated to have sex with her. That was easy. Getting past her walls wasn't. No matter how he tried, Lizzy held herself at a distance. She allowed him inside her body, but her heart and soul remained impenetrable.

This was a whole different type of seduction. Way he saw it, there was a difference between intimacy and *intimacy*. Fucking her, even getting her to come, wasn't enough anymore. He wanted all of her, everything. To touch her in every way, to claim her body until they truly became one. Until there was no going back, no separating, not ever again.

Fuck her? He was going to do so much more than that. He was going to brand her. To knock down those damn walls and reclaim his Elizabeth. One inch at a time.

Lizzy fumbled with the key in the lock, turning it. Spinning on her heels, she fell into Ty's arms, grappling to twist the knob behind her and shove open the door.

"Careful now," Ty warned as they stumbled into their hotel room, the deep timber of his voice careening down her spine.

With what? Her heart? Her body? Not tonight, no thank you. She was throwing caution to the wind . . . herself at Ty.

"Jus' get in here and hurry!" A martini-flavored hiccup escaped her. "I'm horny."

A growl of appreciation rumbled from him. "I think you've had one too many."

"Or one just enough." Her hotel key dropped to the floor and she nearly went with it. "Don't complain. Geesh!"

Catching her by the waist, he prevented her from toppling over. "You're lucky you're so cute when you're sloshed."

Ty crooked her head to the side and kissed her neck and collarbone. She was so hot, starving, and his lips were like a sex toy in their own right. The way he licked at her mouth, suckled her lower lip sharply. Tingles exploded over the swelling flesh, running straight to her pussy, igniting her body, and Ty drew harder. Pure glorious torture.

"Mmm. Don't stop." Blinded by the dark, she used him for balance and kicked off her shoes. They flew across the room, creating a bang as the hard soles hit the wall.

Rotating in his hold, she pulled at the stretchy fabric of his T-shirt, guiding him to the bed. Forget his mouth—erotic as it was—at the moment there were other, bigger, *longer* parts of him that she was compelled to put into use.

Lizzy could scream from the intense desire controlling her body, the way she felt so *out* of control. She was on fire. Her pussy soaked. Ready.

"God, Ty." Wanting to devour him, she attacked him with her mouth. Her tongue plunged inside his and his lips claimed her hungrily, latching on.

Every second seemed an eternity, but far too glorious to take lightly. Life didn't get any better than this. Kissing him, she slid her hands around his neck, and his fingers pinched her rear, lifting her.

His hard cock pressed against her lower belly, promising ecstasy. God, she couldn't wait to have him buried deep inside her, pumping in and out.

Sliding her hands down, she pushed them under the hem of his shirt and up to his chest. Her fingertips encountered coarse, curling hairs as she explored his muscles, the way his abdomen flexed under her touch, the way his pecs were so well-defined and rippling. How strong he was.

God, he'd never felt like such a man. She'd never felt like such a woman.

She urged his feet backward, and in three steps, they bumped into the side of the bed. Ty gave a little tug at her waist and together, they fell onto the mattress. Their bodies bounced in unison, their chins collided, and her cry of laughter pierced the air.

His fingers danced along her sides, tickling. Teasing. Curling against him, Lizzy giggled and wiggled and forged her way into his jeans through the zipper.

Ty groaned, his hands falling away from her.

Her thumb brushed the delicate skin of his hard cock, stroking. It was amazing, this piece of her man, and she wanted to—

Ty pulled her hands from his pants, rolling away. "Get those clothes off, woman." His command was gruff, impatient.

Forget that. For once, he could do the work. Lizzy stretched like a cat, watching him.

Ty crawled from the mattress, turning on a bedside lamp. Standing, he kicked off his boots and stripped off his clothes.

Retrieving a box of condoms from the end table, he pulled out one of the small foil packages and ripped it open. He rolled the rubber into place and turned back to her. "I thought I told you to get undressed?"

"You always make me undress myself," she complained, throwing her arms out. "Ravish me."

God, was that really her talking?

"Oh yeah?" Reaching across the bed, Ty grabbed her by her ankles and hauled her around. His movements were rough, brisk. In charge.

Not wasting a second, he tore open the fastenings of her jeans, peeled them off, then tugged her shirt over her head.

At his mercy, she lay there in only a bra and panties. With narrowed, appraising eyes he glared down at her. "Lizzy?"

She opened her mouth, but nothing came out. She didn't know what to say, couldn't think of anything but his cock driving into her, easing the ache that was consuming her very mind.

He swept his fingers over her belly, leaving a trail of hot sensation. With a moan, she lifted her bottom toward him.

"If I do anything you don't like, just tell me to stop." His warning rumbled through her, making her stomach flutter and her loins burn.

Anything?

Had *anything* ever been more of a turn-on than the deepness of his voice, the questions his statement left behind? *What* things would he do to her?

At the moment, she wanted everything he had to offer.

"There's nothing I'd want you to stop doing," she promised him on a breath. "I want it all."

He made a small sound of pleasure. "We'll see."

Lizzy looked at him and realized quite soberly that there was something different about Ty. Something domineering and dangerous.

And when he said *anything*, he *meant* it.

She gulped, her body trembled. Tilting her hips, she gave herself up.

Fisting the side of her panties, he yanked hard, tearing them apart. Her pelvis lurched and she cried out in surprise. The fabric burned at her skin, a strange sort of pleasure and pain that left her lower half undulating, on fire . . .

"You know what I want?" Seizing her upper thighs, Ty tossed her over roughly. "I want to hear you begging me."

Umph! Her face thunked into the mattress as he forced her knees to the bed and her bottom in the air. "Ty!" she protested, trying to turn back over.

"It's hard for you, Lizzy, giving me control, isn't it?" Forcing her back down, his palms slid over her bottom. "But you like it, don't you?"

As if she was going to answer that question!

But her body did—her libido screamed *yes, yes, yes!*, her muscles became tense, her arousal hummed through her, drawing her like a cord running from her heart to her cunt, stretching and pulling.

Suddenly, he smacked her ass sharply, making her jump from him. What the—

But she couldn't deny her response. Her pussy flooded, her bottom instinctively rose for another.

"Ty!" She wasn't sure if she was complaining or obliging him by begging, but she didn't say stop. Didn't want to.

She'd heard about women who enjoyed being spanked in the bedroom. She'd been intrigued, curious.

She didn't understand, but the way his smart smack on her bared butt made her feel . . . Her very gut told her she wanted it, wanted more.

He climbed onto the bed, positioning himself over her.

"Spank me more!" she found herself calling out. She presented her bottom, wiggling it.

Oh God, was she really saying that?

And enjoying every second of it?

"You like my hands on your sweet ass?" *Smack!* "You need a good spanking, baby?"

"Yes!"

"Damn." His fingers flexed into her skin, as if he was grasping for control, then left her. *Smack, smack!* "You were naughty tonight, Lizzy. Drinking like you did." He slapped her bottom again, then again.

Each time, the muscles of her rear contracted and released, a new zing of arousal shot through her pussy. Higher and higher her body climbed, rising above rational thought into a realm of pure pleasure that went beyond reason.

On and on, Ty continued the sensual punishment, reminding her both physically and verbally that she'd been bad, that she wanted to be bad.

Showing her just how good bad was.

Dizzy, she closed her eyes, whimpering and moving against him with every stroke of punishment. He was right—she didn't want control. Didn't know what to do with control. She wanted him to possess her body, her mind.

Ty's hands claimed her ass one final time, landing softly, squeezing and kneading the stinging flesh. His thumbs dove between her cheeks, pressing her anus as he bent and buried his face between her legs.

Claiming her clit, he drew on the tense bud. Suckled and nursed her desire. Explored her ass, stroking the sensitized skin.

Her cunt felt so empty, her arousal so extreme. Her anus twittered.

Lizzy gulped, nervously wondering, hoping. She wanted to know more than what a spanking felt like. There were other things, dirtier things.

Would he do them?

"Ty?" she asked. "I think I want . . ."

Thank God, she didn't have to say it. His thumb pressed inside the tight ring, stretching the virgin hole. His fingers spread her crack, exposing her to the air. To his touch . . . and his mouth.

He nuzzled her slit with his nose, licked around his hands. Ate her out so thoroughly, from anus to pussy, she was ashamed by the way her body sang in response. She'd never been touched this way before, so intimately, so completely. And if it weren't for the booze, she wouldn't allow it now. Or would she?

"I'm going to make your body mine," Ty swore, as if he could read her mind. His hot breath blew into her cunt, his nose nudged her rectum, sealing his words. "All of it."

At that moment, Lizzy knew there was no going back. No getting hesitant. No resisting.

Only the deep need for him to keep licking her in this unique way. Driving her higher.

To her disappointment, he moved away, shifting onto his knees. His hands slid over the mounds of her ass, up her back, to her bra fastening. Undoing the hooks, he let the garment fall away. He palmed her breasts, pressing and massaging them as he aligned his cock at her slit.

Slowly, he sheathed himself in her pussy, until she was filled completely with his length and breadth. Amazed by the way she felt—even needier, hotter. So damn compulsive.

Her hips bucked and she ground herself against him. "Hard and fast," she demanded.

But Ty didn't obey, didn't let her even have that much say in their lovemaking.

He took her slowly, moving in and out, pressing deep, exploring, circling, driving her wild. His every movement seemed calculated, like he was intentionally driving her nuts and enjoying it.

She was going wild. Tears of ecstatic frustration filled her eyes as Ty moved one hand down, encompassing her body in order to play with her clit. To tease her unmercifully. With his free hand, he continuously pinched her nipples, alternating between her breasts, tweaking and twisting.

Oh God. *More, more, more!* All she wanted was for him to ram into her. To take her like a caveman.

Was he going to make her beg and plead?

Of course he was. He'd promised to.

Her vaginal muscles clenched him, held him securely so that she could enjoy his every measured stroke fully. *More, more, more!*

And then all at once, without warning, Ty answered her silent pleas, thrusting into her, fucking her hard, shaking her to the core. The bed lurched as he suddenly began throwing himself into her body, slamming his cock deep, deep inside her.

His hips jabbed her ass; the mattress wept under the punishment. Harder. Faster. Her world spun, her body cried until she was sure she couldn't take any more. Until she was soaring and falling all at once, her pussy convulsing around him as she came and came and came.

Still he fucked her, forcing more, demanding everything from her body. Milking little earthquakes from her cunt. Over and over.

Her knees weak, she buried her face in the mattress, whimpering. She couldn't breathe, could barely hold herself up as she met his every plunge, propelling herself against him.

"Ty!" she called on a high-pitched squeal.

His answer was a grunt. He buried himself deep inside her and she collapsed, only half-aware as his hips twitched against her.

A moment later, he pulled out, moving to the edge of the bed. Her knees fell out from under her, and lying flat, Lizzy twisted her neck and watched him.

His breathing was heavy, his actions slow. He peeled off the condom, tossing it in the nearby waste can. Picking up the tissue box on the end table, he wiped himself clean.

Then he got out another condom.

Oh God. Again? More?

More, more, more!

Ty crawled back onto the bed, returning her to her ass-in-the-air position. "I want all of you," he reminded her.

She wasn't sure she could take any further loving, but the moment he touched her, her body awoke. Obeyed his sensual commands. Opened for him.

But it wasn't her pussy he aligned himself with, no, his cock nudged her bottom, preparing to enter her there. His fingers gathered cream from her dripping cunt, spreading it along his cock. Over her anus.

His palms flat on her butt, he held her steady and pushed into the tight hole.

Lizzy closed her eyes. Ty was making her his, claiming all of her, and she'd never been so turned on by the thought of belonging to a man in all her life. She was meant to be Ty's, her body was meant to take his in every way. Her heart couldn't fight it any longer.

Lizzy let go of everything but the curious way his cock felt buried in her anus, the way his fingers felt like electricity on her sensitized skin.

Another orgasm was building in her, growing and expanding, and Ty was nourishing the feeling, making it bigger and bigger with every pump of his hips, every stroke of his immense cock.

To think, two days ago she couldn't come at all without toys. Now she was going to with him . . . like this.

The feeling was unlike any other. Intense. Sharp. Slightly painful. But oh so wonderful.

One hand slid up her back, taking her hair in hand. He held on, rode her like an animal riding its mate. His other hand found her pussy, exploring her folds. With one finger, he flicked over her clit,

traced her labia, then he pressed all four digits against her moist-
ness, palming and rubbing her cunt.

His hip thrusts increased, becoming faster. Needier. It was
gritty, dirty, raw. Everything between them had been stripped away,
all the hesitation and uncertainty and emotional mistrust deleted,
leaving only the most primal of feelings.

Her body snapped, her pleasure exploding, radiating through
her—the hot, consuming ecstasy of an orgasm. Ty joined her, driving into her one final time.

Together, they collapsed on the bed. Neither uttered a word as
Ty rolled off her, pulling her into his arms. Talk wasn't necessary.
At that moment, everything was perfect.

Silently, he held her, his shallow breaths fluttering over her head,
blowing her hair. The scent of their lovemaking wafted through the
air, thick, *telling*, and Lizzy was certain she'd never smelled anything so erotic.

The buzz from all her drinks earlier still hummed through her
body, warming and mixing with the aftereffects of her orgasms.
Slowly, Lizzy's consciousness began to fade away and she drifted off
into dreams of Ty, of the way he touched her body . . .

seventeen

The day promised to be beautiful. One to remember.

Ty was up with the birds, showering as the sun rose. After last night, he was high on life, feeling like the world's most manly of men. Feeling in *love*.

He dug out a pair of black jeans and his new Buffaloes T-shirt from his duffel bag. Dressing quickly, he sat at the small hotel table and combed his hair, watching Lizzy sleep. Could she get any sexier?

Wearing neon green panties, she was curled in a ball, the blankets wrapped around those legs he so admired. Her gentle snores filled the air, and her hair stuck straight up.

It took all his willpower not to hop into bed and wake her up—with his tongue. But after last night, she deserved her rest.

Drunk or not, the way she'd responded had been amazing. Mind-blowing. So damned hot.

Lizzy didn't have a clue what she did to him. The way she made him feel—like an animal. Uncontrollable.

Even now he was growing hard for her, heating with the potent desire to claim her body over and over.

How could he ever get enough?

But he didn't have to worry about that anymore. Lizzy was his.

So she liked toys . . . *he* was the first *man* to bring her to the ultimate pleasure. And the way they'd made love—there was no going back now. No clamming up or holding back. No putting up walls.

Way he saw it, what woman could shut out a lover who'd spanked her? Taken her in the ass?

Okay, maybe it sounded a little crude when put that way, not as intimate as he actually saw the acts they'd experienced. But he was sure Lizzy would open up more now—sexually and emotionally. How could she not?

He just hoped this trip brought her what she was searching for. That it was worth it. And when it was over, they'd be inseparable once again. Forever this time.

Ty wasn't sure exactly what he'd do when he arrived in Shot Creek, Tennessee, or how he'd feel. Sending cash to his ma was one thing, but facing his dad? And Lizzy's parents? Shit.

Not that his parents were near as bad as Lizzy's, but he had no respect for them, for their way of life. Dad was a drunk who spent more money and time on booze than he ever had on his family. And his ma? *All* that mattered to her was her soaps—she hadn't cleaned house, had never kept a proper eye on him. He'd run wild, unsupervised, his whole childhood. It was no wonder he'd always managed to find trouble so easily.

And yet, Ty knew it was he who'd be condemned. He was a stripper;

he'd been to juvy. He'd taken an underage Lizzy and run away with her.

Yeah, he'd done the right thing, taking her from the abuse, but they wouldn't see it like that.

And he didn't want to hear it.

Maybe he'd just wait in the car. After all this time, he hadn't planned on any family reunions. Some things were better left alone.

With a moan, Lizzy tossed in the bed, pulling Ty from his thoughts. He stretched and waited hopefully for her to awaken. She didn't, instead rolling over with a snort.

Jesus, he needed to put his mind on something constructive. He couldn't just sit here, staring at her and getting horny, not any more than he could take worrying himself.

Standing, he decided to get his books and laptop from the car. Get to work on his English report—he might be down two courses, but he still had two to save, and with his teachers allowing him to e-mail his papers, he didn't have a single excuse in the world for not acing them.

Burying her face in the pillow, Lizzy licked dry lips. God. She was parched. Hungover. Her head was pounding, her thoughts swarming.

Flashes of the previous night flickered through her mind, forming one big embarrassing mess: slurring words, stumbling in the hotel room. Begging Ty to spank her. The ways he'd . . . made love to her . . . if you could call it that.

And the orgasms. Wonderful, huge, repetitive orgasms . . .

Oh man. What had she been thinking? Worse, what was *Ty*

thinking of her? And damn, he was some kind of perv! Sure, she liked her toys, but this was entirely different. She would've never guessed he was into such kinky sex . . . that *she* was.

With a groan, she pulled the blanket over her head, wishing she could disappear.

"You awake?" she heard him ask through the thick comforter. "Have a headache?"

"Yeah," she mumbled. *My ass hurts too.*

"I figured you would." Heat flooded her face as he pulled the blanket down. "Two aspirin and a glass of water."

Sitting on the edge of the bed, he held them out to her and she accepted the pills, taking the water to wash them down.

He stared at her, his dark and sultry gaze never wavering. His eyes analyzed her, waiting . . . for what?

Spank me more! Lizzy's face blazed as she washed down the bitter aspirin, finishing the water to the last drop. *I think I want . . .*

God, not only has she enjoyed his spanking, she'd practically begged him to put his cock in her rear end.

She handed him back the empty glass and turned away, wishing she could have stayed hidden under the blankets.

"Lizzy?" His hand went to her hip. "You okay?"

Of course she wasn't!

She shrugged. "I guess."

"You guess? Hey, that was some night, wasn't it?" His hands slid over her bottom—the bottom he'd *spanked*—slowly, reminding her.

Like she needed a reminder!

"The orgasms were great, weren't they?" His voice dripped with cool confidence. Smugness. "See, I told you I could get you there. Not a single toy involved."

"That you did."

But not normally! She'd been drunk . . . he hadn't played fair! And was he *bragging*?

"I'm going to get you there again this morning," he promised, even more arrogantly. His fingers danced over her skin, traveling from her rear to her chest. He cupped the weight of her left breast, squeezing the nipple. Making the bud hard. "And again later and after that . . ."

Like she was going to let him do those things to her twice! Sure, she'd enjoyed them, had come immensely, but . . . but . . .

It's hard for you, Lizzy, giving me control, isn't it?

No man *controlled* her . . . not her body, not her heart. She should have never given him that privilege. To do so was playing with fire.

"Ty . . ." What did she say? That she'd been so screwed up, she would have enjoyed anything he'd done to her? That she didn't care for the idea of so thoroughly giving herself to him, of being at his mercy?

Hell, maybe he couldn't get her off at all!

"You know, we have lots of catching up to do," he added. "I can't even remember the score now."

She rolled back over, forcing herself to look at him. His eyes shone with pride, devouring her as he continued to tweak her nipple.

Whatever. She so wasn't impressed, even if tingles were awakening throughout her body, flooding her pussy.

"I was drunk last night, Ty."

"I know."

Her annoyance peaked. She lifted her brows and looked at him with wide eyes. "So, don't you think that had a little something to do with . . ."

"I think you finally let go of some things that were holding you back. Let yourself enjoy sex with a man, for once." His hand dropped from her breast, ran down her belly to cup her mons. "And now that you have, we—"

Shifting her hips, she avoided his touch. "I don't think so, Ty."

He pulled back, looking at her through narrowed eyes. "What does that mean?"

"It means I don't think you made me come. The alcohol did," she snapped. "And I don't think I'll be getting that carried away for some time. And no, I don't secretly want you to control me."

"That was just a bedroom game." He looked confused and angry, sounded desperate. His hand snaked around her hip, grabbing her ass, harshly squeezing it while his eyes searched hers for a response. "And you do. You like being dominated. Admit it."

Lizzy fought back tears, refusing to agree with what he said. "No."

The truth was, she did want sex. Orgasms. *Ty*. She just didn't want to wake up feeling like she'd been stripped of her soul—the very core of her being bared, exposed.

It hurt too much. Was too embarrassing.

"You know what, Lizzy?" He stood up, his hands clenched at his sides. His jaw steel. "You're just afraid. Scared to death to trust me. To let me back in your life. Hell, anyone." He began pacing, back and forth, strutting across the small room as his fingers flexed and clenched. "You're just so damn self-reliant. Why need a man? You've got a sex toy! Well a sex toy can't love you, Lizzy."

One thing was for certain—toys didn't make her feel as *badly* as she did right now.

"Maybe I don't want love," she whispered. "Maybe I'm incapable of it."

"You're lying. You're just scared." Ty stopped in his tracks, glaring at her. "And I'll prove it."

"Oh?" She tried to sound coy, unimpressed.

Unsuccessfully.

"I won't sleep with you again. Not until you're *truly* ready to be with me, to give yourself like you did last night, heart and soul, no regrets. And no alcohol."

"Yeah right, you can't keep your hands off me." She found herself daring him. "That's why you came along."

So why was she suddenly feeling so desperate? Regretful? It wasn't as if she wanted a repeat of last night!

"Try me. We leave in half an hour." He went to the table, plunked in the chair, and hit some buttons on his laptop. Ended the conversation.

And that's when Lizzy realized she didn't want it to be over. She just had nothing else to say.

Ty shut down his laptop and folded the lid shut. Gathering his books, he slammed them together and crammed them into his book bag, then slid the computer in on top.

He hadn't made her come? He couldn't believe her! He didn't *get* her!

After last night, he'd been so sure, so looking forward to the new them.

But the letdown was just like yesterday. She teased him with her body and her heart then pulled away coldly, like the sex was nothing. Like *he* was nothing.

And he was going to prove to her just how wrong she was. She couldn't push him away if he wasn't pushing himself on her, which only left her with one option—*she'd* have to fight for him.

Ty battled rising anger, impossible needs. He couldn't make

Lizzy love him, couldn't make her feel a damn thing, but he was pretty darn certain she already did. Always had. She just needed to stop hiding—from him, from what they had, now and in the past.

Hard as it was, he just had to walk away, at least from the sex. Life had turned her cold and indifferent and she was determined to stay that way. But no matter what she had in her head, her body spoke to him. Told him of her needs. Her desires.

And no matter how hard she tried, she couldn't deny those feelings forever, especially not if *he* were denying *her*.

His bag packed, Ty sat in the chair and rested his forehead in his palm. Maybe he was as confused as Lizzy. He loved her *so much*. All he wanted was for them to be together. To be happy. For years, there had been this aching gap in his soul, this burning for her sweet laughter in his life again, her innocent smile. But things just weren't the same. He'd fooled himself into believing sex would bring them closer, but it hadn't. Rather, it was Lizzy's way of holding him at bay. Keeping him out of her heart.

Well, he was sticking to his guns. He really wouldn't touch her again. He'd take her home, let her face what she needed to face and be there for her.

He'd be her friend.

And if Lizzy wanted more, that was up to Lizzy.

Rising, Ty slung his bag over his shoulder and stalked from the room. He'd wait in the car, listen to some tunes. And hope like hell he could clear his mind before they left.

eighteen

Not sleep with her again? *Please.*

The atmosphere inside the Trans Am was tense, wrought with unsaid feeling. Unfinished business.

Sitting with her arms crossed, Lizzy fumed at the things he'd said to her this morning. The way the words stung, cut right through her.

Where did he get off anyway?

Ty glanced at her yet again. He cleared his throat. "Want to turn the radio on?"

His gaze lingered over her legs and then finally jerked to her face.

Lizzy crossed her legs. "No."

See that?

He couldn't keep his eyes off her. He wanted her. She could see it in his every move, the way he looked at her, dark and tortured. Penetrating.

But she wasn't giving him the satisfaction. No matter how much she reciprocated his desire. No matter how many times scenes from the night before played through her mind, driving her crazy. Making her wet.

Spank me more!

A wave of heat smacked her in the face. Her mouth went dry. Her nipples became hard.

Squirming in the vinyl seat, she cracked the window. They'd been riding like this all day, straight through Kansas and into Missouri. Their travel time was great, probably because neither one of them wanted to stop and face another hotel room.

How was she supposed to feel? He'd spanked her, fucked her ass! Taken advantage of her drunken butt in every way.

And he wanted bragging rights for making her come?

Wincing at the crudeness of it all, Lizzy wound the window down the rest of the way, resting her arms and chin on the sill. Wind whipped at her face, blew through her hair.

God, she had to stop thinking about it.

But she couldn't. Her mind replayed flashes of the night before over and over. His cock stretching her, filling her, his promise to make her completely his; the way her pussy had shuddered and convulsed and she'd welcomed the notion of belonging to Ty.

Completely his. Perhaps that was the part that both bothered and intrigued her the most. After all that had been said and done, she still wasn't certain she ever wanted a serious relationship. What if—

"Lizzy?"

Pulling her head in, she sat back. Her mouth was pasty, her eyes arid. "What?" she asked, blinking.

"Going to have to stop for the night. I need a rest," he told her. "We'll make it the rest of the way tomorrow."

Great. A knot formed in her throat as she nodded in agreement. Just what she didn't need. How could she face . . . the bed?

"Don't worry," Ty interjected into her thoughts, as if he could hear them. "I'll be getting us each our own room."

Taking the next exit, Ty pulled into the parking lot of Major's Hotel. Stones and debris from the broken pavement pinged off their wheel wells; the sign overhead blinked and fizzled out.

A single-story strip of rooms wrapped around a closed, inground pool, and the grass needed mowing. It wasn't exactly the Ritz, but she'd seen worse. After you've slept on the streets, a roof over your head is a roof over your head. No matter how much money she had, that appreciation had become a part of her.

"The area is pretty remote," Ty said, keeping the engine running. "But we can drive farther on, try to find someplace better."

She could see it in his eyes—he was aching. Needing to get out of the car.

The fool. He should have accepted her offer to drive, but as always, Ty had to be in control of his car. Or rather, his baby. Men.

"As long as there are no roaches," Lizzy pushed her door open. "This is fine—probably ten times better than the place we're headed to."

She didn't see herself sleeping anyway, despite separate beds.

Fifteen minutes later, Ty unlocked the door to his room. Carrying his duffel, his books slung over his shoulder, he pushed his way in, wondering if she'd come around tonight. Just how long it'd take.

After the way she'd turned so cold on him this morning, he refused to dance to her tune. It wasn't just her heart at risk in this little game she was playing, but his as well. He just couldn't keep being pulled close then being pushed away by her.

It was good for them to have a little breather. He couldn't help but think he was trying too hard to be with Lizzy, that he needed to give her space to want him.

Ah well, at least this way he'd get his juvenile justice report proofread and zipped to his teacher. Maybe he'd even get his paper for English completed as well—if he could keep himself awake long enough. With the way they'd been going, he needed to catch up on sleep too.

Ty set his belongings on the bed and went straight for the bathroom. Stripping, he cranked on the shower and stepped under the warming water.

Lathering up, Ty washed quickly. He'd been hard on the gas pedal today, making every mile count, and it was almost eight. Damn, he ached. Exhaustion tugged at him.

If he was going to drive like that again tomorrow he didn't have too long before he needed to hit the sack, but not before he got as much work done as possible. His deadline was looming, threatening him, and it would feel glorious to get the majority of the work and worry off his back.

Three minutes later, he stepped out, refreshed. Toweling off, he slipped on a pair of boxers and nothing more, then sat on the bed and dug out his laptop.

That's when it started.

Bang. "Oh, Chuck!" *Bang, bang.* "Oh yeah, that's the spot!"

Ty laughed at the sound of the headboard slamming into the wall opposite his, at the sexual moans and groans.

Good grief. How long was this going to last?

Ty tried to get back to work, opening his file and reviewing the last sentence he'd written on his examination of juvenile crime and punishment throughout history.

"Oh, oh, Chuck!" Pleasure howled from the woman.

She was certainly enjoying herself.

Just like Lizzy last night. The thought made his cock twitch. With a sigh, he set the computer aside and rested his head on a pillow, resolved to listening to his neighbors get it on. How long could they go at it anyway?

It wasn't hard to imagine the hot, sweaty, dirty union that was taking place. The woman on her knees, the man's cock plunging into her wet pussy. So hard, so fast.

Bang, bang! "Chucky!"

Ty couldn't help but wonder if Lizzy could hear. Then again, of course she could—as luck had it, she was right on the other side of the two rooms.

What was she thinking right now? Was she as turned on as he was? Perhaps she was masturbating?

He couldn't resist picking up the motel phone, calling her cell.

"Ty?" she answered immediately, as if she'd been clutching her cell in hand.

"So, all settled in?" *Bang, bang!*

"Yep," she answered quickly—too quickly.

"Watchin' television?"

"Yep. The weather."

Yeah right, not with Chucky oh-oh Chucky in the background. Ty could hear the truth in her voice—she was getting the same show as him.

"So, what'll it be like tomorrow?"

"Nice. Sunny and warm."

"Perfect. Get some rest, call me if you need me." Ty hung up. The weather, his ass.

Bang, bang! His cock grew hard, heat flushing through his body. Ironic, wasn't it?

Separated as they were, both listening to the sound of neighbors screwing like wild animals, remembering how they'd fucked the night before.

Because he knew it was on Lizzy's mind—just as it had been on his all damn day. He knew her well enough that he could see it in her eyes, her every movement.

Well, he hoped this was driving her crazy. Making her want sex, want him. Making her face her demons.

Thump! "On top!" the man commanded.

"Yee haw!" The woman squealed. Five seconds later, the banging resumed, faster, louder. Unrelenting.

Ty chuckled. Now that was what he was talking about! Jeez, they were lucky the bed didn't collapse. Maybe they'd come sliding right through the wall.

"Woman, fuck me like you mean it!" *Smack, smack!* "Don't you dare slow down!"

The sound of the spanking clapped through the air, sharp and distinctive.

"Oh, Chuck!" *Bang, bang!* "Harder! Spank me harder!"

The banging and creaking became more rapid, the woman pealing out in whimpers and cries as an orgasm took her.

For a moment, all was quiet.

A knock sounded on his door.

Standing, Ty crossed the room. Either it was the manager, mistaking him for the source of all the commotion, or all the sexual noise had driven Lizzy out. To him.

He hoped the latter.

Using the door to block the fact that he wore nothing but boxers and had a steel erection, he slid the chain free and cracked the door open.

"Hey," Lizzy said, breathless. She pushed her way inside, taking the door from his hands and shutting it. Leaving him exposed. "I thought you might—"

Her gaze drifted over his body, noting his lack of attire, gaping at the tent in his boxers.

"Let me back on top," Chuck demanded loudly. "I'm going to do you in that sweet ass of yours."

The bed creaked. A moan filled the air.

Lizzy's face turned red, her hands began shaking. She looked more nervous than a virgin about to be deflowered.

Could this be it . . . was she coming to him? Really ready, so soon? He'd figure she'd hold out a bit, but then, he hadn't been counting on Chuck.

She tucked her hair behind her ear, swallowing deeply. "I thought you might like to go get something to eat."

"Lizzy, we already ate," he reminded her.

The woman screeched. "Fuck that ass, baby!"

"I have to go," Lizzy blurted.

"Wait!"

With that, she disappeared, leaving Ty disappointed. And hard, so miserably hard.

Oh yeah, fuckmefuckmefuckme!" the woman squealed. "*Oh, Chuck!*"

Lizzy pressed her back to the door of her room, breathing heavy.

What the hell was wrong with her? Why was she quivering? Why had she fled like a coward?

Why—after all she and Ty had done together—hadn't she just hopped on him and rode like a cowgirl? Taken what she wanted like the bold woman next door?

"Spank my ass, Chuck!"

Smack, smack!

Tears welled in her eyes as she remembered. *Spank me more!*

Oh God, Ty was so right about her.

Her nipples were hard. Desire dripped down her legs, made her loins fiery hot with need. All she could think about was Ty and how it felt to have him do those things to her. How wonderful and glorious coming was, how intense being with him like that had made her feel.

Why had she pushed him away this morning? Why couldn't she go to him now, apologize and be done with it? *Why?*

Clenching her pussy muscles, she tried to make sense of herself. She was so confused, so angry and sad all at once. Sometimes she could swear she was possessed by some sort of man-hating demon that wouldn't let her get close, wouldn't let her . . . love.

And she just wanted it out. Just wanted to exorcize the monster. To be at peace, to be with Ty.

"That's the spot, Chuck! Rub that pussy! Make me come!"

Oh God, why wouldn't they shut up? Just shut the hell up!

She ran to the wall, banging on it with her fists. "Stop having sex!" she screamed.

Laughter answered her. Moaning.

A sob caught in Lizzy's throat and she slid to the floor, the tears coming heavier and heavier. Lying down, she curled in a ball and cried like she'd never cried before.

She was miserable. Horny and unhappy, and yet some deep, ugly part of her refused to let her seek relief. Refused to let her be free.

Refused to let her forgive Ty.

Damn him! How could he have left her on the streets like he had? What if her adoptive mother hadn't found her and given her a home? She would have sold her body, become a whore at sixteen!

All because she'd trusted—Ty.

How could she do so again?

Ty—the happiness he presented—was all she wanted, all that she needed. Yet so terrifying, seemingly impossible to truly have . . .

She hiccupped, trying to catch her breath. *God!*

A week ago, she would've sworn being normal in the bedroom was all she'd ever want. Now, she knew—it wasn't enough.

It was only the beginning . . .

nineteen

Smelling his breakfast even before it arrived, Ty looked up from his English report. Balancing a breakfast-laden tray, his waitress made a beeline to his booth.

Finally. His stomach rumbled in agreement.

After a night of hard work, he was starving. To his satisfaction, he'd managed to complete and zip off his juvenile justice paper just after midnight. A little more research and his English paper would also be complete. He'd be home free, and even better, he'd thought of a way to make up for his two failed classes. Rather than take a summer break, he'd sign up for a couple Internet courses, boost his credits. Best of all, he could do so from Aspen. Assuming he could afford it . . .

"Here you go, hon." The older, Southern-accented waitress who reeked of too much perfume set his scrambled eggs and ham on the table. "Anythin' else for you?"

His mouth watered. "This looks excellent. Th—"

The diner door jingled then opened to reveal his pink-haired princess.

"Thanks," Ty finished, his food forgotten.

Mesmerized, he watched as Lizzy walked toward him. The way she moved, the way she looked, something about her—she was different today.

Her hair pulled back, she wore little makeup and a simple white T-shirt. An old pair of jeans clung to her curves, molding her hips and thighs, and her black combat boots had been replaced with Nikes.

It didn't matter how she was dressed, she always looked sexy as hell. But he didn't get it. Today they'd arrive in Tennessee. He'd figured she'd have put on something nice. He had.

The stress of having to face his parents again had him in his newest jeans and a nice button-down shirt. If he had to go back there, he'd be damned if he handed his pop anything to pick about on a silver platter.

Lizzy paused at the counter, leaning against it and talking to the waitress.

Pushing his books to the side, Ty drew his steaming breakfast in front of him. The salty scent of fried ham wafted in his face, so pleasing to his soul it was a turn-on.

Course, around Lizzy almost everything was a turn-on.

God, he was hungry. He took a big bite and chewed the cheesy eggs slowly, wanting to enjoy every last nibble. It wasn't often that he had this kind of breakfast. Normally it was just cold cereal, since there was no one to cook for him and he definitely didn't have enough culinary skills to handle anything beyond boiled eggs himself.

Lizzy turned and walked down the aisle, holding a steaming cup. Silently, he nodded toward her.

"How'd you guess?" he asked.

The diner was across the street from their hotel. This morning, when he'd risen along with the sun—and well before her—he'd been unable to resist.

"I know how you love your coffee while you read. Always the first thing you do."

So she'd noticed. "My favorite time to work."

Ty took a sip of his coffee, rinsing down the eggs. Used to be he could sleep all morning and half the afternoon, but the older he got, the earlier he rose. That quiet time before the day's start, when his mind was fresh and clear, always seemed like the best opportunity to get his studying done. Then it was out of the way and he didn't have to worry about remembering to get to it.

"How'd you sleep?" Like he didn't already know. That damn couple had been at it until two a.m.—hence his ability to stay up so late working.

Ty took another sip, looking at Lizzy to gauge her reaction as she slid into the booth across from him.

His appetite vanished.

"You've been crying." His heart kicked in his chest, adrenaline rushed through his body. There was no mistaking the puffiness around her eyes, the way they were red and vein streaked. "Are you okay?"

God, he hated to see her torture herself as she did.

"I'm fine." She shrugged him off.

Fine? She was lying.

Damn it, if she was upset, why hadn't she returned to him? Allowed him to comfort her?

"You're not." Ty leaned across the table. "You look like a wreck."

"It was just a hard night, okay? But I'm over it."

Hard indeed. He'd spent the majority of the night strongly tempted to jerk off and trying to distract himself. It sure wasn't any fun listening to the neighbors fuck like animals while his lover slept in a separate room.

But it hadn't left him in tears.

"You should have called my room. Come over."

"I did, remember?"

"And then you fled like a scared cat."

"You refused my dinner invitation." She cleared her throat. "No offense, but I realized you were the last person I wanted to be alone with."

Ouch. He didn't need a magnifying glass to read between the lines. She was saying *he* was the reason for her tears.

That stung. The last thing he wanted was to hurt her. But if she cared enough to cry, why was she putting herself through this?

Clenching his jaw, Ty pushed the menu he'd saved across the table. "Get yourself some breakfast."

She pushed it back. "I'm not hungry. I'll just take coffee."

Ty motioned to the waitress. "The lady will take eggs and bacon, over easy."

"That'll be about ten minutes." Retrieving the menu, the waitress disappeared.

"I said I didn't want anything," Lizzy hissed.

"You obviously don't know what you want. Or what's good for you."

"Don't be a jerk, Ty."

He was being the jerk?

They sat in silence until her food arrived. Ty tried to take another bite or two of his meal, but even the ham tasted like crap.

"There you go." The waitress placed the hot plate in front of her. "Get ya anything else?"

"No," Lizzy told her stiffly. "Thank you."

She didn't touch her breakfast, just sat there staring into the black depths of her coffee, looking troubled.

"What are you going to do, Lizzy, if you get there and don't find the resolution you're looking for?" Ty asked. Because he knew damn well she wasn't going to get it.

She was setting herself up for a hell of a downfall. More disappointment and heartache, when that was the last thing she needed.

Lizzy picked up a spoon and scooped some sugar in her coffee. "I'm not looking for a resolution."

"Then what are you after?"

She poured in creamer. Her spoon clanked against the porcelain as it swirled round and round.

"Peace," she said finally, seeming satisfied with her answer as she repeated it. "Peace."

"Why do you need *them* for that?" He was beginning to think the only one torturing Lizzy was Lizzy. She didn't need permission from her ex-parents, from him, or anyone else to be happy. Didn't she know that? "Look at you. You're beautiful. You're independent and individualistic and well educated. You own your own club and—"

She shot him a look, her eyes blue stones, hard, defiant . . . dead serious. "I can't explain it, Ty. And it's not just them. It's you too. I don't know . . . I just need to face some things, I think."

A knot formed in his throat and he gulped it down, plagued by the thought of her being so angst ridden. By the fact that she'd stayed up all night crying. That she hadn't asked him for comfort, that she held him so far at bay. Didn't she know she could've leaned on him, that it didn't always have to be about sex? He would've gladly held her, distracted her, helped her . . . was he so terrible?

"Lizzy . . ." He reached across the table. Her hands encircled her coffee mug and he wrapped his around hers, gently hugging them against the warmth. "Whatever you're looking for, whatever you need, you'll have me."

"I know." She smiled and her face lit up for the first time in two days. "Thank you."

"What do you say we hit the road?"

The sun was fading into the horizon in a glorious show of purple and orange as they crossed into Cocke County, Tennessee. After a traffic jam and an overheated engine, Ty had suggested stopping for the night, but Lizzy just wanted to get the visit over with. There was still some light to the day and she'd lost all her patience in that hotel room last night.

She rested her head against the glass, taking in familiar sights as they drove closer and closer toward home: miniature towns, picturesque farms, rolling mountains just budding with the green of spring. She'd forgotten how beautiful Tennessee was in the early spring.

To her surprise, a new development had gone up not far from her hometown, brand spanking new houses, suburban curb appeal. And a Wal-Mart! Incredible!

She just couldn't believe she was here after all this time. A nervous twinge fluttered through her belly as they rode into Shot Creek. The tiny town had doubled in size, though it was still a speck compared to Los Angeles, where she and Ty had escaped to. Many

of the older buildings had been fixed up, making the previously ne-
glected main street look brand new.

Boy, a lot of changes had occurred in the years she'd been gone.
The question was, had they also happened to her parents?

Why was she even getting her hopes up?

Lizzy released a sigh of frustration and looked to Ty. He was
gripping the steering wheel, his knuckles white. He was apparently
just as nervous as she was, the anxiety between them growing with
every second they cruised closer.

Barely two miles from start to finish, they left Shot Creek behind, and Ty turned left onto Barrel Road, which led past a trailer
park and up the mountainside.

"Looks like Wal-Mart created quite the boom," she observed as
they drove past the half mile or better of row after row of new mo-
bile homes.

Ty glanced out the window. "It's something else, isn't it?"

"Can you imagine having a store so close when we were kids?"

Ty grunted. "Our parents never had money anyway."

True, that. Sadly true.

The mountain grew steeper, the trees thicker, and the homes
less frequent.

Ty hit a bump, jarring them. "Damn it!" he swore. "Not too sure
about this."

Neither was she. It was sunset, and she'd forgotten how the
hanging branches of the thick forest created spooky shadows and
made everything so much darker. Maybe they should turn back,
wait until morning.

To that effect, maybe she should dye her hair back to normal
first. She'd pulled her unruly mop back, tried to dress casually, but
nothing could hide the pink.

Pink that surely her stepfather would make into the joke of the day.

Lizzy had to bite her tongue; force herself to remember that what her parents thought of her meant nothing. That she *wanted* to do this. Get it over with. Tonight.

God. She felt sick.

The farther they drove, the less of a road the road became. More like a dirt path, riddled with potholes, rougher than ever, grown in with thick brush and a mix of pine and hardwood trees. It was hard to imagine anyone lived up such a trail.

And maybe they didn't. For all she knew, they'd find their childhood homes abandoned. Her parents dead.

Ty hit another bump, this one harder. "That's it." A string of curse words heated his breath. Applying the break, he put the car in park. "It's too rough. We'll have to walk from here."

Lizzy nodded silently, too overwhelmed to talk. Maybe they should have checked in town first, asked around.

But even if her parents weren't here, she wanted to see the house she'd grown up in, needed to walk by the creek with Ty one more time, to remember.

Shouldering her purse, she climbed out of the car, reminding herself she'd ventured through these dimly lit woods without fear as a child. Surely she could do so as an adult.

The dusk air was cool, crisp and filled with a symphony of crickets, the occasional hoot of an owl. She laced her hand in Ty's, holding on to him as they managed their way uphill over the last eighth of a mile.

Instinctively wanting to be done, to beat the night that was rapidly settling over them, she walked quickly, dragging Ty along and covering the distance in little time.

Together, they turned a bend and came to two dirt driveways—her parents to the left, his down a small hill to the right. Lizzy stopped and stared, discouraged.

The house was still occupied—and her parents hadn't changed a bit. Under the black, crisscross shadows of the tree branches, it was clear—her stepfather was still a lazy drunk, her mother was still trying to pretend like planting flowers and collecting knickknacks and cleaning house made everything pretty.

Laundry hung on the line. Beer cans were tossed about the un-mowed lawn—in sharp contrast to her mother's pristine flower beds. *Jesus*. Was that old motor still hanging in the tree out front? Her stepfather had used the big oak to heft it out of a failing '75 Chevy truck when she was thirteen. It was rusted, the rope hanging on its last thread. Not a very good birdhouse, if you asked her. And right underneath it, Mom had stationed a Welcome sign.

Lizzy marched on, feeling like a soldier walking straight into hell.

Some things never changed. In fact, it looked like they'd only gotten worse. *How* was this going to bring her peace? She must be certifiable.

"You sure, Lizzy?" Ty's hand took her arm. "Things don't look any better."

Despite her shaking legs, she forced her best smile. "I survived them as a kid. I can handle this."

She had to, and now, not later. She didn't know why, she just did. Maybe it *was* resolution she wanted; maybe she just needed to know. But she'd come this far and she intended to face her parents tonight.

With a deep breath, she stepped onto the rickety porch. The rotting wood shifted under her weight, flashing her back to her childhood.

That step had been on its last leg for too many years to count.

A skinny, sad-looking orange cat brushed her calves, curling around her feet and mewing as she approached the door. Greeting her.

Lizzy had to look twice at the booted white feet before she realized. *Jinkers!* She didn't believe it! It was *her* cat—her mother had kept him!

Bending, Lizzy picked him up, snuggled him to her chest. "Do you remember me? Huh? You remember me?" she cooed, scratching his neck.

He was so old, his hair falling out. The poor baby.

"It's my cat," she told Ty, looking at him. "I can't believe it. He was still a kitten when I left."

"You better knock." Standing at the rear, Ty held his hand at the small of her back protectively. Lizzy closed her eyes, wishing his simple touch could make everything safe and all right. Then she wouldn't have needed to do this.

God, she was trembling. Never more thankful to have Ty with her. If it weren't for him, she'd never have made it this far. She'd have turned and run. Stayed trapped inside of herself—afraid to live, love, and be with a man the rest of her life.

But that was all about to change. She had to change it. Starting here, starting now.

Cuddling Jinkers, Lizzy knocked.

Her insides curled into a giant knot and Lizzy mentally commanded herself not to run. *Stay, stay . . .*

Who would answer? Please, God, don't let it be her stepdad. Let him be not home. Maybe he'd actually gotten a job.

Footsteps approached the door and the porch light flicked on, illuminating them. Metal scraped as the lock was undone.

The door swung, leaving her face-to-face with her mother. A whoosh of relief exhaled from Lizzy.

"Elizabeth?" Her mother's hand went to her mouth, her wedding ring glistening in the porch light. "Oh my."

Stupid, quarter carat hunk of junk! Lizzy wanted to rip the ring off her finger, throw it to the ground, and start stomping.

Her mother had ruined her life the day she'd married that bastard!

"You okay?" Ty whispered in her ear, holding her even closer.

Get it together, Lizzy told herself. Swallowing, she nodded and blinked back tears.

God, she almost didn't recognize the woman standing before her. All of her hair had turned from a beautiful chestnut brown to white, her once smooth skin wrinkling and beginning to spot with age.

Forty-three. Her mother was forty-three, yet she looked so much older. She was so frail. Beaten down by life.

Talk, Lizzy chided herself. *Say something!*

"Hi, Mom," she forced out. It felt as if her throat were swelling shut, like she was going to choke to death if she tried to talk more.

"I can't believe it." Reaching out, her mother touched her hair, then quickly retracted. She stared as if she was seeing a ghost, her gaze sweeping over Lizzy. Analyzing. Disbelieving.

Thank God she'd disposed of the violet contacts, Lizzy thought, never feeling more awkward in all her life.

"Mrs. Richard," Ty said, sounding smooth. Confident.

Her mother's gaze lifted.

"Tyler Black." There was no missing the sternness in her voice, the displeasure in her mother's tired blue eyes. Eyes everyone told Lizzy she'd inherited. "You're lucky you're too big for a whoopin', though I'm tempted to try anyway." She dropped her hands to the side—hands that were shaking almost violently—and stepped aside. "Well, come in then. Can't stand here with the door open, letting in bugs."

The hole inside Lizzy's chest grew wider. That was it? *Come in then?* No hug. No excitement. She was more worried about bugs getting in her damn house?

Lizzy clutched Jinkers against her chest. Ty was right. She shouldn't have come. She'd been stupid to think this would bring her anything except pain.

Ty hugged her shoulders, pulling her against him as they stepped into the foyer and he shut the door behind them. The small room was dim, illuminated only by the reflection of light from another room, and the stench of tobacco was almost overwhelming, despite that fact that it was a smell she was used to from the club.

Lizzy glanced into the living room, shocked by the large shadow she saw standing against the far wall. A big-screen television? How could they afford that?

"I didn't think I'd ever see you again," her mother said, her voice hushed, restrained. She glanced at the entryway to the kitchen, then at Lizzy again. "They told me I couldn't."

What?

"*Who* told you?" The question burst from Lizzy, louder than she intended.

In the kitchen, she heard a chair creak, then footsteps.

The cat leapt from her arms, fleeing.

"The people who adopted you."

"You knew about that?"

Thunk, thunk, thunk. The heavy clank of boots beating the

wooden floor announced her stepfather, a sound she remembered all too well. One that sent a chill down her spine.

"Of course we knew. Had to agree to it, now didn't we?" Joe's loud, overbearing voice boomed into the room, inflicting instinctual fear into Lizzy. "We were all too happy to give you away. Pain in the ass."

Lizzy winced, but stood tall. At least Joe wasn't drunk.

"Joe," her mother admonished in a weak voice. "Please."

"Oh . . . *you* wanted to tell her about the money?" He chuckled, practically pushing her mother out of the way, so that he stood right before Lizzy. "I'll admit, your mother was less willing than I was. It took some dough to convince her that her first daughter wasn't worth fighting for. Nice hair," he added. "Always knew you were a crazy freak."

"Hey," Ty barked in protest. "Don't talk to her like that again."

"Or what? You'll take her away once more? Boohoo."

"Or I'll do what I really wanted to do to you all those years ago," Ty threatened in a cold voice that would scare the pants off any psychiatrist.

She'd never heard him sound so mean and didn't want to know what action he might have thought of taking back then. She leaned on her heels, pressing her back into his chest, telling him silently that she needed him, needed him to get it—and to keep her—together.

Ty's arms tensed around her as she searched her mother's face.

The money? What did that mean, anyway?

Nausea rose up in Lizzy as she saw the truth—shame and guilt, palpable in the way Mom stared at the floor, hid behind her ass of a husband.

So *she* was the source of the damned big-screen television? God. How? Why?

But deep down, despite her confusion, Lizzy knew. There might have been lots of prospective men willing to toss out a ten or twenty for her body as a teenager, but there was only one person that would have given real money to have *her*.

"Lance Cross paid you off." It was more a statement than a question.

Jesus. She didn't know who to be more angry at—her adopted family or her real one.

"You don't understand." Her mother protested, moving around Joe, looking at Lizzy desperately, begging with her eyes.

Oh, suddenly she cared? Lizzy stepped back, pushing herself farther into Ty's protective embrace, wanting to hide.

"I don't," Lizzy agreed coldly, casting a glare at her stepfather. "I was better off anyway."

"Mrs. Richard." Ty's hand grasped Lizzy's shoulder, giving her reassurance. "Why don't you make Lizzy understand? Explain yourself."

"Yeah, Amelia," her stepfather chuckled. "Explain yourself. Please."

He said it like a dare, like a *threat*, silencing her mother.

"So the prodigal daughter returns." With a scoff, her stepfather walked from the room. "Better begin the feast, Amelia."

The fridge opened, its hum filling the air, succeeded by the pop of a beer tab.

Tense quiet fell around them, closing in, saying more than words ever could. Lizzy battled a hundred raging emotions, still hoping, still wishing.

But all the while knowing better.

What had she expected? A change? Perhaps an apology?

No and double no. Damn, it was so simple. So childish. All she really wanted was their love. Why did that feel so out of reach?

"Mom." The ache in her was growing and growing, making her feel hollow and empty inside. Dead. But no answers, no excuses presented themselves. "I was a fool." Breaking free of Ty's arms, Lizzy fled.

Bastard! Ty's jaw clenched, the overwhelming desire to rush into the kitchen and pound the life from Joe Richard pumping through his blood, intoxicating him with adrenaline.

It took all his strength to stay where he was, to fight for what Lizzy truly needed.

Through narrowed eyes, he stared down Lizzy's mother. God, he wished he could shake some sense into her. Make her care. "That's your only daughter, and I guarantee this is your last chance."

She lifted her hand to her mouth, her whole arm convulsing violently. What the hell was wrong with her? He'd never met a woman who shook more than Mrs. Richard.

"I don't know what to say to her" was her pathetic excuse. Her eyes shot nervously toward the kitchen. "I was so happy that she'd found a good life."

"And yet she still came here, still needed to see you," Ty ground out. "I told her not to."

"I can't talk with him around. I just can't." With one last worried glance to the kitchen, the frail woman stepped past him, onto the front porch.

Ty followed her.

At the end of the road, in the ever-darkening shadows of the trees, Lizzy stood tall, with her back to them, unmoving. Like a statue, a tribute to all that life had made her—hard as stone, impenetrable.

Mrs. Richard watched her longingly and suddenly, Ty saw something in her hunched shoulders he'd never recognized before. Regret. Love. Lizzy's mother did care, but she certainly had a funny way of showing it. Like she was afraid to—no surprise there.

"It took a lot of courage for Elizabeth to visit," she said, reaching in the side pocket of her flowered housecoat and pulling out a pack of menthol smokes. "But you're right; she shouldn't have."

It was too late for that. Lizzy had traveled far and she couldn't turn back now and leave things unfinished with her mother. Ty knew if Lizzy left here like this, she could forget all about the so-called healing she was searching for. And peace? No way.

She'd spend the rest of her life tortured by unanswered questions. Afraid of love, unable to trust.

Ty stepped away as Mrs. Richard lit up, amazed by how the unhealthy act steadied her hands.

"As much courage as it took Lizzy to come here, don't you think you could—just once—be there for her? Love her like a mother should, more than yourself?" Ty didn't mean to be rude, but the truth was the truth. "She didn't ask to be born, didn't earn the life you gave her. She *is* better off now and I guarantee you this, she won't return here twice."

To his surprise—and relief—Mrs. Richard silently acknowledged his harsh words. Her eyes welled with tears. "There's so much I have to tell her. But I don't think she'll listen long enough, and I know I don't deserve the chance."

"Just try," Ty encouraged her. "With your heart."

"Don't let Joe bother us. Or . . . anyone else." With a flick of ashes, she stepped down from the porch. Ty glanced through the screen door. *Oh boy.* Ty grinned wryly to himself. Just what he always wanted—the satisfying possibility of putting that bastard in his place.

Not that he needed a confrontation, much as he might enjoy one. He'd already had enough trouble in his life, and he sure wouldn't want a fight to be the way his parents discovered he was home.

Nonetheless, he crossed his arms, guarding his station as Mrs. Richard walked gingerly down the dirt drive to Lizzy.

He'd give them a few moments and then they were out of here. Because of the trees, it was getting really dark, really fast, and Ty didn't feel like they were safe.

He glanced at his watch, giving them ten minutes. After that, anything else between Lizzy and her mom that might need to be resolved could be discussed tomorrow, somewhere else, away from Joe, and in the daylight. *If* the two of them had anything left to say to each other.

twenty

Lizzy didn't have to look to know it wasn't Ty approaching her—it wasn't Ty's walk. Her mother had always walked on air, barely making a sound, like she thought too much noise was dangerous. Lizzy supposed it was, if you spent your life hiding from reality.

"Elizabeth?" her mother asked softly, clearly afraid to approach. Well, she ought to be.

Lizzy clenched her fists at her sides, trying to stop shaking. At that moment, standing there in the darkening woods, listening to the lonely call of a hoot owl, Lizzy had never felt so angry. So frustrated.

So completely, utterly lost.

Why? Why—after her mother had just disregarded her—did she want to talk now? Enough had been said, hadn't it?

"I'm sorry to have bothered you." Turning, Lizzy forced a smile. "We'll be going now."

Her mother gaped, silent. What, did she expect a hug? Too late.

Walking past her, Lizzy looked to the house and found Ty leaning over the porch railing, bravely waiting within reach of her evil stepfather.

In the large front window, the glow of the television illuminated the living room and the low sound of talking hummed through the night.

Bastard! After years of abuse, he'd been awarded a large-screen television. It wasn't right!

Her hands started shaking all over again.

She really needed to leave now, before she did something crazy. Like smash the TV. With her stepfather's head.

"Ty?" Lizzy called. "I'm ready, let's go."

And hurry.

"Elizabeth, please," her mother admonished, following on her heels as Lizzy turned again and headed toward the car. "There are some things you deserve to know."

"No." What she *deserved* was to be free . . . for once in her life!

"Elizabeth." Her mother's hand caught her upper arm, tenderly encircling her biceps and squeezing. Unwilling to let go.

Lizzy blanched at the intimate touch. "Let me go."

"You act as if *I* were terrible to you."

Lizzy turned accusing eyes on her. "Weren't you?"

"I'm not to blame for his actions."

"Of course you are." Let her deny it all she liked, there was no one more to blame than her mother. She could have stopped her stepfather! "I was your kid, *your* responsibility. So thanks for the happy childhood. Now let me go."

To her surprise, her mother shook her head, and held tighter. "There were good times too. I know you haven't forgotten. Remember the button box you used to play with at my feet while I sewed?"

Lizzy softened at the recollection, allowing her mother to tug her closer as she continued.

"Remember the popcorn strings we made at Christmas and the stories we used to make up when you couldn't sleep and the—"

And the undeniable comfort of her mother's arms, wrapped around her, hugging away fear. The first dress Lizzy had made on her own, at her instruction. The unforgettable sound of Mom calling her in for a home-cooked dinner.

Staples of her childhood.

Emotion flooded Lizzy as more powerful memories took over, reminding her that for every good moment there was a bad one.

The back of her stepfather's hand across her face. Stinging words.

Love and hate. Fear. Frustration.

Such desperate need.

"Stop it!" she cried out. Wincing, she twisted her arm free of her mother's touch. She *needed* no one now, needed only to get out of there, to escape just like she had all those years ago.

"Ty!" Lizzy called again, louder this time. Why wasn't he coming? "I want to leave!"

With a silent nod, Ty stepped down off the porch. He dug in his pocket, pulling out his keys as he walked toward them, down the lane that seemed to stretch farther and farther with his every step.

"Elizabeth, if you would just—"

For once her mother wasn't giving up. But why bother?

It was just too late.

"Five minutes ago, you had every opportunity to share whatever you needed to." Lizzy hated the coldness in her voice, the reality that she'd returned to make peace and she couldn't get past her hatred. "Let's face it, Mom. You don't want me around."

"I've always wanted you with me, Elizabeth. I can't stand that you think differently."

"You *sold* me." She whirled around, searching her mother's face for some sort of regret. Something, anything that would give her reason to listen. To hope.

And she found it—tears shining in her mother's gaze. *Tears.*

"And that I won't make apologies for, Elizabeth."

Disappointment all over again.

"Apologize? Of course not. Not you." Lizzy practically fell into Ty's arms as he walked up to them, taking her into his embrace, clutching her.

"I'm sorry about a lot of things, Elizabeth. Very sorry I let your stepfather treat you like he did. Sorry I even married him. Sorry I wasn't stronger, that I just can't be," her mother told her in a near whisper, quietly admitting the truth, clearly ashamed. "But not for taking that money."

Lizzy lifted her head, disbelieving. An actual apology? Perhaps the first ever, she thought sarcastically.

Very sorry. Wasn't that what she wanted to hear? Why did she suddenly feel so very sardonic?

She was really, really trying to be mature about this. But she didn't feel mature. She felt like a kid again, a sad kid . . .

But no longer helpless. Strong enough that she simply didn't have to tolerate the pain.

"Give her a chance, Lizzy," Ty encouraged, his words hitting home. "You can't get past something you keep running from."

He was right, of course. She might not have to abide with any of this, but she needed to face it.

Isn't that why she'd traveled all this way? To settle things, at least in her heart, once and for all? She couldn't do that if she left.

And her mother *had* said she was sorry. Maybe Lizzy had told herself all along that she wasn't searching for an apology, but the truth was, it meant a lot.

"Okay." Lizzy straightened. "Let's talk."

Relief washed over her mother's face, instantly replaced with wrinkles of worry. "Like I said, there are some important things you ought to know," she repeated. "But now isn't the time."

All that, for a dismissal? Lizzy swallowed. "Then when will be?"

"Tomorrow."

Lizzy shook her head. "I can't come back here again. I won't."

"Oh." Disappointment, uncertainty, echoed around them.

"Why don't you two meet for dinner?" Ty suggested. "It's been a long time since you had a burger at Diggy's Drive-In, Elizabeth."

"Sure," she agreed, looping her arms in Ty's, leaning on his strength. "I'll be there at five tomorrow."

And then her mother did what she should've done in the first place. She pulled Lizzy into her arms, hugging her.

With a kiss to Lizzy's cheek, Mrs. Richard turned and left them, disappearing into the house.

"Ty?" Lizzy whispered, watching her. "I just want to stand here a moment."

The low rumble of her parents talking filled the quiet night.

Ty's gut clenched. He didn't know what she was waiting for, but *he* knew what he expected. Instinctively, he listened for the sounds of an ensuing fight, prepared to stop it if he had to.

Instead, the lights flicked off, leaving them in total blackness. Lizzy leaned closer. "God, it's dark. How are we going to make it to the car?"

"I have a flashlight in the trunk. Let me get it." Had he been thinking earlier, he would've brought it along. Night had fallen over them so quickly. Ty'd almost forgotten how fast the thick mountain woods could swallow you whole.

With a gentle squeeze, he released her. "Stay here. I'll be right back."

"No, Ty," she started to protest. "I want to go."

"Hey." He brushed his fingers over her cheek, speaking softly. "Just trust me?"

Trust him. Not easy, not for her, as simple of a request as it was. Yet to his relief, she closed her eyes and nodded. "Okay."

"Don't move an inch." Juggling his keys in his hand, Ty managed his way down the lane, barely dodging potholes, and tripping over a few branches before he thankfully made it to his car safe and sound. He fumbled with the keys, searching for the keyhole, and unlocked the trunk.

Taking out the flashlight and a six-pack he'd picked up earlier, he flicked on the yellow beam and hiked back up the drive, taking her hand in his and squeezing. "Come on."

"Where are we going?" she whispered as he led her away from the car, across the Richards' yard and into his parents'.

"Shhh." Ty flicked the flashlight back off, not wanting to alert them to their presence. When he'd set eyes on the lane home today, for the first time in so many years, his true feelings had hit hard. Indifferent as he was to his folks, he really missed them.

Family was family, and maybe a bad one was better than none at all. But that didn't make the thought of facing them any easier. In fact, he was more nervous than ever at the thought of putting his heart on the line, asking for forgiveness.

He wasn't certain he could.

Guilt chewed at him and he glanced at the rear of their single-story cabin house, thankful to find all the windows dark. What would his father think to know his son had tramped through his backyard, without so much as a hello?

He'd be angry, just like he undoubtedly already was over so many other things.

But his parents could come later. Lizzy was all that mattered right now.

And the last thing she needed was more stress. Or to be trapped inside some stuffy hotel room. No, not tonight.

He found the small opening in the woods at the rear of his parents' yard he was searching for and, flicking on the flashlight, he led her on the trail they'd used often as children.

"I'm surprised this isn't grown in." The small beam of light led their way as they quietly navigated the downhill trail. He brushed aside a branch and held it for her. "Long as we've been away."

"It's weird," she agreed, "almost as if someone's been using it."

"Maybe my dad, for hunting." Taking her hand, Ty helped her over a downed tree. "There's no one else who'd come down here."

The air turned fresh and moist, filled with the sound of the babbling creek, and the trees thinned, giving way to a tiny clearing. Together, they walked to the edge of the water and stared into the dark depths, their shadows glaring back at them. Ghosts of their childhood.

"It's been a long time." Ty dropped the beer to the ground and took her hand. "But it still feels the same."

"Magical," she whispered. "Remember when we used to pretend we were king and queen of the mountain and this was our moat?"

Ty looked up at the huge weeping willow tree standing on the high ledge overlooking the water. "And that was our castle."

Pulling her with him, he ducked under the hanging branches, and sat down beneath the old tree. They lay back in the tall grasses blanketing the ground, cushioned by their thick growth.

Tiny stars and a half moon shone above, filtering through the branches, creating glimmers in the sky.

Crickets sang and a gentle wind whipped around them, blowing the frayed rope they'd once used to swing off.

Ty exhaled. *Instant peace.*

Lizzy said nothing, but he knew she felt the same way. Could hear it in her breathing.

"Hard day." Ty flicked off the flashlight, leaving them in the dark. "You okay?"

"Yes. No." She sighed as Ty pulled her into his embrace, so that her head rested in the crook of his arm. Her fingers hooked in the buttons of his dress shirt, resting over his heart. "I am now."

"Good." Cracking open a beer, he handed it to her. She took a sip and passed the can back. "What about you?"

"Tomorrow's another day," he answered thoughtfully, taking a sip. "And I'm ready."

"You're not scared about facing your parents?"

"Terrified." He handed her back the half-empty can. "But it doesn't change a thing. I think I have to."

"Mmmm." Sitting forward, she took a drink, then returned it to him, resting in his arms. "Ty?"

"Yeah?"

"We had our first kiss right here."

"I know."

"Kiss me again," she breathed. "Just like you did back then."

"My pleasure." Tangling his fingers in her hair, he lifted her head, kissing her softly on the lips.

She opened for him and he swept his tongue alongside hers, enjoying the gentleness of it.

Despite the bitter taste of beer on her breath, she was so sweet, so much everything he'd ever wanted. *His Elizabeth.*

He'd sworn never to let her go and he hadn't. But he'd almost lost her, and he couldn't stand the thought of that happening again.

Ty's stomach muscles quivered, his heart ached. The kiss became harder, more intense, their lips and tongues tangling together as they rediscovered each other. And for the first time since they'd reunited, their embrace was anything but sexual. It was sensual, soul-awakening.

Pure love, shattering though them.

He could've kissed her like this forever, could've made love to her until their bodies fused together, but she'd said to kiss her like he had back then. And back then, he'd been too damn scared to continue.

Maybe he was a little too scared to continue now.

He could hardly take being rejected by her at all, but especially not here. Not like this.

Breaking free, Ty lay back. His hand smoothed her hair as she rested against him.

Taking the last drink, he crumpled the can in his hand and tossed it aside. He opened another, saying nothing, not needing to.

Together, they rested there in silence, sipping beer, remembering. For once, not thinking of the bad things, but the sweet memories they'd created at this creek. The support, the love.

The everything that they were to each other—then and now.

twenty-one

Tap, tap. Tweet, tweet. Tap, tap.

Groaning, Ty yielded to the morning symphony of birds and an annoying woodpecker and opened his eyes. Sunlight streaked down through the treetops, beams of golden light casting long shadows across the moist forest floor.

Beside him, lying on her side, her knees pulled to her stomach, Lizzy slept soundly underneath the protection of his leather jacket, on the thick, creekside grasses. Dewdrops glimmered on her nose and she still clutched an empty beer can.

Ty peeled it from her fingers and gathered the trash into a pile.

He hadn't aimed for them to spend the night at the creek. It'd gotten mighty cool overnight, though thankfully they'd had each other for keeping warm. He might as well take advantage of the situation. Shoot, he'd always loved his mother's home-cooked, mouth-watering pancake and bacon breakfasts . . .

And he couldn't put off the inevitable any longer.

There was no sense in avoiding his parents. Sooner or later, they'd find out he'd been here—the Richards *would* tell them—and he just couldn't hurt them like that.

Hurt them. That was what changed everything for Ty. Last night, as he'd crept through their yard, he'd realized it—that he would, he *could*, hurt them. Someone who didn't care, didn't love, couldn't be hurt.

All these years, certain he was hated for taking Lizzy and running away, he'd told himself they were better off having nothing to do with each other, that Pop didn't give a hoot about him anyway.

That he didn't need either of his parents in his life.

But he'd been lying to himself. Easing the guilt, the shame he felt every time he thought about facing them.

He and his parents had their differences, sure didn't see eye to eye, but he wasn't some dumb-shit kid anymore. He was a man now.

Man enough to go home.

Standing, Ty stretched his hands above his head, moving from left to right, pulling the ache from his muscles. God, the ground was hard on a back.

And beer was hard on the bladder.

Finding an out-of-the-way spot, he relieved himself, then headed up the trail. Five minutes later, he stood at the woods' edge, watching his father tinker with an old, rusted push mower.

"Goddamn piece of shit!" Pop grumbled and cursed in his usual manner, grabbing his beer and disappearing into the shed.

Ty couldn't help but smile to himself. Still fighting the mower, still drinking before breakfast. Pop hadn't changed a bit.

Swearing with even fouler words, his father came back out carrying a clear plastic jug half-filled with yellow liquid—gasoline, Ty'd guess. He poured some into the carburetor and gave starting it another try.

The engine puttered and strained. Failed.

More nasty language filled the air. "Emily?" Pop hollered toward the house. "You got breakfast—"

His father's words fell away as he glanced in Ty's direction. He froze and stared in disbelief, years of wondering etched on his sun-leathered face.

Ty's chest grew heavy, anticipation and uncertainty squeezing at his heart. What if his father told him to get lost? What if he *did* hate him?

And what had happened with his family all these years? Who might be sick, passed on?

Tap, tap, tap. The woodpecker hammered at a tree behind him. A hundred questions hammered in Ty's head.

He forced himself to wave. He couldn't just stand there, looking stupid. And he couldn't run, not now.

Shoving his shaking hands in the snug pockets of his jeans, Ty crossed the yard, coming to stand before his father. He swallowed. "Hi, Pop."

Age had wrinkled his skin, grayed his hair, but his eyes were as black and sharp as ever.

For a moment, they just gawked at each other, silent. Then to his surprise, his father stepped forward, pulling Ty into his arms. Embracing him.

Ty had never felt such relief in all his life. It was as if two cement blocks had dropped from his shoulders, freeing him. He felt lighter, happier. He felt loved.

God. Ty hugged him back with everything in him. Until that very moment, he hadn't realized just how heavily his estrangement with his parents had weighed upon him. How sad he was, how much he missed them.

"Boy, where the hell you been?" His father's palm clapped his back and he withdrew, holding Ty by the shoulders and analyzing him from head to toe. "You look healthy."

"And you sure as hell don't." A wry grin curled on Ty's lips.

He couldn't help but pick. It had always been that way between them.

"Ah," his father complained, "you sound like your mother." He glanced in the direction Ty had come from. "What the heck were you doing walking out of the woods?"

"Lizzy and I spent the night down by the creek. Fell asleep by accident."

"Lizzy? You mean Elizabeth?"

"Yeah, Pop. Elizabeth."

His father nodded, solemn faced and contemplative for a moment.

"Awful cool for sleeping outside. Where's your car?" he asked, looking down the drive.

"Down the road. Wouldn't make it up—too low for all the potholes."

"Still driving that Trans Am I got you?"

"Wouldn't dream of selling it."

That brought a smile. "What are you doing—"

The back door slammed, interrupting his father's question.

Ty turned around to find his mother clenching the rail of the small, rotted wood back porch, gaping like she'd seen a ghost.

Ty supposed, in a way, she had. One jerk of a ghost.

Gingerly, she walked down the stairs. The wood creaked with her every step, and Ty found himself grounded and gawking.

His mother. God, to think at one point he'd convinced himself he'd never see her again.

What in the hell had he been thinking?

She was as beautiful as he remembered, small and slim, with raven hair that fell past her waist. Hazel eyes that sparkled.

"Ty?" she questioned as if she were seeing things.

Ty went to her, offered his arms.

And she slapped him. Slapped him right across the left cheek, hard enough to make his eyes water.

"Where have you been?" she demanded. Her foot pounded the grass like that of a child throwing a fit. "How could you! Sending me cash like I'm some sort of charity case! Not even writing!" Then she pulled him into her arms, hugging him so hard it hurt, crying.

Ty blinked the eye on the smarting side of his face. Mom had always gotten right to the point—and she'd learned a little too much from *Dynasty*.

"Guess I deserved that." Ty returned her embrace, inhaled the scent of home that he'd so missed—warmth and baking bread. "I'm sorry, Mom."

A *whoosh* of relief exhaled from him. If that was the worst of it, it proved what a fool he'd been. Lizzy had no idea the favor she'd done him, dragging him to Tennessee. He just wished she could've found what he had—an end to more than a decade of running.

"Cash?" Pop asked from behind them. "What cash?"

Ty couldn't help but chuckle.

Ack, roots."

Later that day, Lizzy gawked at the reflection staring back at her in the mirror of their hotel bathroom. She needed to do something about her hair and soon, before she looked worse than a bottled blonde behind on maintenance.

But what?

On one hand, the pink coloring no longer felt right. Awkward, as if she'd outgrown it.

Or the other hand, she was determined to be comfortable in her own skin. To be herself. Not let the pressure of wanting to impress her mother, or Ty, or anyone, especially not the male gender, get to her.

Too late.

She pulled at a strand, not sure how to dress, what to wear, what she'd say tonight. She stared in the mirror and faced a woman she didn't know. Somehow, she'd lost confidence in the self she'd created, the thoughts and feelings she'd known for so long.

Last night had changed her. Who knew, maybe she'd been changing all along. Maybe coming home had done it, maybe it'd been Ty's kiss under their willow tree. The beer?

Now that was wishful thinking.

But she just didn't feel the same, not about Ty, not about her parents.

Not about life.

She couldn't put her finger on why, or what, she just felt new. Weird, and not in her usual way.

A knock sounded on the bathroom door. Ty peeked in, his dark eyes sweeping up and down her. "How's it going? You've been in here awhile—you've got a half hour before you need to meet your mother."

Lizzy groaned in dissatisfaction. "My hair."

"What about it?" Ty walked into the bathroom, suctioning her back with his front like he loved to do. Wrapping a strand of neon hair around his finger, he twirled and tugged it, studying her reflection. "It looks fine to me. I like it down, all frizzy."

"I'm thinking about dying it." Relaxing against him, she rolled her shoulders, trying to release the tension.

Ty patted her arm and tugged her to her side, so that her head rested against his chest. "To what?"

"Something normal." Listening to his steady breathing while she practically held her own, she looked at their intertwined feet and waited for his reaction.

What would it be? Would he jump to tell her to change? Probably.

Most definitely.

No one liked her hair. Her sister had been after her to go brown since the moment she'd put the pink in; her dad had a hundred jokes about Loony Lizzy and her crazy hair. And her stepfather . . . he sure had shared his opinion yesterday. For that matter, even strangers laughed at her.

But *she* liked being pink. Most of the time.

"Mmmm," Ty murmured, still twirling her hair round and round, tugging at her scalp. Lifting the bulk of her curls, he kissed her gently, trailing his mouth along her neck and creating shivers that raced down her spine. His lips suctioned her skin, tasted her, and his hands played with her hair.

Sensation pooled in her pussy, making the flesh swell with desire, and she swore even her hair was getting horny.

"*Mmmm* isn't an answer!" Lizzy ducked from his hair and mouth attack, play-slapping his chest. "Out with it! You think I should change it, don't you?"

"Nope. I think you're sexy." His mouth chased her down, reclaiming her neck, suckling and licking from her ear to her collarbone.

"With pink hair?" she challenged, not quite sure she believed him. After all, one of her prime reasons for dressing so outlandishly was to avoid men.

And jeez, if he found her desirable even like this, she was hopeless.

"Pink. Blue. Orange. You're sexy."

"What about lime green?" she dared.

"Whatever."

That deserved a kiss. Twisting around, she stood on tiptoe and planted her mouth to his, kissing him for all her hair was worth. Letting her tongue slide into his mouth as she slid into the hope that maybe he'd let that little swear of his go and decide to seduce her.

Hell, maybe she'd seduce him.

Lizzy kissed him deeper, wanting more, needing the connection they shared, needing the sparks that erupted in her body, a distraction from reality.

Ty suckled her tongue, pulled at it until she could rise no higher on her toes, until she had to fall back or climb right up his front.

Her descent to flat feet sent her crashing into the sink behind her and Ty's arms quickly steadied her. "Whoa there."

Whoa, her. Did she really think she could kiss him like that and not start trouble? No matter how much she wanted him, she wasn't about to give him what he wanted.

A pleading for a spanking. And worse.

Uh-uh. Ty was just going to have to come around, realize that was never going to happen. No matter how long he made her wait or how horny she became.

Obviously more composed than her as he fished in his pocket, Ty brandished a silver chain holding a sole key. "The spare to my Trans Am, milady."

Lizzy laughed. First the kisses—she completely blamed him for her advances—and now his car? "Someone trying to get into my pants?"

Perhaps regretting his decision to cut her off? Oh, please!

"You know I'm not." He made a *tsk-tsk* sound. "I much prefer the notion of you getting into mine."

"Oh." And wasn't that tempting?

All too much.

Lizzy toyed with the notion of telling him that she was ready, that she truly wanted him, heart and soul. Of giving him everything that he wanted. Of begging him to do the same.

Spank me more!

She'd thoroughly deserve it.

She closed her eyes, overwhelmed as her heart pounded against her ribs, her clit pulsed between engorged, wet labia.

And how close she came . . .

Close. But no cigar.

"Yeah, I know you want in these jeans, Lizzy," Ty toyed, attacking her neck again, sending aftershocks straight to her pussy. "And it's so fun to torture you."

An orgasm was trapped in her cunt, demanding release as she leaned into, then pulled away from his sensual attack.

Damn it! If she weren't about to meet her mother, she'd run to the car and drag out her toys. Fix the problem he'd created.

Yes, she blamed him—the bastard *knew* what he was doing! How crazy he was making her!

"Fun? No, it's not!" Lizzy twisted away from him, encountering her reflection once again. Seeing herself, her need, her pink hair—her fears.

And suddenly she wanted nothing more than to stay with him. She was worried, anxious about tonight, and all she wanted was to bury her face in his chest and hide, lose herself in the way he could make her feel.

Scary as it was to admit, begging for a spanking was nothing compared to facing her mom again.

"Ty?" she whispered.

"Yes?"

"Maybe you should come with me."

"Nervous?"

"Very," she admitted.

"Your mother clearly has some things to get off her chest. I think it should just be you and her tonight, on even ground." Ty dangled the key in front of her, and she took it. "You'll be fine."

"You're probably right." With a sigh, she jiggled the key as if shaking off her silly overreaction. She was fine, she could do this. "So you're seriously going to let me use the Trans Am?"

"Yup."

"Wow. It's your baby."

"I trust you, Lizzy, and *you're* my baby." He kissed her forehead gently. Sweetly and unseductively as ever, the show-off. "As long as you come back in one piece, I'm happy."

twenty-two

God, she couldn't believe she was actually here. That Diggy's was *still* here.

Pausing halfway into the parking lot, Lizzy put the car in neutral and stared up at the treasured childhood memory. Like the creek, this was one of the few places where she hadn't felt invaded by her stepfather. She and friends used to dance to the oldies, get high off milk shakes and penny candy . . .

She could still taste the sweetness, feel the excitement. Curious what was playing, she opened the window a crack and breathed in moist air.

"With a love so rare and true, oh, Peggy . . ." Buddy Holly's "Peggy Sue" blared from the speakers overhead, making her smile to herself. It was one of her mother's favorite songs. She'd probably selected it from the jukebox—which meant she was here. "I want you, Peggy Sue. Oh, Peggy Sue, Peggy Sue . . ."

It was hard to believe she and Ty had walked the three miles between their houses and here, taking a shortcut through the woods. She wished he were with her now, but he was right—she needed to do this on her own.

Returning the Trans Am to drive, she gave the outside of the place one last look-over. Black-and-white checkered moldings and flashing neon signs confirmed the restaurant's age—straight back to the early 1950s, when it had seen its grand opening. Many of the old advertisements still hung in the window, tributes to a simpler time.

You still couldn't drive in and order—the order speakers had been damaged in an electrical storm and the overhang was roped off in favor of rows of picnic tables, a problem that had existed as far back as Lizzy could remember.

Nope, Diggy's Drive-In hadn't changed a bit. And with any luck, they still had the best root beer floats in all of Tennessee.

Her mouth watered at the thought. At least she had something to look forward to this evening. At this point, she knew better than to be hopeful where her mother was concerned. After a lifetime of disappointment, it wasn't realistic to expect much from the woman that had allowed her to be abused then had sold her like an animal.

And yet, despite everything, regardless of knowing better, Lizzy couldn't temper the flicker of wistfulness, the idealistic notion that maybe they could get past everything and move on. Be friends. Maybe Mom could visit her in Colorado, away from her stepdad. They could shop together, cook a Thanksgiving dinner or something. Act like mother and daughter should.

Silencing the childish notions, Lizzy slid Ty's Trans Am into a parking slot, put up the window—it looked like rain—and double-checked that all the doors were locked. He'd given her his trust with this car and she'd be darned if anything happened to it.

It was no wonder Ty loved the vehicle. All she could say was *what a ride!* Being in the driver's seat was a whole different experience from riding as a passenger.

Fast and smooth, tickles still fluttered in her stomach from the way the car took a corner, the quick way the engine seemed to take off at the slightest touch of the gas pedal, accelerating to illegal speeds in a heartbeat.

Maybe she'd buy herself one—hot pink, of course.

Dropping the keys in her denim bag, she slung it on her shoulder, and rose from the vehicle. She bumped the door shut with her hip and crossed the cloud-shadowed parking lot. The air was heavy, laden with humidity, and in the distance, a darkening sky threatened. Oh yeah, April showers—it was going to storm bigtime. Lizzy just hoped she beat the bad weather home. Not to mention how relieved she would be to get this meeting behind her and move on.

Mustering all of her anger and resentment to the surface—it was the only defense she had and a well-practiced one at that—Lizzy pushed open the left side of the double glass door, looking around. "Peggy Sue" ended, replaced with Elvis's "Don't Be Cruel." How appropriate.

Craning her neck, Lizzy spotted her mother's unmistakable restrained white hair. In the farthest corner, she waited in a booth with her back to the door. A spiral of smoke rose up from the table—leaving it assumable that she sat in the smoking section. How appetizing.

Lizzy's very heart quaked, her hands trembled, but she forced her feet to move, to quickly cover the distance between them.

"How much?" Lizzy demanded, cutting right to the chase. "How much did my adopted parents pay to have me?"

Nervous, not giving her mother an opportunity for a hug, she slid into the vinyl-covered booth and sat down, only then catching sight of the young lady sitting next to her mother. A preteen—thirteen, maybe fourteen.

An eerie, uncalled-for shudder racked Lizzy's spine. Who was the girl? And why in hellfire had her mother brought her to *their* dinner?

Lizzy looked at them questioningly, noting how all the blood had drained from her mother's face. "Perhaps we should order first, Elizabeth," she suggested, taking a slow drag of her menthol and tapping the ashes in a tray.

What the hell . . .

And wasn't smoking illegal in restaurants now? Damn one-horse town.

"I'm not really hungry," Lizzy snapped. She could feel the sarcasm seeping from her pores, the disappointment making her physically ache.

One opportunity, one chance to make things right, and her mother was *babysitting*? Not to mention she was killing the kid with secondhand smoke.

Lizzy might have sworn to herself not to get her hopes up, but she'd broken that vow from the get-go. Big-time. *God.*

Menus lay on the table and Lizzy took one, spinning it over the cracked Formica. She couldn't help but stare, wonder at the teen's presence.

Blond and small boned, the girl gawked at Lizzy with huge gray blue eyes, eyes that reminded Lizzy of a ghost, eyes that seemed to follow Lizzy's every move without exhaustion.

She might even be older than Lizzy's first guess—her breasts were certainly past budding—but if she was, she had a small bone structure for her age. So babysitting didn't even make sense.

Lizzy ought to walk out. She'd never been her mother's first priority and obviously she still wasn't. But she couldn't leave, for her own sanity.

Questions. Lizzy had so many and she needed answers. Real, honest answers and no excuses.

"I didn't come here to be social. Or for a meal," Lizzy said, her voice strained. "And since you brought her along, I at least deserve an explanation, not an empty look. Who's the kid?"

And please, have a good excuse, Lizzy added silently.

Cocking her head, she studied her mother, searched for some sort of reaction or reason. Her tightly braided hair allowed a full view of the way her face wrinkled in disappointment. The sadness in her eyes, pulling at her lips.

Her mother opened her mouth then shut it, but still she gave no excuse for the child's presence.

What had she expected? A happy get-together, menial chitchat? A child—even a teenager—had no business being present for the conversation they *were* going to have.

"Fifty thousand," her mother blurted. Her hands were shaking as she took another drag.

So that was the price tag on her?

Burning heat rose to Lizzy's face. Anger . . . embarrassment? She wasn't sure. But having a number put on your life sucked.

"I may not have done right, raising you," her mother continued, "but the day I took that money from Mr. Cross, I did."

"How can you even say that?" Yet, Lizzy knew it was true, knew that even as painful as it was to accept, the best thing her parents had ever done was give her up.

"Mr. Cross is a good man and you deserved a new life, not to come back to Shot Creek." Reaching across the table, Mom laid her hands on Lizzy's twirling menu. Their fingers brushed, then connected. "We both know your stepfather has his way about him. You're not his true daughter, and he always had it out for you. I saw no good in you returning to that, for you or us."

Pale with worry, her mother glanced at the girl next to her, as if making silent apologies.

"Then why take the money? Why not just sign the papers?" She felt cheap, used, betrayed. As much as she wanted to, Lizzy just couldn't find peace in her mother's explanations. Thus far, they didn't add up. She just needed more than what she was being fed. "And what about *you*?"

Mom looked taken aback. "What about me?"

"All that money and you stayed with the bastard?" Lizzy hissed, then she realized what she said and bit her tongue. "I'm sorry," she told the girl. "I'm not used to watching my mouth."

"No problem," she spoke for the first time. "I'm used to it."

Lizzy blanched. "Well, you shouldn't be." She knew what being raised like that felt like. "And whoever she is, Mom, she shouldn't be with you now, hearing this."

Pad in hand, a waitress chose just that moment to walk up to them. "Hey, ready to order?"

All of them sank back in their seats, as if caught—even the kid.

Impatiently, the waitress—Ruby, her nametag read—chewed at the end of her pen and waited for one of them to respond. Lizzy cleared her throat.

"I'll just take a root beer float," she spoke up, unable to keep herself from staring. The buxom brunette couldn't be more than seventeen, eighteen years old.

It could've been her. Not with the knock-you-down breasts, of course. But had she stayed, Lizzy probably would've worked here. Saved for a car. College. A way out.

Was this girl doing the same?

Big tip, Lizzy promised herself. She'd leave a tip big enough to send this girl to the moon.

"What size?" the waitress asked.

Lizzy smiled to herself. "Large." And she'd enjoy every drop, appetite or not.

"I'll take a water," her mother chimed in, pushing the menus into a pile at the end of the table. "And a salad. Savannah?"

Savannah. Odd . . . Lizzy remembered her mother once telling her she'd almost been called Savannah, but her renegade Yankee father had protested use of the former Georgia capital. Not that he'd stuck around long enough to use her name.

"Cheeseburger and fries. Ketchup on the burger—nothing else."

The waitress walked away, and Lizzy turned to Savannah in surprise. "That was my favorite meal here, when I was a kid."

"Just ketchup too?"

"To this day." She gave a pretend shudder. "Pickles and onions and mustard—"

"Gross!" Savannah finished for her.

Lizzy glanced at her mother and noticed her smiling inwardly as she finally crushed out her cigarette. "You two have a lot in common."

But why? Who was this girl?

The mood turned serious again. "Mom?" Lizzy asked. "I'd like an answer. With that kind of money, why'd you stay with him?"

"You can't help who you love, Elizabeth." She sighed at the truth of it, clearly searching for the right words, something that typically evaded her mother. "But I wasn't about to let losing you be in vain."

Well, that's news. Mom officially had her attention. Her interest peaked, Lizzy sat forward, folding her hands on the table and waiting. "Okay and . . . ?"

"Mr. Cross visited me one evening while your father was passed out, and something told me not to involve him. And I didn't need to either, since he's not your real father."

"Thank God for that. And so?"

"For my own good, I took Mr. Cross's offer and signed the papers and waited until the check was safe and sound, deposited in my own account I opened at a bank two towns over. Felt guilty as sin, like I was betraying my husband, but I knew that I had to be strong." A tiny smile of bemusement twitched on her mother's cheeks, hinting at how proud she was of herself for the bold action. "Then your stepfather and I, we had a little chat. Oh, you should have seen him turn colors!" Her hands clapped down on the table, applauding herself.

All of her blood dropped to Lizzy's toes as she imagined the thought of her mother standing up to Joe. *"And?"*

"Lizzy, things are tough at times, but they're working out," she practically pleaded for understanding. "It isn't like it used to be. I haven't heard him so nasty until the day you showed up."

"So I take the blame." Lizzy glanced at Savannah, increasingly ashamed that the kid was hearing all this. And why? Her mother still hadn't explained Savannah's presence. Deliberately so it seemed, just as it seemed her mother wanted the girl to hear all this.

"The blame? Not at all. He's angry at you, Lizzy, because in the end, you won." Her mother's gaze begged for empathy as she pulled out a second smoke. "Oh, Lizzy, I'm sorry. I want you to know: Even before the money, there was a change in Joe. Your leaving did something to him. I think he saw himself for the first time."

Lighting her cigarette with her always-nervous hands, she drew a long puff that seemed to instantly steady her shaking.

"Mom—" Lizzy started to protest—the incredulousness of it all, the little girl's presence . . . suddenly she just wanted to leave.

"I know you don't believe this," her mother interrupted, continuing, "but Joe does love me. He loves his daughter too."

"I'm not his daughter." The words were bittersweet in her mouth. She didn't know who her birth father was and as a child, she used to imagine him coming to her rescue, how good and loving he would be—

"No, Lizzy," her mother's voice adopted an insinuating tone. "*You're* not his daughter . . . and I'm not talking about you."

What? Lizzy jerked her head up, looking at her mother, then to Savannah. What she saw was a smack in the face.

Eyes expectant, they were waiting for Lizzy to finally grasp the true point of this meeting, and suddenly, she did.

Of course her mother wasn't talking about *her*. She was talking about Savannah. Her little sister.

Oh God. Lizzy choked back a sob and tried to make sense of it all, but her mind was such a mess.

Her sister?

The waitress chose that inopportune moment to deliver their order. From a wobbly tray she could barely balance, Ruby lifted Lizzy's whipped cream-peaked, cherry-topped drink and placed it in front of her. "One root beer float and . . ." Savannah's plate clanked on the table, sliding over the Formica to her little sister. Lizzy studied the cheeseburger. "Just ketchup . . ."

Just ketchup. Damn, come to think on it, they even looked a little alike.

And suddenly, Lizzy realized—it was Savannah who was visiting the creek, taking refuge in her and Ty's special spot. That's why the path had been so clear. Her old hiding place, *her* little sister.

"And your salad, ma'am," Ruby lowered the tray, and her mother took the bowl, setting in front of her. "You need anything else?"

"No, thank you." Mom stamped out her cigarette. "Just the bill."

Lizzy had to know, couldn't contain herself. "Does he hit you?" she blurted out, asking Savannah directly.

Taken aback, the girl appeared offended as she shook her head no, glancing at her mother—*their* mother—for reassurance.

Lizzy did the same.

"Lizzy, I haven't and I won't hide the truth from Savannah," she said. "I decided when Mr. Cross contacted me and I was forced to give you up that you both deserved two things—a better mother and honesty about it all."

"Don't you think . . . she's a child, Mom . . ."

"In a harsh world. Better she knows the truth now than to get smacked in the face with it later on in life like I did. Imagine if I hadn't told her about you, how hard this would be. She knows who her father is, who he was to you. I'd like her to know her sister."

Lizzy's hands started to shake, her mind was spinning. It was all too much. She took her straw, plunging it into her shake, swirling it round nervously.

God, she felt like she was losing her grip. Hearing things. She'd certainly never heard her mother so bold, so strong.

She wished . . .

"Did you . . . did you know you were pregnant when you took

the money?" Lizzy heard herself asking the question distantly, like she was in a movie, going through a role.

"Yes."

"When I left home?"

"Yes."

Yes, yes, yes . . . The truth echoed in her brain.

"Okay." Lizzy bit her lower lip until she felt it swelling in the vise grip. It was all so much to digest. Everything was clicking into place, and yet she felt like she was falling apart.

Trying to calm down, Lizzy pushed her glass aside and clutched the table. She couldn't even drink her float. She had too many questions.

But she just couldn't ask them, couldn't face anything more. She looked at her little sister, suddenly seeing herself, at her mother, for the first time realizing she did love her. That Mom had done her best as a parent, even though she'd sucked.

How could home be such a hell? How did they go on from here?

Lizzy had never felt so stripped to the core. She couldn't be angry at her mother any longer, couldn't hate her. She was pathetic, but she wasn't that way on purpose.

Clearly Mom was trying to be better for Savannah. And by giving Lizzy away, she'd tried to provide her firstborn with a better life. Evidently, she had realized her mistakes and was making an effort not to repeat them.

Taking that money, working things out with Joe, Mom had done what she had to, what she thought was best for everyone.

But what was left? Reuniting as a family?

Fear struck Lizzy hard and she stood up quickly. She could never consider Joe a father, never interact with him pleasantly.

But Savannah did. Lizzy had seen it in her eyes when she'd asked if Joe hit her—her sister loved her dad. And Mom loved him too.

Joe, Savannah, Mom, they were a family, blood related and clearly content with their relationship. So what was she doing here? Stirring up bad feelings? Ruining everything? She didn't belong, she never had. That was reality.

"I have to go." Fighting a breakdown, she slung her purse over her shoulder. Unzipping the pocket, she fished a twenty from her wallet and tossed it on the table to cover her shake and a little extra for Ruby. "I'm sorry."

"Wait." Rushing to her feet, her mother caught her arm. Their gazes locked in debate. "I've made apologies for a lot, Elizabeth, but don't forget, you're the one who ran."

"I escaped," Lizzy whispered bitterly. The truth was sour in her mouth, acidic and eating away at her. Would she ever get past it? Ever stop feeling the sharp pain of her childhood?

She pulled at her arm but her mother refused to let go. This time.

"I chose to let you be where you were best off," she reminded her tenderly. "*You* came back."

"I know." Tears started streaming down her face, and her mother released her.

Saying nothing, Lizzy dropped her arm to her side, but she didn't walk away. She couldn't. She only knew that she couldn't stay.

"So now you're leaving again?" The question came from Savannah, who was crying herself.

Lizzy looked at her newfound little sister, seeing the disenchantment turning down her mouth, clouding her eyes. The wet trails streaking her cheeks. The need.

The question loomed around them, and Lizzy knew, had it not been for Savannah, she might have done just that—she would have gone and stayed gone, angry at no one but herself. Afraid.

But this time around, she couldn't do that. She knew what it was like to be a little girl with a broken heart and she wouldn't do that to Savannah.

"No." Lizzy forced a smile and wiped the tears from her eyes. "I just . . . I need some time, some space. I can't think."

But she *was* running . . . hiding . . . escaping in the only way she knew, except this time, she *knew* she was coming back.

Why? WHY? The question pounded in her mind, her very heart as Lizzy clutched her purse, walking briskly through the diner.

Why had her mother had another child? Why did her mother's reasons for staying with Joe and selling her like livestock make so much sense, when Lizzy *knew* she was so wrong? Smart wives leave abusive husbands and mothers don't sell their children! There was no excuse worthy and yet Lizzy knew those types of expectations of her mother were unrealistic.

She should, she *would*, forgive her, if only she could stop being so pissed-off. God, she'd stayed away so long, wasted so many years being angry and indifferent.

Why did she still *want* to be that way? Why couldn't she allow herself to forgive and forget?

So many questions, so many answers . . .

But no peace. Never peace.

Lizzy shoved open the glass, ad-covered door of the diner with a

jingle and fled into the parking lot. Dark and stormy clouds threatened overhead, a light rain misting the air.

Frantic, she dug through her purse, finding Ty's key ring buried
at the bottom. Unlocking the driver's side, she flung open the heavy
door and tossed her bag to the passenger seat, then sat. She started
the Trans Am's engine with a roar, and the rumbling sound fueled
her overwhelming desire to escape.

Backing out of her spot, she cranked the wheel around, speeding
out into the road.

She just wanted to *go*, to get out of there, to outrun the twisting
in her gut, the confusion in her head.

Lizzy pressed the gas pedal to the floor, flying down the road.
Trees whizzed past her, thunder roared, and lighting flashed. Rain
pounded down on the windshield, making it hard to see.

But she just couldn't slow down—couldn't go fast enough, far
enough.

She saw the water rushing across the road too late, panicking
and slamming on the brakes as her tires hydroplaned. In a split second, she lost her thin thread of control, sending the vehicle spinning off the road.

Her scream echoed in the vehicle's interior as the car crashed
into a tree and her face struck the steering wheel, her last thought
being of Ty.

He'd trusted her with his car and she'd let him down. How could
he ever forgive her?

twenty-three

The last remnants of the storm rumbled through the night, like a deliberate backdrop to the sad country song playing on the radio. Lightning flashed in the distance, illuminating the edge of the woods.

Reaching forward, Ty tugged at the seat belt to give himself some space, and flicked the dial off, leaving them in silence. He glanced at his pop, who drove with both hands on the wheel. Ty thought he should say something. He wanted Pop to know it was good, being out with him like this, but damned if he could put his feelings into words without sounding like a sissy.

Instead, he cleared his throat. The wrong move. Uncomfortable uncertainty filled the cab of the truck. Darn it, if he had nothing to say, he should have left the radio on.

Then, like a foghorn blasting out in the quiet, his father farted. Both of them shared a knowing grin, and the awkwardness vanished.

Maybe words were unnecessary. And his father could provide all the music they needed.

Tempted to undo his pants, Ty relaxed and opened the window a few inches, inhaling a breath of fresh, moist air. After e-mailing off his English report, it'd shaped up to be a real nice evening between him and Pop—dinner at an all-you-can-eat restaurant two towns over. They'd stuffed their guts on barbequed shrimp and rare roast, talking about nothing in particular—fishing, Mom's fried chicken, the new town water treatment plant. And to Ty's relief, his father had even resisted drinking.

Unfortunately, that had been all they'd talked about. Whenever his father asked him about his life, Ty sidestepped the questions like he was dancing around a rattlesnake.

No way had he told the truth about what he was doing—the stripping or college. He couldn't rightly explain how he was paying for school without mention of the dancing, and Ty was pretty damn sure the truth would push his father away.

Not that they were even close to *close*—that would take time, if ever.

"So . . ." Ty began again, glancing at Pop, but the sudden flash of red and blue lighting up the cab shut him up. *Cops?*

"Looks like an accident up ahead," his father noted. With the grinding of gears, the squeak of old brakes, his father slowed down his truck and shifted into the single lane letting traffic by.

"What happened?" he wondered. From the amount of emergency vehicles, someone had gotten hurt tonight. *Who?*

Instantly his mind flashed to Lizzy, but he quickly dismissed the thought. It couldn't be her.

Right?

Yet something in his gut flared. Clutching the door handle, he sat forward to stare out the front window as they passed a fire truck, allowing them full view.

Shit, no.

"Stop the truck. Pull off!"

God damn it, it *was* Lizzy! That was his car, his goddamned car *wrapped around a tree!*

Before his father could pull off the road, Ty leapt from the cab, leaving the door hanging open. Recklessly, he dodged in front of the still-moving truck and raced onto the scene.

"Lizzy?" he hollered out. "ELIZABETH!"

For God's sake, where was she? What the hell had happened?

He never should have let her drive his car! It was too fast, she was too upset with all that was going on. He should have listened to her, taken her himself!

"Lizzy?" he called again. His heart was racing a mile a minute, his skin sweating with fear.

"Sir? You can't—" A policeman tried to stop him, but he barreled forward.

"ELIZABETH!"

Let her be okay! She had to be—he *couldn't* lose her! Not again!

"Oh God. Ty?" Her voice was small and muffled. Several people around an ambulance moved out of his way and Ty rushed passed them.

Ripping off a blood pressure monitor, Lizzy leapt from where she was receiving treatment on the vehicle's bumper. The blanket around her shoulders dropped to the ground.

"You okay?" Ty took her in his arms roughly, kissing the top of her wet head. She was drenched from the rain, quivering. "Are you okay?"

She nodded against his chest and sobbed.

"You scared me to death." He squeezed her tight against him, pretty sure *he'd* hug her to death. In the face of losing her, holding her had never felt so good. "What happened?"

"I'm sorry, Ty." She hiccupped. "I wrecked your car."

"I noticed." His whiskered chin rubbed against her slick strands of hair as he kissed her head, relishing the soft feel of her, her fruity scent, everything about her. He could have lost her! "I should have driven you myself."

He was growing angrier by the second—at himself. Why couldn't he *ever* manage to take care of her, to look out for her? Over a decade ago he'd sworn to do just that, yet it seemed he was constantly slipping. Lizzy had been hurt and he could've prevented it. Again.

It was no wonder she couldn't trust him. Perhaps he was asking the impossible of her.

"Are they taking you to the hospital?" he asked. Tilting her chin, he inspected her face, noting a nasty knot on her forehead. Jesus.

His fingers roved over the bump ever so gently, gauging its size, and she winced. "Ty, I'll pay for the damages, I promise."

What? He couldn't believe she was even saying that. "You think I care about that car? I *don't*."

One of the EMTs behind him cleared his throat, and a policeman stepped forward. "You two can talk on the way, but you better get going. Just to be sure—"

"I told you, I'm fine!" Lizzy burst out. She pulled free, walking away from the ambulance and the staring eyes and flashing lights, heading down the street.

She was refusing treatment? What was going on in that stubborn head of hers?

"I don't know." Struck by confusion and worry, Ty faced the cop and two waiting EMT workers. "Give me a minute. I'll get her." He jogged to catch up with her. "Lizzy!"

"I've been trying and trying to call you." She was crying, sobbing uncontrollably as she walked briskly down the road, past where his father was parked.

"I was out with my pop." Ty shot his father a glance—he leaned against the side of his truck, watching the whole fiasco, to Ty's unease. "Lizzy, you need to let them take you to the hospital. I'll go with you."

"I'm fine." She kept right on walking as if she had somewhere to go, besides down a dark road, away from everybody. Away from *him*.

Really, what was she thinking?

"You're not. You're soaked to the bone and you could have a concussion or worse. You're acting crazy!" Catching her arm, he hauled her to a stop. "Enough!"

"Why do you care?" Wailing, she struggled from his hold and stumbled away. *"Why?"* she demanded again. "Give me an answer!"

The question wouldn't leave her alone, wouldn't rest.

She knew she was acting crazy—she'd never felt crazier in all her life, and it wasn't the freakin' bump on her head.

Didn't he see, didn't he get it?

"Lizzy, don't be ridiculous." Again he claimed her arm, firmer this time. His eyes said it all—she was scaring him. Well, good. Let him be scared. Let him wonder! Let him know what it felt like!

"Come on," he pleaded, "we can discuss whatever is bothering you later. For now, go to the hospital. Just in case."

Determined to free herself, she jerked her arm vigorously. She wasn't going. Not with him, not with them. If she got in the ambulance right now, she'd suffocate. Even now, out in the open, it felt like the walls were closing in on her. No, like she was being driven out. Forced to look at things she had no desire to see.

She just wanted to be back at her club in Colorado, listening to loud music and fending off men. With a vengeance.

"Lizzy, you're creating a scene." Ty forced her closer, trying to hide that she was fighting him. "Stop, before they think you're drunk or something!"

Like she cared!

"They already breathalyzed me." She didn't give a hoot who was staring, what they saw, but still, she lowered her voice. "I wrecked your car. You should hate me!" she ground out.

Maybe something was wrong with her, but all she knew was that she was *pissed*! Pissed because she was so confused, because rightfully, she should lose his trust. And she wasn't!

Even without him saying it, she knew. Ty would forgive and forget. He'd hand her the keys again tomorrow in a heartbeat.

What the hell was his problem?

"That's what you're upset about?" he ground out between clenched teeth, holding her firmly. Anger radiated from him, but for all the wrong reasons! "You think I care about that damn car? Lizzy, *please*."

"Of course you do! That car is your life!" Why couldn't he admit it? She'd screwed up royally. That car was his baby, his pride and joy.

"Lizzy, you're my life." He pulled her against him, pressing her face against his chest. "All I care about is that you're safe."

Another sob racked her. When Ty pulled her into his arms this way, she *felt* so very safe. So protected, as she always had. It was out-landish! How could she feel so very secure in the arms of a man she didn't trust? Of a man who'd betrayed her?

Ty was acting like he didn't even care about the car. Despite everything, he was here for her, loving and understanding. She didn't deserve it, didn't deserve him!

She *couldn't* give him the same, *never* had. When he'd screwed up, she'd sworn never to let him forget it and she hadn't!

God!

The past was always there, reminding her. Flashes of fear and doubt tortured her, screamed at her to run.

So she did. Needing to escape, she wrenched and twisted her body free. But Ty would have none of it. From behind, his hands caught her upper arms, and he whirled her around, giving her a little shake. "Damn it, why are you doing this, Lizzy?"

She squirmed out of his grasp, but didn't bother to flee. He'd only catch her again. "Why did you leave me?" she demanded.

"What are you talking about?"

"You abandoned me!" she accused. "I was cold and hungry and I almost sold my body, just to survive! To some dirty old man! I was scared! Terrified! I *needed* you!"

He yanked back like he'd been struck. She watched the pain and regret flash in his eyes—hopelessness and defeat.

"Lizzy . . ." He swore under his breath, clenching his fists at his side. "What happened?"

"It was raining all the time and I was so sick. I needed to see a doctor and I . . . I was so hungry I would have done *anything*."

"God, honey, I'm so sorry. I had no idea."

"Of course you didn't! Don't you see?" she wailed. "You were gone!"

Pain etched on his face, he stared at her and said nothing—there was nothing for him to say. But she had plenty of words for him, stored up for what seemed like an eternity.

"You had no *right* to take me. You couldn't care for me. What were you going to give me after a *stolen* engagement ring? What Ty?" She slammed her hand into his chest, shoving him backward. "*What?*"

He caught her hand and held her at bay. "What do you want me to do? Just tell me how to fix this and I'll do it."

"Just leave me alone!" She regretted the words the moment she uttered them, knowing that wasn't what she wanted. Hadn't been all along.

He dropped her arms. His eyes fell, the look of a man beaten, of a soul smashed. "I can't be any sorrier than I am. I wish I could take it all back, but I can't. You know I never intended to disappear on you."

Just like she'd never intended to wreck his car.

"I was so scared," she whispered, more to herself than him. But wasn't she always?

Not when he was holding her, she knew that, deep down inside herself. And suddenly, that was all she wanted—for him to hold her soundly and never let go.

But she'd told him to go, and she could see it in his gaze, hear it in his breathing.

For once, he was going to do just that. She'd pushed him to the point where he really believed she wanted him to leave.

She opened her mouth, wishing there was something she could say to change it all. Instead, she stood there, gaping like a fool, shivering and breaking down. Raw and unable to simply ask for his love.

With a silent nod, Ty took off his leather coat and wrapped it around her shoulders. Then he walked away, leaving her standing there alone. Alone, as she had been for years.

God, what was wrong with her?

Sliding her arms into the sleeves of his coat, she wrapped herself in its warmth, inhaled his scent. Buried herself in the security the coat left her, realizing only Ty could make her feel this way, so certain, so treasured.

And yet she drove him away. Accused him. Refused to let him in.

Tears poured down her cheeks, fell to the ground amidst pounding raindrops. Memories inundated her mind, reminded her of years of misgivings and doubt, even before Ty. She didn't trust him, didn't trust anyone. And it wasn't him, it wasn't any of them.

It was her.

Rain poured down on him, cold and stinging.

Embarrassed, smarting from his head to his heart, Ty made arrangements to have his car towed, and stood back, watching as the EMTs finally collected a defeated Lizzy into the ambulance.

She needed him, but he couldn't be there for her. She wouldn't let him, and that was nothing new.

He'd never felt so damn helpless in all his life. Worthless. He hated hearing what she'd been through, hated that he'd caused it all. She'd almost sold herself, for God's sake!

She was right not to forgive, to mistrust him.

Ty watched the emergency vehicle doors shut and he closed his eyes at the sight.

He was disgusted with himself, with the turn their life had taken long ago. But what could he do? He couldn't change things. The past was the past and it didn't seem she would ever let it go.

He knew one thing for damn sure—he'd never do anything so stupid again. Money and things weren't worth the trouble they caused. In the end, his desire for a better life had cost him *Lizzy*. And it had almost cost her something far more precious.

"Sir?" a man barked, making him jerk open his eyes to find one of the EMTs standing before him. The vehicle's engine rumbled as it waited for rubberneckers to clear out of the way.

"She okay?" The question was a gut reaction.

"A likely concussion, but it could be worse. Only a CAT scan can tell for sure. She asked me to give you this."

Before walking away, the EMT handed him a set of keys—*her* keys. To her house, to her vehicle back in Aspen.

Ty juggled them in his palm. Now why did she want him to have these? They were hundreds of miles away from . . .

Then it hit him.

She was giving him her trust, just as he had given his to her.

Folding the keys in his hand, he gripped them for dear life. The metal dug into his fingers as he called out to the emergency worker, "Wait up!" He motioned to his waiting father to follow and began jogging toward the ambulance, toward what he prayed was a new them. "I want to ride with her."

twenty-four

The ambulance's engine rumbled impatiently as the rear door swung open.

"Ty." Lizzy smiled on the inside and out. The knots in her stomach unfurled.

She felt safe again.

The look on his face—relief, washed with joy—said it all. Ty'd gotten the message she'd sent with the keys.

Maybe it had been the bump to her head or her near breakdown. Perhaps finally finding the answers she'd long sought by facing her mom. But it was like she'd had a mirror held to her very soul and she'd seen the reflection: a two-year-old child crying for the father that never came home.

Long ago, her life had been split into puzzle pieces, stuck in a box, and shaken rudely. But the shaking had stopped. Everything fit into place now. She finally got it.

She couldn't have trusted Ty, couldn't have trusted anyone, not when she didn't even trust herself. And it was no wonder—she was always screwing things up, *because* she didn't trust.

It was time to let go, namely, of control. Good things and bad happened in life. She couldn't stop them, could never have complete run of her world. The only thing she could do was change how she saw matters.

And she saw herself with Ty. Happy, trusting . . . even climaxing.

"Hey," he said softly, sitting down on the bench. His left hand clutched her keys, holding tight, just as he'd always held tight to her. For heaven's sake, this man had waited years to find her! Plenty of women would love to have a guy like him, but he'd never even considered getting serious with someone else.

How could she have doubted him? *Why?*

"Hey," she whispered back. Suddenly, she was so happy she knew she must be glowing.

He brushed his fingers over her mouth. "That's good to see."

Sensation erupted along her lower lip and she smiled further. "It's good to feel."

"And how's your head?" With his free hand, he smothered hers, the embrace warming her with a comfort she could only find with Ty. He was her rock.

"I'm fine, I promise."

"Just get checked out, in case."

"I am." She quieted a moment, in awe at the words on the tip of her tongue. "Ty?"

His brows lifted in question.

Was she really about to say it?

Yes . . . *yes, yes, yes!* There was no way she couldn't tell him, no way she could avoid the compelling feelings. She wanted him to know what was in her heart. Wanted to hear him say the same.

"Ty, I *love* you." Her fingers tightened around his as she searched deep in his fathomless eyes. Eyes that were haunted by past pain, but light and renewed by her words. "I love you," she said again, with conviction that could never be doubted.

"I love you too." Lifting her hand, Ty turned it over and kissed her palm sweetly. *"Always."*

Three hours later, Ty's father dropped them off at their hotel. Thanking him, Lizzy waved good-bye. Ty lagged behind, exchanging a few words with his dad.

Letting herself in, she went to the bed, sitting on its edge. Aspirin had done the trick. Her headache was gone, and there was no concussion to be concerned about. She was fine. No, better than fine.

She was in love. And ready, more ready than she'd ever been, for anything.

Though it was late, she wasn't tired. In fact, she'd never felt more awake. Desirous heat warmed her all over. Her skin felt like it could conduct electricity.

There was only one thing in the world she wanted right now—to make love to Ty. Real, honest, gritty, and raw *love*, no holding back.

She was ready to confess and explore.

With a wry grin, Ty walked inside, shutting and locking the door behind him. "My dad said to tell you he likes your hair."

"First time I ever heard your dad say anything in good taste." She laughed. "You can tell your dad he's in luck—the hair is staying."

"I'm glad." Ty stripped off his shirt, revealing the hard muscles of his back. "Brown is too boring for you."

Her eyes traveled over his well-defined shoulders, along the indentation of his spine, and her mouth watered. God, she wanted to dig her fingers into his flesh, hold tight.

"It's nice, getting along with Pop like this," he continued, kicking off his shoes. "Not that I think it'll last. We'll always have our differences. But it's good, the estrangement being over."

"Yeah," Lizzy agreed, thinking of her newfound sibling. Something inside her lifted and she realized how great having something positive about home to look forward to felt. It made all the difference in the world. "I'm really glad I came. I needed to."

"And you have a little sister to pick on now."

She'd told Ty about Savannah at the hospital, practically shocking him from his shoes.

Lizzy grinned at the thought, but even more so at the idea of having another friend like her sister Elisa in her life. She needed all the loved ones she could get.

Following suit, she unlaced her boots, tugging off the right one as she spoke. "You know, I might ask my mom to let Savannah visit me in the summer."

"That's a great idea." He plunked down beside her, creating a lurch in the mattress. Taking her left foot, he gave her boot a final yank and threw it aside. "Man, after tonight, I'm not sure how I'll ever fall asleep."

"Who said you're getting any sleep tonight?" she said seductively.

His amusement filled the air. "Mmmm. No man in his right mind would argue with a suggestion like that." Hooking his arm around her shoulder, he tugged her against him, so that she hugged the side of his chest. He kissed her cheek gently as she looked up at him. "So I must've lost mine the moment you told me you love me."

What? He better not dare!

"You're denying me?" She wouldn't stand for that, not as long as she'd suffered, wanting him terribly, but emotionally incapable. Now that she was ready, she was *ready*. Wildly ready, and only one thing could satisfy the fire burning in her.

His cock, hard and long and thrusting.

Lizzy slid her hand down his lower back, snaking between denim and skin to tweak his rear end.

"Hey!" He jumped three inches off the bed, landing with a bounce. "What was that for?"

"What wasn't it for?"

"Vixen." He cast falsely disapproving eyes down on her, eyes that danced with good humor and affection. They warmed her with the intense feeling of love, of *being* loved. "You're playing with fire."

"Fire? Hmmm, sounds dangerous. Not at all boring." And the thought of him losing control was pretty damn sexy. "Perhaps I should put out your *fire*."

He chuckled in delight. "Who are you?"

She looked up at him with pouting lips. Pleading eyes.

Still, he hesitated. No kiss, no sweeping her back onto the bed and making furious love to her.

She couldn't bear it if he turned her down tonight—she needed to seal her feelings, to finish off that last hanging part of her that wanted to doubt them. She needed forever with urgency. *Now.*

"Ty," she breathed, fingering the tiny curling hairs on his chest, scraping her nails over his nipples in promise of the wildcat she'd be. "I *really* want this—you. You said I had to come to you, to really want you, and I promise, I do." She sucked in a sharp breath, finishing with, "I promise, I'll enjoy it to the very end."

An orgasm was a lot to commit to—how could she be sure?—but she *had* to.

"Wow." He cupped her head with his hands, holding her gaze, looking at her like she might be an alien. "But, I'm worried about your head."

Not *that* again. "The doctors said I was *fine*! Just a bump. Oh!" With a hearty shove, she pushed him back on the mattress, climbing over him. "I'm not a doll."

"You used to remind me of one—a porcelain doll," he told her in an amused voice. "But that couldn't be. You must be made of rubber."

Huh? Her legs straddled him, squeezing firmly so he couldn't throw her off. "Rubber?"

"Despite everything, you don't break, you bounce."

If only.

Her head fell forward, drooping. "I don't know that I agree with that. I was pretty broken."

"*Was.*" His hands encircled her waist, supporting her, just as he'd always supported her in life. "But the past is the past."

How right he was.

"And from now on, I'm leaving it there," she vowed. She leaned forward, kissing his face with tiny, succulent kisses and crushing her breasts into his chest, rubbing and teasing, determined to arouse him. "I meant what I said, Ty. I love you."

Her nipples had turned into tiny rocks of desire, tight, constricted, screaming to be sucked.

And her pussy . . . she was so tingly, so wet yet searingly hot. Her clit pulsed in readiness.

Normally, it was a feeling she'd try to resist, to hide from. But oh, how she was relishing it this time. How good it felt to be comfortable, not to fear—only to desire, to love.

She sat up straight, so that her jean-covered pussy pressed into his bare chest, and he gave her bottom a little smack. "I know that you love me, Lizzy. I've always known."

A tiny grin curled on her lips. "You should have told me."

"Oh, I think I gave it some effort!" He slapped her ass again to enforce his words. "Stubborn woman!"

"I really want to be with you. Tonight." Circling her hips, she rubbed her pussy over him, whimpering. Pleading.

She wouldn't accept being denied. Now that she knew what being pushed away felt like, it sucked. Royally.

"Persistent, aren't you?"

"I learned from the best," she reminded him. "Ty, I want to make love to you. I want you to make me come. To do those things to me that you did the night I was drunk . . . but I don't want to be drunk." She pulled back, so she could stare into his eyes. "I want to feel *everything*."

That did the trick. With a groan, he threw her over and rolled her onto the mattress beneath him. His body pressed against hers, his hard-on riding her cunt through her jeans, his chest flattening her breasts.

"Congratulations!" he all but growled. "You've convinced me. You're ready, and I'm going to give it to you."

Her heart kicked in her chest excitedly, took off so fast she thought it might run away.

And then she remembered. They couldn't do it, not yet!

She slid her hands between them, pushing at his chest. Shoving him off. "Wait."

twenty-five

"*You* tease!" Disappointment rumbled from Ty as he flopped onto the mattress, his arms spread open. "You've got to be kidding me!"

Lizzy scooted from the bed. "Not in the least!"

"I might just have to spank you again." His eyes followed her, questioned her.

Accused her.

But he was wrong. She wasn't pushing him away. This was about something else entirely—something fun, something he was going to enjoy thoroughly.

"Maybe." She lowered her tone sultrily. "Truth or dare?"

"Dare."

"You didn't even hesitate." Lizzy stood, waving at him to follow suit. "Come on," she urged, "get out the game we bought. Play with me."

"Play with you?" His chuckle was devilish—and delish. He took her hand, simultaneously pulling himself up while tossing her back onto the mattress. "Gladly."

She landed with a thunk.

"Don't you dare move!" he threatened, and winked at her. "You're not allowed to leave the bed."

She watched as Ty crossed their tiny, poorly lit hotel room and rummaged through his duffel bag, knocking clothes to the floor as he dug the game out from the very bottom.

"Here it is." He held Confessions and Explorations in the air, waving it like he'd found gold. "Unfortunately, we left your other toys in the trunk."

"Oh, we won't need those. Not tonight."

All she wanted was his cock—she'd had enough plastic to last a lifetime.

Blinding hot excitement and mind-spinning curiosity rushed through Lizzy as he came toward the bed.

She didn't know what to expect as he tore the plastic wrapping off the game, as well as the cards inside. To allow room for him, she scooted back, sitting cross-legged, and he placed the board before her. Unfolding it, he put two card piles in its center—*Confessions*, red cards with black hearts, and *Explorations*, black cards with red hearts. Each pile of cards matched spaces on the game board—and there were far more explorations.

Next, Ty opened the tiny pack of game pieces and Lizzy cracked up. Pewter boobs and penises—*four* each. She'd never seen anything so crudely hilarious in all her life.

And the sheer number of them left quite a bit to the imagination—she couldn't picture so many people being sexual with each other at once! She wouldn't want to do something like that—not on her life. All she wanted, all she'd ever wanted, she had right here with her now—Ty.

"I'll go over the rules."

And I'll break them, Lizzy thought with a smile. Nevertheless, she nodded in agreement as he unfolded a white piece of paper, reading silently.

Just to see, Lizzy pulled a red card. "Tell your lover your favorite thing about kissing," she mused. With a smile, she lifted her eyes to Ty. This was going to be fun. More romantic than she expected. Definitely intimate.

"Eh, eh." Dropping the instructions, Ty took the card from her, sliding it underneath the rest of the pile. "You have to roll the dice."

Lizzy wrinkled her nose at him. Darn, she'd really wanted to hear his answer, and to give hers—she *loved* when he nibbled and sucked at her lower lip. Just the thought of it made her pussy quiver with anticipation.

Speaking of which, her jeans were now soaked at the juncture of her legs. She needed to get them off, fast, before the wet rubbing drove her insane.

Picking up the dice, she tossed them onto the board. Four. She moved her tiny tits four spaces and placed the game piece on a black space. An exploration, already? Just her luck.

"Pick a card," Ty urged impatiently, sitting on the edge of the bed. The mattress shifted with his weight, knocking over her piece.

She shifted it back. "You're next," she reminded him, lifting a card. She flipped it over and read silently. *French kiss your partner in the place of their choice.* "Oh boy."

"Lucky you." She showed him the card, which he read quickly.

"You know where I chose. I want my cock kissed, Frenchy."

"Ty!" But she was grinning ear to ear as she climbed off the bed, coming around to his side. "Remember," Lizzy told him in warning, "you'll be in this position soon enough!"

"I can't wait," he murmured, scooting so that he pivoted on the edge of the bed, his legs dangling over, his feet braced toe first against the floor.

With a flick of her tongue, she wet her lips and knelt between his knees. Eagerly, Lizzy undid the button, then the zipper, of his jeans.

Good thing for both of them that she loved the taste of his dick. She took his half-mast cock in her hand, pulling it free from his boxers and resting it against her cheek. He was aroused, but not fully. Still soft and warm and smelling of man—pure, sexual, indescribable maleness.

Inhaling, she took him in her mouth, *kissing* him fully. Her tongue wrapped around him, swirling and loving as he expanded, lengthening to his full size.

She suckled his tip, made him groan with pleasure before she began pumping him into her throat, taking him from mushroom head to the base of his cock, her tongue whirling and licking unmercifully.

She waited until he was groaning and tangling his fingers in her hair and at his hardest—his cock so big she could no longer take all of him—and she let him go.

Clutching the tops of his knees, she pushed herself up.

"Hey!" he protested.

"The card said kiss, not blow," she teased him naughtily. "Your turn."

"First," he suggested, his finger sweeping over the soaked *V* of her jeans. "Let's get rid of these clothes."

Her cunt shuddered and Lizzy quivered inside. "Good idea," she managed to say. Her legs suddenly felt so weak she could've dropped to the floor.

Taking her shirt by the bottom, she stripped it off, all the while aware of Ty's studious gaze, the way he watched her every movement, drinking in the sight of her bared flesh. And she loved it, wanted to dance and spin and give him the show of a lifetime. There was no nervousness as with all the times before and she adored how comfortable she felt, taking her bra off, letting him gaze upon her fully.

His eyes were like cameras, flashing, remembering. He'd seen her breasts plenty of times, but she'd never felt so exposed and appreciated.

Lizzy returned his dark stare, enjoying the moment as she undid the fastening of her jeans, opening them. No hesitation—only anticipation. Flutters of desire and uncertainty of what was to come burst within her—along with faith that she would enjoy this, no matter what happened.

Peeling down her pants, she kicked them off and bent, removing her rainbow-toed socks. Left only in her thong, she bravely turned, exposing her backside. Sensations unfurled in her lower stomach as she used her thumbs to pull it off too, dropping it to the floor, then straightening.

"God, you're beautiful," he whispered. "Come here."

She went into his open arms, and he kissed the pert nipple of her left breast, laving it with his tongue, licking around her areola, over the pinnacle of its center.

The tingling bud constricted and pleasure traveled along her spine as he drew it into his mouth, suckling, drawing sharply. She moaned aloud as a new gush of desire poured forth from her.

If she didn't kill the ache in her soon, she'd climax just from his touch. God, did he have any idea how expert his lips were?

Most likely.

His hands cupped the underside of her breast, molding and massaging the flesh as he flicked the tight knot in circles with his tongue.

Definitely.

"Delicious," he complimented.

"You too." Lizzy's back arched and she leaned into him, whimpering as she imagined him doing the same thing to her pussy. Loving it, so *thoroughly*.

She was wet nearly to her ankles by the time he allowed her to pull her chest away from his torturous mouth. Tracing her fingers over his short, sun-bleached hair, she held him at bay. "That wasn't part of the game."

He licked his lips. "I couldn't resist. And I still can't."

He tugged her to him once again, claiming the opposite breast, nursing the increasing feelings in her. Making her wild, making her want more . . . much, much more.

"I must protest." Again, she withdrew, backing up and putting distance between them. "Your pants are still on."

And how she wanted him naked—ready and willing for her to jump on and ride.

Then again, no, she wouldn't . . . she was enjoying this, every moment. No rushing, no running.

Ty stood and took a step forward, his body bumping into hers, his bared cock nudging her belly. But she refused to let them get carried away—she needed to enjoy this. Every moment of the game.

She again put space between them, watching him as he had her.

"Where do you think you're going?" His dark gaze held her in place, refusing to allow her to back up any farther.

alyssa brooks

Hungrily, she drank in his tanned skin, his defined muscles, appreciating him fully. He was a beautiful sight, physically perfect for a man.

It was no wonder people paid to see such a fine specimen, but God, how she hated the thought of other women looking at him. She reached out and touched his biceps, squeezing. "All mine," she claimed.

"All yours," he promised impossibly, sliding down his pants and boxers and walking free of the garments.

They both knew she had to share him—*for now*—but hopefully that could soon change. It wasn't as if he liked stripping or that she couldn't offer him another way.

His hands claiming her shoulders, Ty took her into his arms once again, hugging her tight against him, their naked bodies flush, their sexual heat searing into each other, marking them as lovers.

His cock lay against her abdomen, pressing into her soft skin, and his nipples smashed into the suppleness of her chest, directly above hers.

He held her just like that, snuggly, unrelenting, and she felt right at home. At *peace.*

They were one, truly meant to be. The only way to be closer to him than she felt right now was to have him inside her, as he was inside her very heart.

His fingers tickled the back of her neck as he kissed the top of her head and she realized he was about to take her against the wall.

"The game," she reminded him. Something this wonderful shouldn't end too soon.

"Right." He kissed her once again and released her, motioning to the bed. He dropped back onto the mattress, picked up the dice, and with a flick of his wrist, rolled.

304

She remained standing, waiting with bated breath. He moved his pewter penis five spaces—another exploration. A surge of expectation bolted through her as he read aloud. "Remove your lover's clothes with your mouth."

"Well darn!" she laughed. "Pick another card."

He lifted a second exploration card. This one he read silently, a dangerous smile lifting his lips.

"What's it say?" she asked in a whisper, knowing instinctively that she was in trouble.

He cleared his throat, his eyes settling on her as he rose. "Your partner's been naughty," he recited. "An appropriate punishment is due—be it a spanking, or other exquisite sexual torment. Remember, pain can be pleasure."

"Oh God," she squeaked. He took her by the arm before she could move away. "Wait! That's not fair—that should have been my card!"

Yeah, she could really see herself spanking *him*. Not exactly sexy, but oh, the thought of his hands on her bottom again!

She *had* promised that she wanted all he'd given her that night she'd drunk too much.

It was just slightly embarrassing, but truly, she did . . .

She trembled inside as he stood in front of her, looking like the bad boy he'd always been. Like he was really going to spank her . . . and enjoy it! It all just seemed so blatant, so matter-of-fact.

And yet, laced with unspoken passion. A thrilling assurance of delights to come.

"Can't argue with the cards, Lizzy. Luck of the draw," he practically hummed with delight. "Hands on the bed, ass in the air."

The jerk! Could he be any cockier about it?

Hazed with lust, his eyes twinkled. Spanking her—that was right up his alley!

He was going to enjoy this—no, *they* were.

Blood rushed to her face, her insides knotted, but she did as he bade, bending and placing her hands at the edge of the mattress. Completely exposed to him, her bottom lifted and waiting.

He positioned himself behind her, his cock dangling in the air and brushing against her moist mound. Lizzy could swear even her pussy hair tingled as he placed his hands on her ass, molding the rounded cheeks.

"Lizzy," he whispered, his voice suddenly filled with indecision. His fingers pressed into her skin, clenched her muscles. "The last time, you pulled away from me. Say you won't again."

Now *he* was afraid, Lizzy realized. Hesitant.

Tears tempted her, but she held back. What had she done? Time and time again, she'd pushed him into a corner, made him fear expressing himself sexually with her.

And that wouldn't do. No more doubt between them.

"Do it," she told him. She pressed her eyes shut. She wanted him to. Wanted this between them—wanted *everything*. "No regrets, I promise."

His fingers slid over the smooth skin, tempting, teasing. The smack came suddenly, but gently. Not enough to make a sound—on her skin or from her—and certainly not enough to cause pain . . . even the pleasing, sensual kind.

She moved against him and another gentle blow—if you could call it a *blow*—came. Torment!

"Perhaps we should switch places," she suggested teasingly, waving her ass back and forth. "After all, it was my card."

"Not a chance," he growled.

"Oh, come on, Ty. If you aren't man enough to spank me . . ."

"Vixen!" This time, he really spanked her, his palm slapping her smartly. Making her rear up. "You know damn well I will."

So he needed encouragement, did he?

Visions of that long night in the hotel, listening to her temporary neighbors get it on, flitted through her mind. The way the woman had cried out. Asked for her man to spank her . . . and more.

She needed to do the same. Wanted them to be like that—a couple of kinky lovers with *no shame*.

"More, Ty!" Again, she wiggled her rear, thrusting it higher, tempting him. "Give it to me!"

The noise that came from him sounded like a wild animal. Both of his hands rained down on her soft skin.

"Yes!" she cried out.

Again, his palms clapped her bottom and a flood of new emotions struck through Lizzy. "Yes, yes, yes!"

Damn, she loved this man. Loved how he loved her, loved how he commanded her body. With every touch, he branded her. Made her quake with thoughts of what he would—and could—do to her.

No other man, no toy, even came close. To say they paled in comparison was the understatement of the century.

She *belonged* to him and she wanted him to know it, to know how ready she was.

"More, Ty," she cried out. Ecstasy jolted through her with his every slap, at the glorious feel of his cock nudging her pussy, coming inside her. "More, more, more!"

His length filled her wet pussy completely and she was lost, spinning and whirling, delirious. Ty delivered stinging blows to her ass alternately. Rapidly, over and over.

"You like this, Lizzy?" he asked, his words rough, barely controlled.

"More!" she insisted. How could she *ever* get enough?

He spanked her harder, tattooed his love on her very heart. Her sensitized bottom burned for him, her anus twittered in arousal. Memories of the last time he'd touched her there seared through her, made her yearn.

"Ty . . ." She rode his movements, not just taking what he was delivering, but demanding it.

As if he could read her mind, his palms cupped her cheeks, one thumb sliding into the crevice. Discovering the quivering bud.

He took her *there*, driving his cock into her convulsing cunt, fucking her ass with his thumb. Lizzy went wild, bucking and screaming out at the orgasm convulsing through her and possessing her body. Every inch of her was on fire, burning with white-hot ecstasy. Searing and soaring.

"Ride it out," Ty told her, slowing his movements, making her pleasure last and last like Doublemint gum, except with the fire of Big Red. "And roll the dice."

Roll the dice? *Now?* He had to be kidding!

But his thumb pressing deeper into her anus, while his free hand smacked her ass smartly, told her he wasn't.

"Roll the dice," he commanded again, his cock surging deep within her, thrusting, so that she had to brace herself from flying forward.

She came even harder and clasped her pussy muscles around his cock to hold on as she picked up the dice. She threw them onto the bedspread, her hand quickly returning so that her fingers could clench the mattress.

"Three spaces—a confession," Ty informed her, leaning over

her and pulling the card for her. "Tell your partner how you felt about your last exploration."

Oh God. She was *still* coming . . . still so hot and wanting more. But how could she ever describe it, put it into words? It was beyond anything verbal.

Instead, she rode out the last remnants of her climax, collapsing against the bed. Ty shifted, taking her legs and flipping her over.

Tears brimmed in her eyes as she looked at him. "I love you. I love the way you make me feel, from my head to my toes. And I promise *never* to be ashamed again."

Climbing onto the bed, he plunged himself between her legs. Buried himself in her love. Four thrusts and he exploded inside her, filling her with his heat. Then he too gave out, falling over her.

She wrapped her arms around him, hugging him tight. "Iloveyouiloveyouiloveyou."

He made a noise of pleasure. Kissing her ear, he whispered, "Marry me, Lizzy."

What? Taken by sheer surprise, she pulled back, staring at him. Their eyes met, locked in place by something inarguable.

Soul mates. She and Ty were designed for each other. Linked forever. How could she not marry him? Why wouldn't she?

The thought of becoming Elizabeth Black made her heart sing. In all this time, despite all that had happened, it was what she'd always wanted, always needed.

A smile formed on her face and she nodded slightly. There was just one little thing.

"Yes," she told him, "but I have a condition."

"Name it."

Lizzy swallowed, knowing it was asking a lot, but also aware of the reality that she had no choice. As much as she loved him, she couldn't marry a stripper. "No more dancing."

He was silent a moment, inner struggles playing on his face before he nodded and said, "Done."

He made it sound like a sealed deal, but suddenly Lizzy wasn't so sure. She could see the questions shadowing his dark eyes, troubles creating lines around his lips.

She touched his cheek, smoothed the concern from his face. "You're worried."

Rolling off of her, he lifted his upper body. His shoulders hunched. "Well, I don't know how I'll pay for school."

"I'll pay," Lizzy said quickly—too quickly. Realizing her mistake, she pulled herself up and wrapped her arms around him. "I—"

"No, Lizzy," he interrupted, his voice filled with pain, disappointed pride. "I can't take your money. I don't want it."

Men.

But he was right. It wouldn't do, *her* paying for *his* education.

"Let me correct myself. *We'll* pay. We'll be married, Ty. It's not my money, not just your future. It's ours." Climbing onto his lap, she looked up at him with a seriousness she'd never thought she'd have about a man. Of all things, she really needed him to agree on this or they'd never work. "No secrets, no surprises. We do it together, and money and pride *never* come between us."

Relief and acceptance washed over his face and he took her by the back of the head, sweeping her into a deep kiss straight from the heart. Their lips meshed together, instantly becoming one in that moment.

"Together," he swore on a ragged breath, breaking free, then kissing her all over again. "I like the sound of that. Together, forever."

"Forever."